AFTER OIL 2
The Years of Crisis

D1572670

After Oil 2
The Years of Crisis

Edited By
John Michael Greer

FOUNDERS HOUSE PUBLISHING
2014

Published by Founders House Publishing, LLC
Cover design by Shaun Kilgore
Cover art © Unholyvault/Dreamstime.com

www.foundershousepublishing.com

Printed in the United States of America

ISBN: 978-0692343951

Contents

After Oil 2

The Years of Crisis

Introduction
The Future We're Getting

By John Michael Greer

A little over two years, ago, in a post on my blog *The Archdruid Report*, I proposed a modest challenge for my readers. The subject of the series of posts then under way was science fiction's role as a sparkplug for the modern imagination, a literature of ideas in which the first rough drafts of possible futures could be brought up for discussion, and I'd commented on the widening gap between the shopworn vision of perpetual progress still being mined by most of today's science fiction and the future toward which we actually seem to be headed.

All through the middle decades of the twentieth century, science fiction bristled with sweeping claims about what life would be like today. Compare those claims to what actually happened, though, and the differences are vast. From jetpack commuting and vacations on the Moon to cures for cancer and household robots who would cook dinner for you and wash the dishes afterwards, any number of grandiose technological fantasies were showcased as the wave of the future, and anyone who questioned them was dismissed as a hopeless naysayer. In hindsight, though, it's clear that the naysayers were right and the prophets of limitless progress were talking through their Captain Astro propeller beanies.

For several decades now, though, the great majority of science fiction writers have gone on as though nothing of the sort had happened. If anything, many authors in the genre seem to have responded to the jetpack future's failure to appear by doubling down, insisting even more stridently on the invincible march of progress and humanity's destiny out there among the stars. I've come to think that this is one of the principal reasons why science fiction, once among the most intellectually stimulating genres of fiction, has lost so much of its edge in recent decades: ignore the future that's actually taking shape, and insist instead on what amounts to a popular folk mythology set in an imaginary Tomorrowland, and your ability to keep breaking new ground is going to be limited at best.

The future we're actually getting, I noted to my readers, has nothing to do with limitless progress; what defines it is precisely the opposite theme. From the depletion of the nonrenewable resources of a finite planet straight through to the remorseless impact of the law of diminishing returns on technological progress itself, the most important drivers of the future looming ahead of us are all about limits. Our collective unwillingness to deal with those hard realities will not make them go away, nor will approaching technology with a cargo cult mentality somehow force the universe to cater to our overdeveloped sense of entitlement.

That was the thinking that was behind the challenge I posed to the readership of my blog. What if, I proposed, we get to work writing science fiction about the kind of future we're actually likely to get—the kind that involves the winding down of industrial civilization, and the difficult but necessary transition from the extravagant habits of the present to the sustainable practices of the future? What if we try telling stories that sketch out the human experiences, tragedies, and triumphs of those futures?

I expected maybe a dozen stories in response. I got more than sixty, and enough of them were of publishable quality that the result was an anthology, *After Oil: SF Stories of a Post-Petroleum Future*, which was published by Founders House in 2013. Clearly there was no shortage of capable writers who wanted to tell stories outside the narrow range of futures that are acceptable to the conventional wisdom of our time.

The one question I had was whether the enthusiasm of the authors would find an equal enthusiasm among readers. Steady sales of that first anthology answered that question, and got me an inquiry from the publisher of *After Oil* about another collection, so I posted a second call for stories. The response from my readers was even more enthusiastic than before, and enough good stories came in that the second anthology promptly mutated into two volumes—the one you're currently holding in your hands, containing stories set in the near to middle future, and *After Oil 3: The Years of Renewal*, containing stories set in the middle to far future.

All the stories in both anthologies are about the hard transition from today's industrial societies to the less extravagant cultures of the deindustrial future. More to the point, they're about people caught in that transition, coping with its crises and living their lives in a world that's drifting further and further away from the jetpack future we were promised toward the future we're getting instead, and discovering—as people have so often discovered—that there are lives worth living and stories worth telling in challenging times as well as in comfortable ones.

—Cumberland, Maryland
8 November 2014

Winterfey

By Grant Canterbury

M om sliced cold chicken into a sandwich and called, "Little Sandy! Tear yourself away from those picture books and bring some lunch down to Dad. He went off this morning and forgot." And so he had, frowning and lost in his unseeing, worried look.

Sandy looked up from the broad foxed pages, full of bright-gowned women swooping with their partners across a great marble-floored ballroom. She was lying propped on dirty elbows, with her stomach on the floorboards and Pan's black hairy bulk snoozing against her side. "Okay." Mom handed her a cloth bag heavy with lunch, and she slipped on her shoes at the door. Pan roused himself, getting a paw print on the page, and followed her out.

"Come right back." Pan trotted at Sandy's side as they passed the Martinez house, Uncle Tanner's, and the last few boarded-up houses and the Space. The breeze was chilly on her light jacket; her breath and Pan's came in strange little gray puffs that faded at their mouths. They meandered out beyond the town and onto the straight line of Fourteen where it cut across the open short brown grass of the high places and began its gentle slope down to the thorny scrub of the creek bottom. A gray shrike watched her from one of the mesquite saplings that had crept into the fields of late, poking up above the buffalo grass and prickly pear. She walked with the dog along the high crown of the road, scuffing the flaked remnants of yellow paint under her shoes. On Fourteen Dad always made Sandy promise to walk the shoulder – he was worried about cars coming by fast – but sometimes that was hard to remember. Really, she could see them coming from a long ways away, and they didn't come along very often at all. Most of a mile to the store, and more often than not no one would pass her on the way.

She watched the steps of her feet as she walked. In the story the chimneysweep boy had had to study long nights over the footprint diagrams of how to place his steps as he danced, just so, to secretly prepare for the ball. She carefully hopped and jumped across diagonal-wise, and the lunch bag drooped lower as she did this. This interested Pan very much, and he let her know about it with eloquent sidelong looks and low whines and wuffs. Eventually he got a loose piece of chicken even though Sandy wasn't really supposed to give it to him.

The sky was crisp, cold, clear. Way out ahead the Rockies rose up out of the plain, never a whit nearer as she walked toward them. She was almost to the store, and there was a rumble and sharp double beep behind her as the gasoline truck turned wide to give her berth and rattled into the gravel lot. Sandy's older brother, Zack, waved to the driver and went to unlatch the tank cap. Dad was there on the sidewalk, talking to old Mr. Zimmer from the Grasslands office. She trotted up and handed him the bag. Dad nodded and sidelong said to her, "You keep to the shoulder going back, Little Sandy. Don't think I didn't see you."

Mr. Zimmer said, "I'm not saying it didn't need done, but this is the fourth year we've been in there. Starting to add up to one hell of a butcher's bill."

Dad said, "Oh, I hear you." He glanced over at Zack.

"With the Army you kind of have to expect it, but even in the Navy, now those Chinese missiles are getting smuggled in, popping up everywhere on the coast, the Antilles approaches –"

"Hang on, I've got to talk with this guy." Dad walked across the lot to the gasoline truck. His face had gone pale and grim. The driver nodded to him uncomfortably. Behind him the black hose wobbled as gasoline sluiced and gurgled through into the tank.

"Any change from what you told me last week?"

"No, I'm sorry, sir. This is the last time we're running this route."

"It leaves my business in a hell of a fix. Isn't there an arrangement that we can make?"

"I can't do anything about it, truly. The company has to pull back. We got told to stick to the arterials."

"This is an arterial. Fort Collins through to Omaha. It's a damn state highway!"

The driver shrugged. "I know. I don't know what to tell you."

"Yeah. Not your fault, is it." Dad scowled and stood with his arms crossed while the driver finished the pumping. They settled up and soon enough the truck was rattling out of the lot, disappearing over the rise to the west. Dad watched it go. He took a push-broom roughly down, a little tremor shaking his hand, and began to sweep grit off of the concrete walkway. He smiled crookedly. "Well Zack, when this tank's dry you could get to take a vacation. Mr. Zimmer. I regret to tell you, but you may be needing to gas up in Greeley in the near future."

"Yes. I'm very sorry to hear that. I suppose I should be off." Mr. Zimmer climbed into his rust-spotted lime-green pickup. He pulled around, then stopped and rolled down his window. "Supposed to be quite cold this week. Did you say you ran a woodstove at home?"

"Yeah. Not that I've been able to get a cord this year. We're burning leftovers at this point."

"Ah… Well, I've been thinking the Corbin Creek parcel is getting pretty thick with mesquite. It could stand to be cleared out before it's choked altogether. And there's a good deal of dry dead wood. It's too bad I have to get the head office to sign off before I can issue cutting permits; seems like that sort of thing can take years. Anyway. As it happens I'll be down in town all weekend, so I'm afraid nobody will be on duty. Back on Monday, right? See you then."

Walking back home Sandy kept to the shoulder. Pan stayed close against her side. No one else drove by.

&

That night Dad and Zack came walking up the road from Fourteen when they'd closed the store, just as usual. But after dinner Mom and Dad spent most of the evening closeted in their room, talking. Dad was worried about the store. Mom was worried about a call she'd had that afternoon over Tanner's shortwave, from her friend Janey Nichols in Ault.

4

Pan whined at the back door, but Mom and Dad didn't hear him. Sandy let him out.

"She said that in Denver they've been going house to house checking the papers of young men. It hasn't been on the news. But now I think, actually that worries me more."

Little Sandy pulled down another big book from her shelf and leafed through it. This one was fairies. An autumn fairy balanced on a nearly bare branch, a curled brown leaf serving her for a headdress, her rusty dress trailing and fluttering in the wind. In May a circle of them held hands and danced beneath the blooming white lilies. And here was a green spruce in the dead of winter, its branches weighed down with thick snow, and from the shadows beneath them the Ice Fairy, clad in palest blue, looked out to meet Sandy's eyes.

"I made damn sure Zack was never in those databases. But he's eighteen. They could still take him. If they come here ..."

Pan had been out for quite a while, and he hadn't scratched at the door. She looked out, didn't see him, and sighed and got her shoes and jacket on again. Outside she called him, crunched across the fallen pine needles in the back yard, and finally saw him standing by the back fence, facing the corner. He was just standing there in the dark. Little prickles rose on the back of her neck as she came up to him, cautiously, talking to him softly. He whined a little when she took him by the collar, then turned himself and came with her slowly back to the house.

Pan went straight back to her room, his claws clattering softly on the wood, and lay down on her bedside rug with a chuffing sigh. She climbed quietly into bed, and put her hand down to rest on his furry flank, and they went to sleep.

❧

Next morning Dad and Zack were up early with work boots on. Uncle Tanner and Mr. Martinez came over to help. Dad filled the chainsaw from a gas can, and an axe and handsaw went clanging into the back of the pickup with an assorted batch of work gloves. Pan wagged his way through the middle of the commotion, feeling fine. Little Sandy tossed pine cones at the Martinez boy Juan – a couple of years older than her – and raced with him down the street as Pan dashed yelping happily at their heels. Mom stood on the porch watching and, as Dad passed her with clippers, asked in an undertone, "Are you sure this is a good idea?"

"We need firewood, don't we?" The heating season wasn't so long anymore – most of the year the rangeland was baked flat under the sun – but she couldn't deny that it was chilly now, and that she always had to cook. In the yards close by there were still a few older trees that shed a dry limb now and then; but if they were to cut them down, heaven help them come the summer heat.

It was a problem then when the pickup refused to start, particularly since the Martinez truck had been repossessed that summer and Uncle Tanner had only a motor-scooter. The pickup hadn't been used for a week or two – Dad had decided awhile back that the gas they had at the station was better used for income than transport. He cursed the damn thing vehemently. Mom went back inside. Mr. Martinez looked thoughtfully at the tires and quietly walked away down the street, motioning Juan to come with him. When Uncle Tanner had raised the hood and clucked over the engine for a while, he thought the battery and starter were actually all right. "Old, but functioning as far as I can tell. I

6

think it's a problem with the engine control unit. There's bad logic in there somewhere."

"Can we get a new logic?" Sandy asked.

"Hush and go play," Dad said.

"Maybe in Denver, for an arm and a leg." They were busy. Sandy slipped away to visit the Space.

What Sandy called the Space had been a huge separate garage of one of the now abandoned houses, high-ceilinged and big enough to shelter from the elements a boat and a big truck side by side. Now it was empty. Its windows were painted over in black. One of them was cracked at the top, and in the summer bats would flutter out of it at dusk.

The doors and lower windows were latched tight. Sandy looked to see if anyone were watching (it was her secret), then clambered into an ancient Russian olive up as high as the upper window, which slid aside enough for her to wriggle through. Inside she found the hand and foot holds on the vacant shelves and workbench, and hopped down to the concrete floor.

Day leaked into the Space through a skylight. The furred shapes of a few hibernating bats huddled in one dim corner of the ceiling. A rosebush had shouldered several thorny branches into the Space through a crack in the siding. In the spring it had borne a few flowers, now long blown and dry.

Sandy had brought a few secret things in here – a white pelican feather that she'd seen fall from the sky; a bulbous, tentacular thing like a dream-ship or a squid, formed from molten lead dribbled into water at a county fair; a picture of a Chinese village painted on a bamboo plate. On a shelf was a crescent-shaped crown of faded foam-plastic and wire, the inducer, which she had retrieved from the bin when Uncle Tanner gave up on it at last.

Tanner had brought the inducer from Fort Collins last year, gleeful at his find. "If we were on the net here you could communicate with anyone in the world, just by thinking about them. When you wear it, it exchanges magnetic signals with your visual cortex and creates a virtuality. See!" He had placed it on her head and adjusted the fit, and she had felt it press and shift coolly against her scalp. Her vision had doubled, or she had found herself in two places at once – Uncle's workshop, and a great phantom array of colorless intersecting lines and arcs, rising to trace a dome overhead and extending out to some far horizon. They swiftly bloomed brighter against her eyelids when she blinked. Uncle laughed at her face as he lifted it away again. "Nothing to be afraid of. They're just sculpted phosphenes. But see, off the net we have no content." Later, when she happened to mention it to Mom, Uncle had come in for a full afternoon of angry threats of reprisal from his sister, so he hadn't let her wear it again, curious though Sandy had been. And not long afterward it had stopped working for him anyway, despite every fix he tried. He'd gone rather quiet for a long time, after that.

Dust motes swam in the cold shaft of daylight. The floor of the Space was broad and open. Soon enough she would be missed. But for a few moments she spread her arms wide and spun round, round, round in circles, precessing around the room in a whirling dance. Her feet scuffed and printed in the dust. Around her the world began slowly to revolve. When she stopped, staggering, she still could feel it spinning on under her feet.

Pan, left alone outside, scratched remindingly at the wall. She hissed, "I'm right here, I'll be out in a minute." This was not satisfactory to him, and he marked his displeasure with a bark. "Shut up, Pan, Dad will hear. All right, I'm coming."

ॐ

Uncle Tanner leaned on the fence with a bemused, dismayed expression as Dad jacked up the pickup. "Seriously? Are we in the Middle Ages here?"

"If you have an alternative, Tanner, let me know."

Mr. Martinez had put in harness his black mare from the pasture by, and contrived to hitch her to a small flatbed trailer that had been sitting abandoned in a nearby lot for some time. She drew it, but both tires were long flat. Dad was swapping them out temporarily with the spare and one tire off the pickup. When they were on, Mr. Martinez clucked and the mare trotted out, looping around the crossroads and back in front of the house. Juan clung to the back of the trailer, whooping.

Mr. Martinez shrugged. "*Mira, ella va bien.*"

"Bien enough, Gustavo," Dad said. "Let's try it then."

The tools and gear were piled into the trailer and they set off. Uncle Tanner muttered something about living this down, and zipped ahead of them on his motor-scooter. Zack and Sandy walked on the shoulder beside the trailer, while Juan sat on the back, eating an apple. Pan watched his chance, and when Juan tossed the core for him he expertly snagged it out of the air with a leap and a snap. "Good one!"

Gray clouds were tumbling fast overhead, and there was a cold wind in their faces. Zack said, "Maybe we'll get snow."

"I hope we do," Sandy replied. "I want to see it finally."

9

"You have seen it before, you just don't remember because you were only one."

"That doesn't count."

Corbin Creek was not too far, just on the other side of Fourteen and down the cross road. Mr. Martinez touched his heart as they passed close to the cemetery where his wife and other son had lain since the flu three years back. The older headstones stood upright with names weathered and blurred, but some newer ones were smooth and black, showing silvery photographs of the departed. The newest were simple stone rectangles, laid modestly flush to the ground and hardly visible from the road. Corbin Creek was dry, as usual. As they went down into the draw the mesquite closed in thick around them, crowding among the few larger, older trees. "It sure has changed since I was a kid," Dad muttered. Uncle Tanner was waiting for them, impatiently, at the old picnic grounds.

Kids were waved back as the chainsaw roared to life. To one side of the trailer they piled silvery deadwood for immediate use; there was plenty enough of that where a tornado had cut a swath two years before. On the other side were stacked lengths of fresh-cut mesquite limbs, to be seasoned next year by the weather. These were treacherous with thorns, and despite their tough gloves every one of them caught stabs and scratches on their hands and arms. "Damn! This stuff is vicious!" Zack cried. "Why couldn't it have stayed in Texas?"

Dad said, "Nasty indeed, but it'll burn well next winter. Mesquite's good for that."

Tired, Sandy sat on an old fire ring. Pan nosed in under her arm. Uncle Tanner stood over them, stretching the small

10

of his back. "He never parts from you, does he? Guess we named him right. Not that either one of you is clean. Little Sandy, you're looking a mite dusty." His laugh creaked, and he gulped from his canteen. "Dustier every day."

When they had finished the cutting and loading, the mare drew the trailer in a half-loop through a picnic space and, walking behind her, they started back toward the highway. Zack said to Dad, "So work's going to be thin at the store, I guess?"

Dad grimaced. "Looks like."

"I might could find work somewhere else. Should I be thinking about it?"

"Could come to that; but I wouldn't want to see it if we can help it."

"There was a bulletin for reclamation workers in Pueblo last week."

Dad laughed harshly. "Definitely not Pueblo. Any hazard pay they offer's there for a reason. Do me a favor and don't even mention that one to Mom. The plume's too close for comfort here as it is. We don't want to see you living in it."

Zack nodded. "I know. It would come with a conscription waiver, though."

"Even so. Let's see if we can work something better than that."

Uncle Tanner rode slowly behind them on the scooter, weaving deliberately back and forth and chatting with Mr. Martinez. Pan started a jackrabbit from the roadside and gave chase in full bark. Hopelessly outdistanced after a few moments, he stopped and ambled back toward them, panting. Sandy fell back to holler at him, and together they followed the trailer back.

They arrived back home with a full load of wood, nobody having said boo to them over how it was acquired. A few pieces of tornado-drift blazing in the stove warmed the house up considerably. Dad and Zack went back out to open up the store for the remainder of the afternoon.

Later that evening, as Sandy was lying in bed with her door cracked open to admit the heat, she heard Mom and Dad talking at the kitchen table.

Dad said, "McAlister's place may need a hand."

"I would not be pleased to give Zack over to a bastard like Joseph McAlister."

"I know. But on the other hand, you think he's likely to stand by and let his ranch help be plucked? He has connections. And back there past the buttes it's his own little kingdom. Not likely that a conscription squad is even going to venture back there."

"Yes… well, why don't you ask Tanner to give him a call? See if it's an option."

"A better one than Venezuela or the Springs plume, eh?"

A couple of days later Uncle Tanner knocked and said he had Joe McAlister on the shortwave. Mom and Dad got Zack and went over to talk. Sandy was not invited, but she was curious. She slipped in after.

McAlister's voice crackled with static. "Listen. I do have a hand who's going off to Nebraska. So I have an opening in February. Not before then. "

Dad looked across the table at Zack, who shrugged and nodded. "Speak up," Mom whispered sharply.

"I'd be happy to start in February," Zack said.

"We'll try you out. I warn you, expect early rising, long hours, hard work. I've seen plenty of kids come here and wash out. If you do, no favors. Got it?"

Zack frowned. "Fair enough."

They talked a while longer about Mr. McAlister's expectations. There were quite a lot of them. Sandy slipped out and went back home. Zack going away... but it sounded like it was a good thing. She sat on her bed and looked through her books while it was still light. The night of the ball... the fairies of spring and autumn, summer and winter. She believed she had seen one once, a glint of light passing among the weedstalks as night fell. Pan jumped up and lay against her for a while to be scratched, and turned his head to nibble affectionately, gently, on her nose.

She woke up late next morning hearing Pan beside her, panting, harshly, as loud as if he'd just run a mile. He didn't stop, and she got out of bed and knelt down by him. "You okay? Come on then, let's go outside."

Pan got to his feet, moving heavily. Concerned, she led him to the back door and let him out. She turned to put her shoes on, and opened the door again to go after him, and saw him collapse in the middle of the yard by the garden bed.

She left the door wide and ran out to him where he lay, and the terrible panting had stopped. There was a tremor in his body, a harsh gagging noise in his throat, and his head moved limply as she cradled him in her arms. She tried to pick him up but he slumped away from her. His belly was strangely swollen and soft.

Soon Mom and Dad were awake, and Zack, but there was nothing they could do either. Pan was dead. She sat there in the dirt with him, feeling a rift opening across her heart, a place that had been inhabited by his warm presence, his lively play and companionship and love, and was now empty space.

ॐ

The ground was cold but not frozen. Dad worked with the spade and made a pit waist-deep. Zack wrapped Pan in an old blanket and set him gently down into the earth with a bone between his paws. They said goodbye and Dad covered him with earth.

Dad said, "Nine years is too young to lose a dog."

ॐ

Her room was empty of Pan when she woke up next morning, late. She came into the kitchen. Dad and Zack were already gone. "I really miss him," she told Mom.

"I know, sweetheart. Mr. Zimmer said it was probably a cancer that grew on his heart. Sometimes it comes sudden like that and you don't know until it happens."

"He was the best dog ever. Is he in heaven now?"

Mom dabbed at her eye and turned away to scour at a dish. "Yes, he was a good dog. But. You know only people have souls, sweetheart."

The storm rising invisibly in her chest stopped her speech. She found herself turning and pawing at the door, slapping against the screen. In the yard she sank down by the turned earth and hugged her knees to her chest. After a while it was cold. She didn't much care.

The door creaked and there was movement on the porch. Mom hesitated there, watched her. "Come back in?"

"Not yet."

14

Later yet, she heard steps coming up the street. Zack was back early, and he didn't say anything when he saw her. He knelt down behind her and put his arms around her and held her there for a long time, rocking a little. His chest was warm against her back, and she felt shivers begin to unlock, and they shook her and turned to sobs that racked her small body. Eventually she was still, and sweating, and cold. She turned a clod of clay in her hand and gripped it tight. It fell away printed with the shape of the inside of her fist. Zack helped her up and they came inside.

The next day Juan found her sitting by Pan again. This time she had put on her warmest clothes and coat, so she could stay out longer. He squatted on his heels beside her. "Okay?"

"Not really."

"*Tengo una cosa.* For you. *Si lo quieres.*"

"*Que es*, then?" she said.

"She can help him, Pan, make his travel. *Guiandolo. Al otro mundo.*" From inside his coat he drew a pale plastic figurine the size of his hand, a skeleton garlanded with flowers. "Santa Muerte."

She took the figurine in her hand, frowning. "Is she good or bad?"

"Not good, not bad. *Pero ella viene al fin de cada vida.* For the travel."

"For dogs too?"

Juan cocked his head, shrugged. "*Cada vida, creo que sí.*"

She nodded. "Okay. *Gracias.*" She set down the figurine by the fence, where it could watch over the turned earth.

Juan gestured with finger and thumb. "*Tienes algunas monedas?*"

There were some pennies in her pocket. Juan took them from her hand and set them down in two stacks at the right and left hands of the figure. "*Santísima Muerte, ayuda por favor nuestro perro Pan. Tiene que hacer su viaje al otro mundo. Guialo, por favor.*"

He sat with her quietly a minute, then rose to his feet and let her be.

࿐

Next evening a call came on the shortwave, from Mom's friend Janey Nichols. She was crying. A conscription squad had just swept in and impressed her son and four other boys in Ault. Just down the road.

Fear moved through the house like smoke. Mom and Dad were arguing in the kitchen. McAlister had been crystal clear about Zack not starting until February.

Sandy sidled into Zack's room. He was sitting on his chair with his elbows on his knees, whittling long ribbons off of a white stick with his pocket-knife.

"I don't want the drafters to take you away. They're going to make you get killed."

"I don't particularly want to go."

"Listen, Zack. I know how to get into the Space. I can show you how. There's a place where no one can see you. I have blankets there to keep you warm, and you can stay there for a long time when they come."

Zack smiled, shook his head. "Little Sandy. I'm not going to hide. It'll be okay. Go to bed."

It was cold in her room. She wrapped up in the blankets and tried to go to sleep. Still no Pan. All dark except for a

16

distant lightpole way out on Fourteen, which gave a bluish backlighting to the window pane. There were shapes on the glass that she had never seen before, white frosty spikes like sharp leaves and flowers. It was like one of the pictures in the book, where the Ice Fairy had reached out a finger to touch a pool of still water and rays of pointy blue and white shapes sprang out across the surface. She thought that they were growing as she watched.

ॐ

Opening her eyes, she saw she was in a tall circular chamber, dimly lit like the Space but immense, and spotlessly clean of any dust. Climbing up the vast walls to the rounded ceiling high above were carved images of roses in red and green. The floor was cool, pale, made of some stone smoother than any she had ever felt. Far away music was playing. A ballroom. As her eyes adjusted to the dimness, she saw that she was not quite alone. Scattered here and there on the expanse of the floor, far far into the distance, there were people, old and young, sitting quietly or patiently lying down with their heads pillowed on their arms. They didn't look at her or at each other. They seemed to be waiting. And not only people; not far away there was an orange tabby cat sitting and licking its paws, there a newborn antelope, and beyond it a sparrow resting with its head tucked under its wing.

Walking out onto the floor among them, she realized that the floor was not uniformly pale and unmarked as she had first thought. There were many large oblong black shapes printed on its surface, as smooth as the rest of the white floor, each as big as her bed or bigger. An old man nodded to her in silent greeting as she passed by, and then looked away. He sat at the center of one of the markings. And looking about she saw that every other person or animal rested within its own black rounded shape.

Not every one of the shapes was occupied; the nearest was not. But when she came closer she saw that there was a lifelike picture traced into it in silvery lines – the image of a spotted horse. In another, there was a burly man wearing a mining helmet; then a frail old woman; a fence lizard; an infant girl. And then she saw the image of the dog, the flopped ears and rough coat and soft muzzle that she knew. Pan. She knelt down and ran her fingers across the image. It was cool and smooth.

The music had become louder. And far away across the chamber she saw a great swaying shape, swinging slowly and gracefully from darkness into some curtain of light falling from above. It was enormous, or perhaps she was very small. Bony arms smoothly upraised, suspended for a moment, falling with wrist inturned in a graceful arc. Silvery bells upon the fingers and ankles rang as they moved. A noseless face with shadowed eye sockets, turning to regard the sculpted roses at one side and another. A wiry flow of something like hair dangling and swaying behind the white dome of the skull. Skeletal legs and feet rattling and scraping upon the floor with each great step, accompanying the rhythm of the music.

Santa Muerte was dancing.

Her body turned and spun across the ballroom, drawing closer, never looking down, unconscious of the girl or of anything but the music and the movement. And with every step her immense bony foot would fall squarely upon one of the black shapes on the floor. The footprints marked for the

18

dance. Closer, towering high above, and the old man who had nodded at Sandy was overshadowed. He glanced up for a moment, without fear, before the twinned pillar of the leg moved toward him and he crumpled and vanished under the foot. She poised and turned on the center of balance and danced on, passing by swiftly with a ringing of bells but with no wind of her passage. The old man was gone, but a silvery portrait of him looked back at Sandy from the footprint of Santa Muerte.

With a leap and a half-pirouette the dancer swung about and passed around toward the other side of the ballroom. And not far away Sandy saw a young man lying on the floor, turning toward her in his sleep. It was Zack.

She ran toward him and shook his arm, but she couldn't rouse him. He only murmured and turned to his other side. – Zack! Wake up! Desperately she grasped his shirt and tried to haul him over from the black stone to the white, but she couldn't move him. He seemed fixed. In the distance she saw Santa Muerte turning again, circling to return. She shook Zack again and, as the music swelled again and she heard the great steps approaching, finally shrieked and fled.

Sandy cowered back against the wall of the ballroom. There was a window there, ringed with white flowers of frost. On the other side a tall lovely woman looked in at her. She was dressed in flowing silks of white and palest blue. Her arms were bare; her hair was unbound and the color of snow. Something wavered and blurred in motion behind her shoulders.

Sandy waved and cried out to her –Can you hear me?

–Yes. I am– and the Ice Fairy spoke her name, a word that Sandy could never after remember.

Sandy dared not look behind her. There was the sound and tremor of immense graceful steps, a rattling and a jingling. She mustered her courage. –Will you give me three wishes?

–Once, Little Sandy, I could give three. But I am not so strong as I once was. Now I can only give you one.

She opened her eyes. It was morning. The frost flowers had covered the whole of her windowpane, and she could not see outside. Mom and Dad were talking in the kitchen.

"Don't worry about provisions. Plenty in the cellar for a few weeks. You may get bored with oatmeal."

"Just as well we brought in the wood when we did, though."

"So you were right."

"Chalk one up for me, then."

Mom cackled. "Have you ever seen the like? Fifteen inches and never a halt."

"So much for global warming, eh?" Dad said brightly. They both laughed out loud at that.

That was how Sandy liked hearing their voices – alternating back and forth in easy volleys, considering problems and working out how to solve them. This morning they didn't sound afraid.

She stepped out into the hall. Zack was standing there, his arms folded, looking out the window of the front door. He cast her a wry look. "You know, I had been planning to go into town and find you some more picture books. For Christmas. But it's looking like I may not have a chance."

Yesterday's fear came rushing back for a moment. But he nodded toward the door. "Look."

White snow was softly streaming down out of a white sky.

During the night it had heaped in rounded cushions on the porch and the railing and the fence. There were a few footprints, already filling with drift, where Zack had gone out earlier and stamped a ways onto the walk. Down the street Mr. Martinez was shoveling snow in front of his house. The fields stretching out from the yard were white, and the snow had smoothed them together with the road, and out on Fourteen—Fourteen was gone. She could not tell anymore quite where it had been. Anyway the falling snow was coming down thick and steady, in gently drifting feathery clusters of flakes, and she wasn't sure she could see that far at all. Out there the horizon had blended with the sky. One thing was certain, though, she realized. Nobody was going to be coming this way from Ault for days or weeks.

In later years that was how she told it to her grandchildren and great-grandchildren, on summer nights after a hard day's ranging, when they would sit with her and the rest of the clan around a little campfire far out on the escarpment. Not that she ever mentioned the Ice Fairy; as she grew that scrap of dream had come to seem a bit silly, and by the time Little Sandy had passed through so many years to become Old Alexandra she had mostly forgotten it. But sure she remembered the snowfall that morning, waking to see how it had come down upon them everywhere from some far place in the sky, making the range all as cold and white as the bright clouds above and sheltering Zack under its mantle for the little space of time he needed.

She never did see another one.

A Dead Art Form

By Calvin Jennings

"Debray!" bellowed Fulton, the echo of his deep voice reverberating up and down the tunnels. "Debray, are you up there? Toss down the ladder! I came all the way from the village in the rain to make sure you weren't dead, and for all that you had better have a cup of tea ready for me! I mean it, you damn Yankee bastard, I'm going to be very fucking upset if you're dead and there's no tea to be had!"

In spite of the acerbity of his words, Fulton's voice was edged with a friendly sarcasm, the kind that develops between two men when they've had years to learn how to rag on each other without causing offence. Because of this Debray took his time in responding, pausing to compose another sentence and then to light the burner for their tea water. With these tasks accomplished he picked up a lantern and headed down the tunnel towards the sound of his friend's voice.

"Okay, I hear your shuffling," continued Fulton. "You're alive. I'm still going to be angry if there's no tea, though."

Approaching the end of the tunnel, Debray looked down at Fulton, who stood some twenty feet below him in a wet raincoat, and with a grimy old duffel bag tucked under his arm. In the thin light from the electric bulb he could see Fulton smile at him as he used his free hand to wring some of the water out of his bushy gray beard.

Debray unhooked the rope ladder and tossed it down to him. With amazing spryness for a man in his mid-seventies, Fulton proceeded to climb it, the arthritis in his knees barely slowing him. When he reached the top of the ladder he extended his hand to Debray, who helped him step off and into the tunnel. They shook each other's hands before letting go and Debray took Fulton's coat.

"I see the rain hasn't yet let up," he remarked as he hung up the slippery, dripping garment.

"Of course it hasn't let up. Why the hell would it let up now? It isn't June on this damn island unless your basement is flooded and your roof is leaking," Fulton muttered, following Debray down the tunnel towards his living quarters. "In all seriousness, please tell me that there's tea."

"Give it fifteen minutes."

Debray's living area was large compared to many of the other rooms carved underneath the mountain, measuring perhaps twelve meters by ten. Fulton sat down at the table and emitted an exasperated grunt, once again wringing raindrops from his beard. The water for the tea was almost ready by that point and Debray remained standing while they waited, even though standing was becoming increasingly difficult for him. Every time he stood, every time he moved, every time he stayed on his feet for more than a few minutes the pounding in his chest returned and his breath became short. If he breathed too deeply he would cough uncontrollably, and if he started to cough uncontrollably he would also become dizzy. So as they waited for the water to boil he tried not to inhale too intensely, even though he felt a cloud of phlegm again growing in his lungs. Yet a moment came when he could not control it any longer and the coughing fit that followed ripped through his body with such force that he doubled over, grabbing the table for support.

After perhaps thirty seconds of hacking and gurgling he managed to subdue the cough. He spit out a cloudy yellow ball of mucus, only to then look up and see Fulton staring at him warily, sizing up the state of his health. Fulton obviously knew how sick his host really was, even though he chose not to mention it.

"I brought your mail for you," he instead remarked in an absentminded tone. "You got a package and don't worry, I made every effort to keep it dry for you." He then produced a thick wad of letters from his bag, followed by a rectangular parcel wrapped in waterproofed materials. Pulling these off, he saw the shipping envelope had a Portsmouth postmark. He knew that it could only be one thing, and so he gingerly tore it open.

Inside was a black rectangular case, the kind of plastic container used to protect videocassettes. It was dingy and well worn, but the label was entirely readable in neat, black type:

UNDERWATER TREASURES OF MOUNT DESERT ISLAND
RUNNING TIME: 52:35:18
1920x1080 (P) – 23.976 fps
LANGUAGE: ENGLISH
AUDIO CHANNELS: 4

Debray smiled. Yes, he had been waiting for this one for a long time. His hands were dry, yet as a precaution he wiped them on a towel and carefully opened the case. Inside was an HDCAM SR videocassette. Considering its age, the tape was in excellent condition; more than likely it had only been played a few times over its life.

"I can see this is a good one," remarked Fulton. "I can also see that our tea water is boiling, so let's perhaps hurry this up."

Over tea the two men caught up, with Fulton providing him all the relevant and irrelevant information from the village. In truth there wasn't much to tell, for the past eight days of rain had kept people mostly indoors. There were, however, press reports about yet another political scandal embroiling the ruling party in Halifax, and despite the unending downpour the bridge to the mainland was now almost fully repaired. Then, with their tea finished, Debray picked up his lantern and beckoned for Fulton to follow him.

The tunnels underneath the mountain were not natural caverns. They had been dug and blasted out by the rebels, who had been given almost four years to work on the project before the old United States government had made a serious move to capture the island. Even with that time the effort had remained far from complete, with only five of the island's twenty-odd mountains having been excavated when the Marines had landed, and with three of those excavations still incomplete at the time. This mountain they were under now – Norumbega it was called – had been one of the smaller efforts, and so it had been fully finished at the time of the invasion. With its network of carefully laid out rooms and passageways, electrical wiring and drainage and ventilation systems, it had remained remarkably intact despite the bombs and shells raining down overhead. The tunnels were all high enough for fully-grown men to walk through, with smooth floors and vertical corkscrew-shaped alleys that had allowed supplies and weapons to be transported on wheels. Following the end of the war a speculator had purchased all of the excavated mountains in the hope of turning them into tourist attractions, but he had found that few people were interested and had sold off all but one of them. Norumbega was too steep and barren for farming or lumbering, and too far from the village for it to be an attractive home, which had allowed Debray to purchase it very cheaply.

At the entrance to the archive Debray put the lantern down and flipped the light switch. His own personal rule was to never bring a candle or a lantern through that door, even though the electricity for the lights was quite expensive. For the benefit of visitors he kept a single bulb burning at the front entrance of the tunnels, but otherwise he mostly used candles and lanterns for his personal illumination. But the archive was different, for candles and lanterns could start fires and the archive was filled with irreplaceable items.

He pulled out his keys and unlocked the door. Entering the enormous, chilly room, the two men gazed upon a collection nearly forty years in the making. Once this had been the sleeping quarters for sixty rebels, their bunk beds stacked high against the walls. Now those same walls were lined with shelves, their contents organized by format and title. On one side were the celluloid films, starting with 8mm formats and continuing to 16mm and 35mm and even one lone random reel of a 70mm print. To another side were the "home" formats – DVDs, Blu-Rays, Ultra 4k discs, videocassettes of every size and format. Still to another side were stacks of hard drives, small projectors, spare parts, splicing machines, batteries, obsolete disc players, ancient televisions and antiquated cameras, all sealed in dustproof containers.

Fulton retrieved the ladder and Debray let his friend make the climb towards the middle shelf, pointing him to where the tape needed to go. But as Debray went to hand it to Fulton he descended into another fit of coughing. His lungs burned with every exhalation and he closed his eyes until it was over with. When he opened them again he found himself staring at the case in his hand, which was dripping with phlegm and dark blood. He locked eyes with Fulton.

"I have an extra," he said in an embarrassed manner. Searching for and finding a case of the same size, he copied down the program information onto the new label and transferred the videotape to its new receptacle. The cassette was fine, none of his bodily fluids had gotten onto it, but Debray was genuinely mortified.

"Yeah, you're not staying here, man," Fulton said to him in the most direct manner possible. "You're coming back to the house and you're staying with us until that cough is under control."

Debray went through the motions of protesting. The archive needed his attention, he said. His work wasn't finished and he was in the middle of too many projects. Yet he didn't put up too much resistance, for he knew that Fulton would insist and in truth he no longer had a desire to stay in these awful, cold tunnels. Yes, his work wasn't finished and yes, he was in the middle of too many projects. Yet he didn't particularly care any longer if he was the one who finished them or even if anyone ever did. His body was overtaxed, his mind was cluttered and his ability to concentrate was waning. His resistance was a mere formality.

"Fine, I'll go with you if it will shut you up!" he finally exclaimed after Fulton threatened to knock him over the head and have him carried back to the village.

∾

They exited the tunnels into the worst downpour that Debray had seen in years and their progress was slow. The wind was howling, the rain was coming down at extreme angles and their feet and pants were thoroughly soaked as they made their way down the winding path through the woods.

Like the other settlements on Mount Desert Island, the village of Northeast Harbor had begun its life as a fishing and farming community near the end of the eighteenth century. A hundred years after it was settled it had started to grow into a summer colony, first as a seasonal getaway for clergymen and professors, then as a haven for Astors and Rockefellers and other prominent families. Now nearly three centuries later it had returned to its roots, for despite its increasing prominence as a commercial port, many of the families still derived part of their livelihood either from tending the land or harvesting the sea.

Unlike Debray, Fulton was not a native of the village, or even of the province of Maine. He had been born in Georgia, now several national borders to the south. As a U.S. Marine during the war years he had been sent to the island as part of the garrison that had kept order there after the invasion. But as the U.S. government itself began to unravel, so did its far-flung military units. "Getting anything out of the government

29

was like trying to get something out of one of those old credit card companies," was the way Fulton had always described it. "Towards the last of it you could barely even get a human being on the phone at the Pentagon." Unable to find a way back to Georgia, Fulton had simply taken off his uniform, walked into the nearest village and asked for a job. Forty years later he was still here, making a steady living repairing machinery and fabricating metal parts and tools for the sailing ships that gathered in the harbor.

Fulton's house was too large for a single-family home, but of course he did not inhabit it alone. Besides his wife the structure was also occupied by his youngest son and his daughter-in-law, plus their three children and eight of Fulton's interns. The couch in the living room pulled out into a bed, and it was here that Debray found himself. For the first two days he was weak, yet he still had an appetite and was able to move about the house and sit at the table for meals. That lasted until the doctor came and saw his condition, ordering him to get into his sofa bed and stay there. Debray – with Fulton's vaguely threatening encouragement – did as he was told, and on the third day he burned with fever and slipped into a delirium.

The days that followed were barely noticed by him, for he passed in and out of consciousness at irregular intervals. Sleep was easy for him in his weakened state, despite the activity around him. The noise from the workshop gave a rhythm to his waking moments as he lay there on his back, listening to the sounds of grinding and spinning and welding and Fulton screaming at the interns to bring him his tea. The rain on the roof, the door to the house opening and closing as customers came and went, the never-ending drone of the weather radio, the scuffle from the shoes of grandchildren who had been cooped up inside too long, these bothered him not at all.

His grip on the physical world wore thinner with each passing day and soon the doctor returned. Debray was vaguely aware that he was being examined, for even with his mind in a far-off place he was still cognizant of the stethoscope's chilly touch and the pinch of the blood pressure cuff around his bicep. The physician administered a drug to control the delirium, and during the ensuing period of lucidity he managed to overhear what the doctor told Fulton:

"There's no sense in putting him in a hospital bed. At his age, in his condition, there's nothing anyone can do," the man explained in a dour voice. "He's got a week at the very most."

So, it was official: he was going to die soon. Well, it was about fucking time, he thought. At this point he was only too happy to cross over to the other side. No matter what waited for him there, at least he wouldn't be here anymore. Nobody cared, and with his end so close he wasn't going to either. Yes, death could come for him any time now, and damn everybody else. Not even Fulton, his best and only remaining friend, understood.

From the youngest age possible to remember, Debray had loved the movies. He had grown up in Northeast Harbor when it had still been a summer colony, and the winters had brought boring, bleak stretches in a depopulated community. He lived for after school and for the weekends, when he could escape to invented worlds. He would watch movies on Netflix and on DVD and Blu-Ray and he would download

31

them onto his iPhone and iPad. When new films didn't interest him he turned to old ones, devouring the classics of every decade going back to the early years of the twentieth century. It was such a wonderful way to escape. His childhood had been materially comfortable, but it would have been psychologically unbearable for him had he not had these to help him cope with the drudgery of school and the never ending pile of homework that stalked him through afternoons and weekends and summer breaks.

After college he had naturally gravitated towards Hollywood, although when he had arrived he had found a city and an industry in deep crisis. Nobody was making a profit except for the biggest names in the business, everyone was trying to get you to work for free, or, if not for free, then for some piddling amount of money. He prostituted his talents for contacts and experience, dodging debt collectors and landlords at the same time. He worked eighteen-hour days on shoots, he spent hours hunched over at his computer editing and sound mixing for projects. He barely paid attention to the problems outside of Los Angeles, to the political dysfunction ripping apart the country or to the epic drought that was slowly killing the southwest. And after years of writing and re-writing his script, of taking meetings and asking – no, begging – for money, he finally got the chance to direct a feature film of his very own. And although that film had not turned out as well as he had hoped and had not received distribution outside of a few festival screenings, he had still been immensely proud of it.

But that had been so long ago now. He had been forced to move back to Maine, back to Northeast Harbor, not long after that. Then the wars came and the island had been taken over by the militia. Debray himself had been a corporal. Not by choice; as an able-bodied islander he had simply been conscripted. He was lucky, though, for he had ended up as a POW after being wounded by a mortar shell. Many of his friends had not lived to see the end of it.

Both his Hollywood period and the war period played through his mind as he lay expiring on Fulton's sofa bed. So did the time after the wars, the time when the Republic had been first founded and he had set about to see what could be salvaged of the film work that he and others had done. He was never able to find a copy of his own movie, but he had collected anything else that he could get his hands on—equipment, tape masters, consumer video products, hard drives, film reels. But the job got harder and harder as the years went on. It had been called the film *industry* after all, and all the complex pieces of equipment needed to produce and to watch movies, all the software and computers and cameras and projection systems, almost all of it had been made overseas, and after the wars it had become frightfully expensive to import what had been needed. Then one by one the foreign factories began to close, and soon there came a day when it could no longer be acquired at any price.

Realizing that his preservation efforts required more time and money than he could supply he had, some five or six years earlier, taken the ferry to Halifax in the hope of securing parliamentary recognition and funding for the archive. He managed to arrange a meeting with a representative named Stockton, MP for the northern district of New Hampshire and chairman for the Committee on the Arts. Stockton was a tall, gangly man in his early forties who reeked of pipe tobacco and inhabited a dreary third-floor office with frosted windows.

Stockton listened politely as Debray made all of the familiar points. He started by asking, in a rhetorical sense, what was culture? Culture was the great conversation between the dead, the living and the yet-to-be-born he explained. It was the conversation that carried on over decades and centuries, which crossed borders and passed on the best values of the deceased nations – the United States and Canada in this case—into the living realm of the new ones, especially their own. He reminded the man of the importance that motion pictures had once had to the two cultures that had preceded them and explained the deplorable state of preservation of that art form. He described the tragedy of digital technology and the film industry's embrace of it. Sturdy, modestly priced film cameras and film projectors that could be used for decades had given way to obscenely expensive digital cameras and digital projectors that required complex and pricey maintenance every couple of years. Stable motion picture film stocks with long shelf lives had given way to less durable videotape formats and then finally to computerized storage on hard drives that had to be constantly maintained and monitored. He told of how many movies had never existed on film at all, how they had been shot and archived on video and had then been left to rot on those same hard drives and imprisoned on cassette formats for which there was no longer the equipment to play. He told of how, even for the motion pictures that did exist on film, that film was often rotting away too.

"Mr. Debray, a seat on my committee is not something that one aspires to," Stockton said in reply. "Nonetheless, I try my best to fulfill the responsibilities that it is tasked with. However, there is scant funding available for an initiative such as the one you propose. Our appropriations for individual projects rarely exceed fifty thousand dollars. Look at it this way - ten years ago we had a cholera outbreak in my district, thousands of people sickened. Two years after that we were at war in Estrie and Labranche's army shelled my district. They shelled it repeatedly. They killed hundreds of my constituents and did millions of dollars in damage and – by the way – they destroyed the drainage systems that had been put in place after the outbreak, the result of which was a return of cholera. And that cholera is still with us, every year hundreds sickened.

"Now you come to me and say you want three million dollars for this project. You seem to assume that I can raise that kind of money from my colleagues. Yet even if I could get them to allocate money for your project, how would I explain to my constituents that, even though I was able to get someone three million dollars to preserve movies in another province, I was not able to get them a comparable sum for the repair of the rest of the drainage systems? And how would my colleagues explain their support to their constituents? Most of them represent districts where there is some other vital need that is only being attended to slowly, if at all.

"No, Mr. Debray, it will not happen. I do understand the importance of your work. If you wish to fundraise for your archive I will be happy to write a letter for you extolling its importance. If you schedule an event within reasonable distance of me I will be happy to speak at that event and extol its importance to an audience. But I can provide no help through parliament at this time. I'm very sorry."

Stockton had a way with words; never before had someone told Debray to fuck off in such a polite manner. Well, no matter, it was over now. He was leaving and he was glad, and with the last bit of energy left in him he opened his eyes and smiled. The years spent building a career that had fallen flat, the years spent trying to preserve what had once been, it was over now. And it had all been such a god damn waste.

≈

At half past two Fulton awoke, feeling the familiar tightness in his pelvis that always manifested itself about this time. He lit a candle and went downstairs to the bathroom, where he urinated with the expected difficulties of his age. Finishing the process, he made a detour into the living room to check on his friend.

Immediately upon entering he knew what he was about to find, for the room had an awful stillness and silence about it that it had not possessed on all the other nights when Fulton had checked on Debray. There wasn't the slightest movement now, nor the slightest sound apart from the rain on the roof. Fulton went to the couch and pulled back the blanket.

Debray's breathing had long since stopped, but the smile was still on his face and his eyes remained open. Glassy and lifeless now, they gazed up towards the ceiling. In death the expression was ghastly, and Fulton used the palm of his hand to shut his pupils and then he sculpted Debray's mouth into a neutral position.

Yes, he thought, it was better that it had happened at night. Not better for Debray perhaps, but better for Fulton, for Fulton would have been too self-conscious to cry if it had happened when the family and the interns were around. But here, at quarter to three, in an empty room, he felt no shame in taking hold of his friend's hand and weeping inconsolably.

"Damn you for making me sob like this, I ought to throttle you for it," he whimpered. And then after some time had passed he broke free of the grip and covered Debray with the blanket. He locked the doors to the room so that no early risers would get a surprise from the body and he returned to bed, tears still welling up in his eyes whenever he thought of the long decades he had known the man.

かな

Debray's will left Fulton with a very unwelcome responsibility:

"To my dear friend Arnold 'Warrant' Fulton I leave the Norumbega Motion Picture Archive, along with the property it sits on, with instructions that he care for it until some individual or entity can be found to take over its operations on a permanent basis."

It was the last obligation that Fulton wanted, so for a time he ignored it and concentrated on other matters, especially the arrangements for Debray's funeral. It was not until a few weeks later that he began to give the task some serious thought.

Fulton knew that Debray had not been alone in his efforts, that there were others out there who ran similar operations. They were listed in Debray's address book, he had been in contact with all of them at one point or another. While none of the other archives were in the Republic itself, a number of them were in other parts of North America. And so Fulton composed letters informing the proprietors of

Debray's death and inquiring about the possibility of their institutions taking possession of the archive's holdings.

As the replies came in over the weeks that followed it became obvious to Fulton that he was never going to disperse more than a fraction of the archive in this way. All of the replies offered praise for Debray and condolences at his passing, but none of them offered the kind of help he needed. Some of the replies cited a lack of space, others explained that they were in serious financial jeopardy and could not guarantee the safety of their own holdings, let alone Debray's. Some of the institutions were interested in taking possession of specific movie titles held by the archive, but none of them could accept the whole collection.

When Fulton had a problem he couldn't figure out, a problem that nobody alive could help him with, he would imagine himself in conversation with those people who were no longer living, people whom he had respected during their lifetimes. His parents, his sister, his dead friends and commanding officers from the Corps, he had asked all of them for help at some point. And now that Debray was dead he could join the chorus. He imagined his friend standing over him while he labored in his workshop, he pictured him walking alongside of him as he trekked into the village to collect the mail. For days he simply did this without imagining a dialogue. He didn't know how to start it until he thought of one question to ask:

"Why should anyone care about the movies any longer? It's a dead art form."

"Because this was an enormous part of our culture," the imaginary Debray explained, and then he launched into his familiar spiel about the conversation between the dead, the living and the unborn. It was all familiar – and banal – to Fulton, so he cut off the monologue and tried a slightly different line of questioning.

"Okay, but why did you care? What did they mean to you?"

"They were an escape," the imaginary Debray responded after a long pause. "They gave my dreams a form. A form for all my fantasies about what it would be like to be a man, to be out in the world, to finally be able to leave this awful place behind me."

"Nobody wants those dreams anymore," Fulton snapped, suddenly angry. "They're dead, and good riddance. Those dreams were always a cruel joke, I'm glad that I lived long enough to find that out. They weren't real. They could never, ever be real. But they seemed real, so real that you believed the promises they made."

Fulton then thought of the glamorous, sexy women that he'd seen in so many movies, and then he thought of the plain, unattractive island girl he had married. He remembered cinematic action scenes, superheroes battling to save the world and sports cars drag racing to techno music, and then he thought of the skeletal automobiles rusting in junkyards all over the Republic. He remembered the antiseptic old war movies that his grandfather had always watched, then he recalled the rebel officer he'd seen in one battle, vomiting blood and desperately trying to prevent his intestines from spilling out of his punctured gut. Most of all, he remembered the promise of a happy ending, without which no movie seemed complete, and which always came no matter how grave the problems of the plot. To Fulton, that was cruelest part of the movies because it was the greatest betrayal, the broken dream that stung the most.

He felt so unexpectedly emotional that he was uncomfortable with himself, and he abruptly ended the imaginary conversation before he could picture Debray's response. He knew he was being unfair to an art form that had been incredibly diverse, and that there had been plenty of movies that had not conformed to those narrow classifications. They had existed, even if he had never bothered to watch any of them when he was younger.

For many weeks he didn't return to the discussion, and perhaps he would never have returned to it at all except for an encounter at a social event in the village. Fulton had trimmed his beard and put on his best suit to attend a wedding ceremony, and at the reception that followed he had encountered an acquaintance of his who had asked how the movie archive was working out with Debray gone.

"What are movies?" asked the man's daughter, who was perhaps seven years old and was standing nearby. Her father then launched into a confusing, convoluted explanation. He started off well enough by describing movies as stories made up of photographs that moved so quickly that they looked like they were really moving, but lost his train of thought when he attempted to provide specific examples, finally asking the child to imagine her school pageant displayed on the video monitor she had seen on a tour of the *RNS Truro*, a naval vessel that had made a port call in Northeast Harbor the previous Christmas.

Fulton could have explained it much better, yet he simply listened to the man's feeble attempts. This was a person who had not yet been born when the last movies had been exhibited on the island, and who had probably been no more than a small child when the Internet had failed and the last television station had ceased broadcasting. The man did not know the language necessary to explain the concept to someone who didn't understand it at all. And that reawakened an idea in him. He returned to the house, gave his interns the rest of the day off and headed off towards Norumbega Mountain.

In the archive he stared at the shelves, his eyes ignoring the video and disc formats – which he knew were completely unplayable to him – and instead focusing in on the 35mm reels, and then in on the wooden crate against the far wall. He knew that the crate held Debray's disused film projector, a device that had never quite worked properly. Retrieving a crowbar, Fulton proceeded to pry open the side of the container, the heavy slab of wood creaking away from the box and falling to the cavern floor with a muffled thud.

This was not a new idea to him, although he had spent months resisting it by telling himself that he knew nothing about the technical work of running the archive. Yet he had to admit that he had spent three decades watching Debray at work here. Surely he had absorbed *something* of that. And so he peered inside the crate and there, wrapped in clear plastic sheeting, was a large black and silver film projector, and taped to the interior side of the crate was a stack of papers. Fulton took them in his hand and realized they were the operating instructions for the projector, along with a set of blueprints for it and a list written in Debray's neat, cryptic handwriting, a list of parts that he had believed needed replacing.

Fulton felt a wave of excitement sweep across him. Yes, it was by no means certain that he could get the projector working again. But the island still had a steady supply of electricity, expensive as it was, and it was entirely possible that he could fabricate new copies of the faulty parts in his workshop. After all, he had tackled tough repair jobs before, and this one could even be a good learning experience for the interns.

"These 35mm films," Fulton began, summoning the imaginary Debray once again. "There are different types on the shelves up there. Which ones can't be projected?"

"Negatives and internegatives," came the reply.

"Which ones shouldn't be projected?"

"Interpositives."

"That leaves regular old prints, the kind used in theaters before everything got computerized," was Fulton's triumphant reply. Yes, he did know a thing or two. He pulled the ladder towards the film shelf and began to climb. Debray had collected hundreds upon hundreds of film reels and many of them were final release prints. Yet he knew that Debray would have been aghast at the idea of projecting any part of his collection, and he knew exactly what the man would have said to him:

"You can't project any of those films, Warrant. I don't have duplicate film copies of any of them, and for all you know each one of those might be the last celluloid copy left in the entire world. If you were damage it that would be it, a part of it would be lost forever."

"How will I damage it? What if I'm careful?"

"It's not just about being careful," Debray would have pleaded. "These prints only have so many projections in them, each time you run one you bring it closer to the day when it will fall apart on you. You understand? Each time you play it you damage it. You might not be able to see it but the damage is there, that scratch at the end of the third reel just got a little bigger, the sprocket holes on reel ten just got a little wobblier."

Fulton replayed these words several times over as he examined the reels on the shelf, then temporarily put them out of his mind. The labels on each canister included not just the title and film format, but also the year of release, the director and the principal cast members. His eye was caught by one that starred an actor he remembered, and so he pulled out the first reel and brought it down. Putting on a pair of cotton gloves just like Debray had always worn, he got out a magnifying glass and began to examine the film. It didn't take him long to realize that it was actually a pornographic film, and that the actor in question looked incredibly young compared to the way Fulton remembered him.

"If I can get that projector working I'll show this one to the men around here," Fulton said to himself. "Discreetly, of course. Hell, I could probably charge double admission." Yet even as he said it he was haunted by the specter of his friend and his adamant disapproval. Debray had been obsessive about protecting his collection, inventing and refining more and more elaborate precautions to keep it all from harm. That was why he had never made any serious attempt to get the projector working, he had had no motivation because he wasn't comfortable projecting any of his films even once. And even with his friend gone, Fulton knew that he would be uncomfortable in doing what he was planning unless he could justify it to himself. Was his idea necessary? Yes, he thought that it was, and he thought he knew why it was, and so once again he summoned Debray before him and asked why it was so important that the prints be kept from any and all damage.

"You'll be risking a lifetime of work. My work. And the work of everyone who made them," he pictured Debray saying. "All of this needs to be preserved for the day in the future when it can be resurrected again."

"I'm two years older than you are – than you were," was Fulton's response. "I could go just as quickly as you did. If I died tomorrow, do you think my wife would care about this place? Do you think my children would? I'll tell you what the future of this stuff is, it's all going in the trash unless someone who cares takes responsibility for it. And nobody is going to damn well care unless they know it has value. Do you know why you could never make anyone care about this place? Why no one ever gave you money to help run it? It's because you have all this awesome stuff up here but you would never show it to anybody. You were too afraid it would get damaged. All of these things that people could have enjoyed were locked away where nobody even knew you had them. The villagers themselves barely even knew what you were up to out here."

A question strayed into his mind: why was it that Debray been so obsessive about protecting his collection from any possible harm? It was a silly question, really, for deep down Fulton knew the answer. After all, Debray had lost almost everything. And he hadn't just lost most of his family, he had also lost his identity. He had dedicated his career and his life to an art form, only to watch it shrivel and die, his own film, the product of years of work, probably gone forever. He could only imagine how much that had hurt him. It wasn't surprising that he had spent the rest of his life frantically trying to protect the works of others. It looked like his way of coping, but he had never really come to terms with it. No matter how he tried to hide it, Fulton knew that his friend had died a deeply embittered man.

Fulton knew that he was bitter too. Maybe not as much as Debray had been, but it was there, sealed deep within him. He too had lost almost everything. He knew that he had stayed in Maine because he couldn't deal with the prospect of going home and facing what was left, or more accurately, acknowledging all of the things that weren't left. He didn't even know where or how his own parents had died. And like Debray, he had lost his identity. It was not just because he had lost his career but because he had also lost his flag, and that had been what had given his service meaning. He had loved his birth country so much, and after all he had gone through for it he would be damned if he ever loved another country that way. The younger generations didn't understand any of that. They couldn't understand it because they had been born into the cold, gray light of reality and were growing up in a world where life promised meager returns from the start. They had no idea what real loss was or what it felt like to be promised everything and then have it denied.

Thinking about these things brought tears to Fulton's eyes, and he allowed them to come, for the concealment of the archive made him willing to be emotional in ways that he would not normally have been comfortable with.

"God damn you, Debray," he cursed under his breath, wiping tears from his eyes and looking over towards his imaginary friend. "The moment that I cross the Styx I'm coming to find you, and when I find you I'm going to kick your eternal ass for putting me through this." He then closed his eyes and banished Debray to the rear corner of his mind, where he would live alongside all of the other ghosts until needed again. And then the tears stopped.

He went back to Debray's living quarters, where he retrieved paper and pencil and spread the projector blueprints out on the table so that he could copy them. He didn't really need back-ups, but doing this would familiarize him with the inside of the machine and make it less likely that he would accidentally damage something when he did open it up. He would do this several times until he felt ready to start working on it physically. And if he could get it working he would watch what Debray had collected, he would find the good ones, the ones that were worth the time of others. And while some of them might represent dreams that deserved to be dead, surely there were at least a couple worthy of a second life.

Then when he found the ones that deserved to be seen he would show them. He would show them to the village, to the other settlements on the island, to the merchant seamen and the navy crews who visited. He would make sure as many people as possible knew about them, and if he was lucky he would find some young person who would be entranced enough by them to take over the work that Debray had started. And if he had to mangle a few irreplaceable film prints along the way that was just how it was going to be. These remaining movies were going to die someday, they could not last forever. And when they did flare to life for the final time perhaps they would do so while providing form to a dream in someone else, just as they once had for Debray.

But of course before he did any of this he was going to make himself a cup of tea.

Byte Heist

J. M. Hughes

My grandpa liked to quote me a scrap of poem by a man named Yeats:

> *...Things fall apart;*
> *The centre cannot hold;*
> *Mere   anarchy   is   loosed   upon   the   world...*

Why he used to say it, I was never sure, but the first line explained my world. I finished cutting the last bolt holding a section of façade to the tower, killed the torch and stepped back.

Boomer yelled: "Watch out below!" As if anyone would hear him twenty or so stories down—as if anyone would be in an active demolition zone. There was only one problem: the facade didn't fall.

I swore a disgusted "damn it" and stepped back up to search for another bolt or tie or anything that was holding that chunk of concrete and granite to the steel. Nothing.

47

"Get the push sticks." I told Boomer. He scrambled off to where we used them last as I pulled off my face shield.

I took a moment to look out over the Sound. It was a spectacular view for early spring. Beyond the patchwork fields of West Seattle stretched the green line of the peninsula and the snowcapped Olympics. The water gleamed sapphire beyond the dirty brown demarcation line where downtown towers marched like toy soldiers into the water. A wedge shaped section of demolished buildings fanned out below, forming a dock built from compacted rubble. A derrick lifted bundles of I-beams, pipe, electrical wiring, and sheet metal into the hold of a Chinee scrap ship taking on another load of Seattle's best.

Boomer returned, dragging the push sticks, and we placed the tips against the wall and pushed. The façade held till we put our backs in it and then it went with a whoosh and a blast of wind followed by the thud of landing.

We looked at each other and grinned. "Ah, Jeb," Boomer said, "you miss this, you know it."

I snorted and shook my head. "Nope."

The quitting horn sounded. Both of us grinned again. We hustled down the tower, leaving everything where it lay for Monday. Boomer glanced back at me as we reached the exit. "Hey! I'll stand you a beer on the ferry! Seeing how this is your first day of hard work in a while, I know you'll be needing it."

"Bite me, Boom-boom." I rejoined; my usual job was salvage foreman, a recent promotion.

Howard, the senior explorer, materialized beside me, "Something for you to see, Jeb."

"What?"

"Ah, better just come and see."

Howard gave Boomer the stink eye when he made to tag along, so I said, "Maybe we can meet up later."

Boomer shrugged, "Sure, Jeb."

I followed Howard feeling a bit mystified. "Yer father sent me for you," he said.

"Interesting find?"

He shrugged and indicated a wagon. "It's a ways."

We rode in silence in the direction of the Seattle Center; the clop of the horses echoed off the concrete necropolis around me, the buildings all in an advanced state of decay and collapse, the streets choked with rubble and new forest taking root on top of everything.

"*Things fall apart...*" Around the Northwest, that seemed to be the truth. Tacoma, Portland, and even Olympia were fine examples, and they were still living cities. All the tall buildings were in bad shape, being demolished for metals, glass, marble and so on. Everything else much the same, as the old'uns didn't build much to last—except trash.

Seattle, though, died a violent death. Seattle was one of three west coast cities that got nuked. Afterwards, the Disorders finished it off. No one knows who started the war. Lots of theories, China and Russia being the most plausible; they went to war on opposite sides over the Siberian revolution, and then North Korea took the opportunity to settle scores.

Chinee ships are still around. Sometimes Siberian freighters show up trading lumber, gas, or oil for scrap; their presence suggests they won. Who knows? Who cares? It's ancient history.

Others say it was all part of the revolution when the United States went under after the west coast bombing, the Break Up. During the Break Up another unknown destroyed the phones and Internet; I don't know who did it or what the real story is, and again, no one really does, as that knowledge vaporized back when, being digital. Most of what I know comes from Mister Granjeans. He was around when phones, radio, TV, internet all just stopped working one day, leaving everyone in the dark news-wise, and then it got real rough— made the Disorders look positively peaceful.

We arrived before a ten-story building set in a plaza: lots of shattered glass on the southwest side, nuke damage. Mashed office junk was scattered around the small plaza from the riots during the subsequent evacuation, and buried under eighty-five years of leaves, weeds, and accumulated soil.

Across the street sat the deceased Seattle Center: this end dominated by late post-modern whatsit construction of sinuous corroded metal, and the skeleton of that tall tower that had been a monument or something, and now was a mass of crumpled steel overgrown and just visible through the forest.

A couple of Howard's crew lounged about looking bored on the steps of the building. "Here?" I asked.

Howard gave a taciturn nod and we entered the building. Standard pre-Break Up joint, peeling sheetrock walls, synthetic carpet, plastic tables and reception counters, all of it pretty bad off, a standard salvage job that we would get to in a few years.

Howard led the way to an elevator bank where a door stood open. We donned harnesses and rappelled down the dimly lit shaft. My curiosity was up now: a parking garage? Cars shielded from the EM pulse, and therefore "class A" scrap? Maybe. At the bottom, we left the rappelling gear and went to a light at the end of a long hall. Dusty signs announced this was a controlled area, U.S. Government Property.

My father, Evan, waited there alone. He looked washed out and tired as he brushed his thin gray hair back from his weathered face. "Jeb, I wanted you here to see this. We were inventorying and found reference to this facility, listed as a FEMA shelter, so we came down. Door's locked."

Not just locked. A biometric lock on a substantial steel door, nothing we could pick or batter our way through, but a torch and tank setup stood next to it.

"Want me to cut it?"

"Yep."

Howard handed me a cutting mask and turned away as I struck a spark. It took a half hour or so to cut through. After that, I took a sledgehammer and knocked it free of the cutting slag.

Inside, rows of desks marched into the darkness and upon each desk sat a monitor and keyboard. "What the fuck?" Dad said, as he moved the lantern about. "It's a computer center of some sort. I was thinking we would find emergency supplies."

We exchanged dumbstruck glances as the amount of computer gear became apparent. We walked on into the dark room till several large flat screen monitors mounted on a glass wall appeared.

"This is some kind of command and control center," Dad stated as he held the light up to the massive monitors.

Howard suddenly touched my arm, "Look," he said pointing into the glass wall.

The wall was transparent and beyond it were racks holding boxes with cables running everywhere in organized chaos.

"Holy Mother Gaia..." Dad exclaimed, "This is a server farm, or something like it."

I glanced around with renewed interest, solid concrete walls, under ground at least forty feet, "These things might be functional," I stated.

"An intact computer center."

We looked at each other, dazed. This could be a big score, as computers in the Northwest Pacific Alliance were an endangered species. Even parted out this would be big, as everything electronic was almost unobtainable. The question was: would we get to keep it?

"Who else knows about this?"

Both Dad and Howard looked at me, realization dawning in their eyes. They stared at each other, "Just us. Rob and Steve know something's up but not what."

"Do we notify Thompson?" I asked; Thompson was the Alliance project administrator for the Seattle Salvage Effort. "If we do, he'll confiscate it."

Dad nodded slowly. "And we won't make a penny off it."

"This could pay off the co-op," Howard added.

I thought about that. Carrick Salvage is a co-operative enterprise separate from our farm co-op, Southworth Grange. All of us were stakeholders in both as one folded into the other. But Southworth Grange was now mortgaged to fund the expansion of Carrick Salvage, and a big chunk of the

Seattle Effort went toward paying the mortgage and to repair things on the farm from tools to solar water heaters.

We were now one third of the way through our piece of Seattle, and we were just breaking even due to expropriation. Thompson expropriated everything, steel, copper, equipment, cars, you name it, he cited the war effort against Zion, or the Brit insurgents up north, or shit, even the Baja Californicators down south. Confiscation is what it is.

We salvaged about 1000 tons a month out of this boneyard in reclaimed metals alone, Olympia's share was 100 tons of metal per month, but in reality, Thompson confiscated 300 to 500 tons a month, and every previous class "A" find had been confiscated. That was the way of it: thievery, graft, corruption.

So why'd we let him get away with it? In a word, nepotism. He was a nephew of the governor, second cousin to the Alliance president, and his brother-in-law was the commander of the army regiment that enforces what passes for law in the Seattle Effort. It was a nice racket.

We all came to the same conclusion. Dad looked at his watch and said. "Let's button this up, post guards and talk it over in the morning."

☙

On the late ferry home Dad napped, and Howard and I bought beers. I took mine out on the forward deck for the air. It seemed to me that a successful heist would have to break into several parts: extracting the equipment under the nose of Thompson and his cossacks; transporting it to a safe location; fencing it, and I didn't know anything about that. Then, it would be a matter of wisely using the dollars earned so as not to attract the wrong kind of attention from Olympia or Portland.

We docked at the Harper pier and got on the Southworth farm bus for late returnees. I sat up front with the teamster, Maya Ramirez. Originally her family were Mex refugees indentured to the co-op; now they were stakeholders. I admired her long black hair and brown eyes while we chatted about the day as she guided the team pulling the bus.

At the farm, three mares had foaled and the sheep were lambing. All of the colts and most of the lambs were pureborn and that was good. The spring wheat and corn were sprouting and the apples trees were setting fruit. I listened politely but let my mind wander over Maya—I was sweet on her and wanted to ask her out to the spring dance coming up on the equinox. As we turned into the village lane I made my move, subtle as usual:

"Mayayouwantotgotothedancewithme?"

Her face wrinkled in confusion as she tried to unmangle what I said. "Un, sorry?" she replied.

I licked my lips and spoke slowly. "You want to go to the dance with me?"

Surprise washed over her and she gave me a sunny look. "Sure."

At our lane she halted the bus. I was going to ride on with her and help settle the horses for the night, as I wanted to be with Maya a while longer, but Dad called me.

I gave her an apologetic smile and said, "Seven on Sunday then?"

"OK, then." She leaned in and gave me a quick kiss on the cheek and I jumped off.

Dad saw it and grinned as I joined him and Howard. "We're going to Mister Granjeans' house for a moment, you want to come?"

I nodded. Mister Granjeans was the oldest person in our co-op and the only surviving founder. He was over one hundred and still all here, mentally and physically. Permaculture farmer, builder, warrior, statesman, mechanic, electronics tech, librarian, teacher, elder: we wouldn't be here today without him.

"We should go now, as he's early to bed these days."

Granjeans lived in a snug strawclay house under a sod roof with three other younger elders. We call it the Elder House: original, right? He was still up when we let ourselves in, and insisted we have some tea, black, since it was last years crop. We settled in around the kitchen table while he busied getting a pot ready. "So what brings you three all solemn looking and such to my house this time of night?" he asked, pouring tea.

Howard looked slantwise at Dad and said, "Evan."

Dad nodded. "Well, we made a find today, was wondering if you could shine some light on it." Dad sketched out the underground bunker and its contents.

Granjeans contemplated for a moment. "I seem to remember them talking about such things, building data mining centers, the NSA or some damn thing. This is probably one of them. Was a student back then at Evergreen College." Granjeans eyed us. "But you all didn't come here to listen to me ramble. You thinkin' about stealing it?"

At Dad's surprised face and our grins, he nodded. "Been reading the financials, andI know things aren't going as well as we projected. How could we figure how much corruption

Thompson would indulge in? So. How are you going to do it?"

Dad looked vague. "We really haven't–"

I interjected: "I have."

Granjeans turned his ancient eyes on me and pushed his equally ancient glasses back up his nose. "Well, boy? Spit it out."

❧

The next morning I was out in the kitchen garden watering, using last night's piss, when a wagon turned into our lane. By the time and the clatter I knew it was the honeybucket wagon arriving for our weekly turd collection. I rinsed the empty piss can out and went to get the turd cans, big, plastic five gallon buckets with lids on tight. Our co-op composts all waste, veggie scraps, meat, dead animals, shit, and more. Composted, it goes out on the guilds or returns as an allotment for our family gardens for soil building.

To my surprise, Maya was driving the honeybucket. I hoisted the buckets in and removed an equal number of clean buckets for future use. "What are you doing, driving this?" I asked.

She looked sad. "Larry's sick, pneumonia, so I volunteered."

"Is he going to make it?" I asked. Since the Break Up, antibiotics were in short supply at best, and pneumonia could be a death sentence.

"He's pushing seventy or so." That was all she really needed to say. In a way it was sad, seeing the first and second generation of our co-op dying off; they had survived so much, but God hunts everyone. We buried them in our remembrance garden, all flowers and bees, a beautiful place.

Suddenly, a great idea popped into my head, being Friday and my day off. "How 'bout I ride along with you, Maya?"

She beamed me a sunny smile. "Wonderful. I kind of hoped I would see you."

I climbed on and we continued collecting turd cans till we finished up at the composting center located in the center of our major farm guilds: rows of wheat, beans, corn all growing fast, not knee high yet, along with plenty of other crops.

Before the Break Up, I'd learned in school, this area was mostly suburban housing and remnant forest, ruined for farming or lumbering or much of anything else. Wheat, corn, tomatoes, peppers and most other things wouldn't grow outdoors here, it was too cold and too wet, but all that has changed. Now Puget Sound gets mild winters, and long, hot, dry summers more often than not. Climate change, deforestation, war, fallout, depopulation, not to mention Carrick Salvage recycling abandoned housing and strip malls, all contributed to the change. It's normal to me, but I grew up here: a bountiful land blessed by the Lady and Lord.

I found it easy to talk to Maya as we unloaded, ignoring the winks and grins of the composters on duty. Suddenly it was noon, and she was dropping me back at my house. "See ya Sunday night," she said, suddenly shy.

I said, "Yeah, till then." She turned the wagon around and headed off for the stables.

☙

I caught up with Dad later at the Grange Common Hall. Once a public school, now it was a multipurpose community center, school, repair shops, and administrative offices. Dad was in his office transcribing a computer-center spreadsheet into a ledger. He looked up from his work, snapped off the one office light, and said to me in the gloom, "Been talking to select members, getting input on our proposal. We'll have to get a quorum together–"

"We're going to have to vote on it?" I replied unable to keep the dismay out of my voice.

"What did you expect? We live in a co-op, just getting quorum approval will knock enough noses out of joint as is."

"But Dad, what we're proposing is essentially illegal—it's stealing. And if everybody knows, someone will blab to the wrong set of ears."

Dad's expression was glum. "I know."

"Then..." I swallowed hard, as I was unaccustomed to pushing my father's thinking when tackling moral conundrums. "What you're saying is forget it, because the risk is substantial. If we get caught, it could mean everything."

Dad sighed, "Yeah, that's true."

"Yet Granjeans was all for it."

Dad gave me a strange look. "Yeah, he is..." Dad chewed on that for a while then suddenly smiled, "Lets go and talk to him again."

On the way I mentioned a thought, "Dad, we have Alliance vested claim in that old shopping center up north, as well as that abandoned government building in Bremerton. What if we discovered all that gear there?"

"Then we parse it out over months or years..." Dad picked up. "Might work."

At the Elder House, Granjeans was tending chickens, clipping wings with the help of a boy. "That be enough for today, Darin," he told the boy when he saw us. "Don't forget to take your share of eggs home."

"Yes, sir," Darin said. "My mama thanks you."

I said, "Hi," as Darin, giving me a quick smile, ran off.

"So, how is the great byte heist coming along?" Granjeans asked.

Dad and I gave each other a puzzled glance, "Bite heist?" I questioned.

Granjeans snorted, "B-Y-T-E, a computer term…" he shrugged, "My attempt at humor…"

Dad took the lead, "Look, I've been speaking to a few selected people about this and the consensus is that we need to gather a quorum to do this, as its basically theft–"

Granjeans cut in. "Only in the eyes of the Alliance."

Dad waited for him to elaborate.

Granjeans motioned for us to follow him into the kitchen garden. He settled us at a table and bench. "Theft. That's a strong word. One might say the Alliance stole it from all those folks who owned Seattle to begin with when they nationalized it." He paused, and looked out across the garden beds. "Still, they'll call it that if you're caught. Right and wrong are always in the eye of the beholder anyway."

At my blank look Granjeans elaborated. "Morals, like right and wrong, theft or expropriation: it always depends on who is in control, which means who carries the biggest stick. In our case Thompson is the biggest stick around.

"So it boils down to this: is it worth the risk? As it is we'll cover expenses, but we'll be left holding the bag for the mortgage. Hard times."

"So how can we judge the risk?" Dad asked.

I interjected, "Seems the first step is to see if those computers work. If they do, they're worth their weight in gold.. If not, they're parts, valuable, but not nearly as much."

"That means the Sisters," Dad stated.

Granjeans nodded, "And something else. We need a partner, someone who knows smuggling, maybe the Morales gang."

Both Dad and I exchanged horrified glances; the Morales gang was the biggest pack of bandits in the Olympic Mountains.

Granjeans sketched an understanding smile. "I know. But they know the underground market for stuff like this. And they're honorable, they will stick to the deal."

"And you know this how?" Dad asked.

"We have arrangements with them, like the other granges on the east side. They shield us from other mountain raiders; in return, we give them food and medicinals. Sometimes we ask other favors, sometimes they do."

"How do we arrange this?" I asked.

Granjeans, winked at me. "I'd ask Juan. He's our contact."

He meant Juan Ramirez, Maya's father.

Dad and I looked at each other, feeling a bit like we just entered the Alice story, with Granjeans playing the white rabbit.

Dad nodded, suddenly understanding. "That explains why all the raids stopped; I never thought our grange patrols were enough to do it." Dad looked grim, "But why is this a secret?"

"Because Portland declared them insurgents and did nothing, so we had to find a hush-hush accommodation, or it would be labeled treason."

"So what about the quorum?" Dad asked then.

Granjeans grimaced, "Would have been better if you hadn't said anything..." he paused to think, "...who knows about this now?"

"Long and Haggerty, kept it pretty general, but let them know the risks."

"So six then? Counting all of us."

"Yes."

"Good, then leave it to me, I'll fix it. You," he looked at me as if judging me, "need to get the particulars arranged."

And just like that, Operation Byte Heist was a go.

Dad turned to me. "Jeb, I'm going to give you the dangerous assignment. Go to the Morales gang and make a deal; I'll do the Sisters."

"Dad, really? We should do this together. You have the experience."

Dad's face became sad, "Son, I didn't want to tell you this, this way, but I can't." He glanced at Granjeans who nodded gravely. "I got cancer."

A cold chill went through me and settled in. I stared at him as it came together, his paleness, his sudden thinness, my promotion, his recent trip. "That's why you went down to Olympia, isn't it?"

Dad nodded, "Went to the hospital. There's nothing they can do."

My mother and sister died when a flu epidemic swept the Alliance, and thousands died. Dad and I survived; now we live with his sister, Deana, also a flu widow. "How long?" I choked out.

"Six months to a year, perhaps more. They said it was from chronic fallout exposure, they're seeing a lot of cancers nowadays..."

For some reason, tears didn't come; I focused back on the job rather than continue down that path. "I'll do it."

Dad watched me, sensing my resolve, and smiled his pride. "Good. I'll go to the Sisters and make arrangements."

Granjeans gave my hand a squeeze. "Jeb, you go to Ramirez. He'll have to go with you for safe passage."

❧

I left Dad at the Sisters and Brothers House in old Port Orchard. Originally they were county buildings, courthouse, or some such thing, but now the buildings housed a monastery, for the lack of a better word.

I said goodbye to Dad as Jose, and to my surprise, Maya waited.

"Just be safe, Jeb," Dad said, all choked up. "Remember, I love you, son."

"And, I love you, Dad," I answered. I felt my eyes growing hot and Dad's were none too dry, so we hugged and quickly turned away. I mounted my horse and rode off. I was afraid to look back.

Maya studied my face as I rode up. I gave her a stoic smile.

"How long will it take for us to find them?" I asked Jose.

"We will ride all day and we will be near, tomorrow we will enter their lands and we will be watched." José studied me, his countenance sad. "I'm sorry about Evan. He is a good man."

"So am I," Maya added.

We rode for the rest of the day, through the village of Belfair, out along the south end of the Hood Canal, a mishmash of submerged houses and poisoned waters. I've been told that the canal, like the Sound, once was a major source of clams, mussels, and oysters, but not any longer: it was dead, stinking, and abandoned.

A convoy of tankers escorted by army gun trucks held us up crossing old highway 101; the truck gunners aimed 50 caliber guns at us as they roared by. It was scary, but fuel oil from the refinery up in Anacortes is gold these days to bandits and insurgents.

We slept that night at the Willows farm—the Willows belong to the Skokomish Grange, which is organized around individual family farms rather than a communal co-op. The current Mr. Willow put us up in the barn, opposite the main house and cattycorner to the farm workers houses inside a stockade of pine logs. "Won't stop raiders with any heavy weapons but we haven't faced any for years now..." he commented, his eyes questioning why we were heading up into the Olympics. "It's dangerous from here on," he concluded.

The next morning we rode into the Olympic foothills entering bandit country. Old maps label this national forest and park. Once a network of roads ran through the whole region, but after eighty-five years of rain and snow only traces remain. We picked our way along a forested path that occasional faded signposts identified as NFS 23. It was still traveled, as both hoof and footprints appeared here and there on soft ground.

Here, the air picked up that crispness you don't find along the muggy Sound. Old Washington reappeared in tall firs, cedars, spruce, maples, and alders that shaded the path into dusk.

Midday the hairs on my neck began to prickle as that watched feeling came over me. Maya, riding beside me, said, "They're here." José nodded confirmation.

Whoever "they" were remained elusive. We rode the entire day, gaining altitude. At dusk we pitched camp making no effort to hide or prepare any defense. After we ate José stated he would take the watch. I bedded down next to Maya who took my hand, "You owe me a dance," she told me with a squeeze, and I realized with a start that today was the equinox.

Two figures materialized at the edge of the camp as I began to doze off. José stood up to greet them as I jerked awake and sat up. José motioned for me to join them. They were two young men, heavily tattooed across faces and arms, dressed in black wool. They addressed José in Mex. José said something back then spoke 'Merican, perhaps for my sake.

"This is Jeb Carrick, son of Evan, of Southworth Grange. He desires to speak business with Chief Morales."

The two studied me for a moment then faded away into the dark. José went to his sleeping bag and crawled in. "Get some sleep, Jeb, we have a ways to ride yet."

"Will they let us meet him?" I asked. José gave me a peculiar smile and nodded.

We broke camp at sunrise. Now we were deep into the mountains, the path twisted and turned, clinging to mountainsides that dropped into forested ravines from which the sound of racing water echoed. Sheep appeared, wooly dots on grassy mountain meadows; shepherds watched in stoic silence as we rode past. Then, from nowhere, tattooed riders fell in around us, silent escorts along our path.

From a ridge top, a valley appeared with a lake in the center. Fields, pastures, and a village surrounded the lake; solar collectors sparkled under the sun. As we rode in, people gathered, silent and solemn, and children peered shyly from behind their parents as dogs yapped. We halted before a long gable roofed building set so low to the ground it required a dormer for the doorway. The interior was not dark, as a row of southern facing clerestory windows brought in ample light. Padded benches lined the walls. Several people sat here watching as we entered, none of them greeted us. A woman standing in the corner with two tattooed men turned and approached.

José stepped forward and they embraced, speaking in Mex so I didn't have a clue what was being discussed. Maya's fingers nervously touched my palm and we clasped hands. The woman saw this and a slight smile crossed her lips, she broke away from José and approached us. Ignoring me, she spoke to Maya in Mex, to which Maya haltingly replied.

The woman switched to 'Merican. "Enough, enough, your Spanish is awful!" She said with a laugh in her voice.

That laugh died when she turned her eyes on me. "I understand you wish to speak to me."

I guess I looked confused, as she laughed again. "I am Juanita Morales, clan chief. You wish to speak to me?"

"Ahh..." I began, looking around, everyone was watching and listening, "It's an honor, my name is Jeb Carrick, but I was hoping we could discuss this in private..."

65

"These," she indicated the other folk with a sweep of her arm, "are elders, my councilors. You will talk before them."

I quickly described my mission. Both José and Maya listened, surprise etching their faces.

Morales' face became still as I talked; then she looked away. "This will require some thought," she nodded at our two escorts. "Put them up in the travelers hut, and see they are fed as guests are." To me she said: "Jeb Carrick, we will give you our decision tomorrow."

⮞

Three days later I was on a tug towing a barge down the Sound, courtesy of the Morales and Bandar gangs and Hoodsport Recycling and Salvage, a wholly owned front operation of the bandits. I was by myself now; José and Maya remained behind to liaison with the clans while I went on to finish the job. I used the tug's radio to call Dad to coordinate efforts, under the guise of loading scrap to ship to the Brits up north.

The clans contributed the barge and tug. The barge contained hidden holds for smuggling. The clans were happy to put their barge to use, though of course there was a price. The computers were useless to them, since they had little or no electricity, but they understood the value in those machines. They were in for a forty percent split, with our tithe to the Sisters being ten percent; we would net fifty percent of the proceeds, if we got out undetected.

The Sound was brisk under gray skies as we steamed southward. An Alliance submarine from Bangor Base appeared, moving toward Sinclair Inlet and the naval shipyard. You saw subs around the Sound; I don't think they ever went out in the Pacific any more, like the supposedly battleworthy Alliance aircraft carriers that never left the shipyard; for that matter, you never see any aircraft in the air either. Still, with what we were up to, a sub out in the Sound was something to take note of, not that I had a clue of what to do about one.

Rain began about noon and increased as the day wore on. The sub disappeared in the rain as we made for the salvage dock. The Chinee ship was gone. More salvage, everything from cars to girders to bins full of scrap metal waited loading.

I went to find Dad. He wasn't in the yard office, no one was, so I went to the stable and checked out a horse. I knew where he would be. As I got the horse, Boomer came in.

"Jeb! You're back," he greeted me.

"Yep," I answered.

He gave me a conspiratorial wink, "Jeb, what's up? Something big?"

So rumors were in the mill—that was inevitable, as we weren't practiced at secrecy—but Boomer is a refugee earning a stake, not a stakeholder, so I shrugged. "Don't know what you're talking about." It was pretty lame, but fabricating lies on the spot is not one of my skill sets.

Boomer grinned at me. "That's okay. I get it, top secret."

"I got to go."

"Yeah, okay."

I rode off in the direction of the Seattle Center leaving Boomer behind. Halfway there I ran into an army squad on patrol.

At the squad leader's "halt!" I dug out my identification papers. He examined them and handed them back, then he wanted to chat.

"We don't usually come this deep into the Effort, but we've had a report of possible squatters in this area," the squad leader stated.

"Squatters? Here? This close to an active demolition zone?" I replied. "Must have a death wish."

"Where are you going?" the squad leader asked me.

I really have to find time to practice lying. "We have an explorer party there," I pointed vaguely toward the Center.

"You mean that forested park?"

I nodded.

"Fine, we'll come along, see what we see."

For a while, I led them in the general direction of our salvage project. I hoped Dad posted sentries far enough out that a close approach would alert them. I didn't have much faith in Dad's skills at obfuscation, so I had no intention of leading them there.

The squad leader was a regular chatty doll named Don Galloway. I learned he was from the east side of Washington, was an army conscript, and glad to be here as he thought this assignment was cake duty. His parents owned a wheat farm near Walla Walla, failing due to the drought. He worried about them, as raiders from Zion penetrated farther each year, torching everything in their path.

About the time I was wondering what to do with them, a wagon turned a corner and Don sent his squad to intercept them. I recognized Rob and Steve in the wagon, hauling a generator. "My explorers," I announced.

When I arrived with Don, Rob shot me a sunny smile. "Jeb, we're done here, none of them worked, so we will be parting them out."

I nodded blankly. Don looked quizzically at Rob. "What didn't work?" he asked.

Rob shrugged. "Oh, we found some old computers in one of the buildings, you got to check them when you find them as a working one is worth real money."

Steve took his identification papers back and leaned around Rob. "What are you doing here?" he asked Galloway.

"Looking for squatters."

Steve pointed toward the northeast. "Over by the lake. I saw vegetable patches hidden between buildings there."

"Well, I guess we'll go and check it out."

We watched as the solders marched off. "That was close," I said after they were out of earshot.

Rob shook his head. "Not really. They've been wandering around now for two days, but we've moved most everything out under their noses."

"You think they're really looking for squatters?" Steve interjected.

I laughed, sounding a bit on edge, "Feels a bit coincidental." I turned back to Rob. "So. The computers are fried?"

Both Rob and Steve shook their heads. "Of course not. The Sisters got them running in a day. Things work fine."

We returned to the FEMA building, rode into the parking garage and down two levels. Here, a crew worked crating the machines as fast as they could cut and build the crates. They were refugees, with guards watching them. My Dad was there; I rode over to where he was talking to a tall woman dressed in the robes of a Green Sister.

I recognized her; she taught classes at the Grange Common Hall, a Sister Kelly. "We must have time to access the servers and see if there's any information on them of value." She paused as I reined up and regarded my intrusion with a critical eye.

"Jeb!" Dad said. "You made it!" He said to Sister Kelly, "Jeb arranged use of the barge with the mountain clans."

"Ahh. I thought I recognized you. Brother Small's welding class."

I nodded , surprised she remembered me. I dismounted and gave Dad a hug. He was startled but accepted it gracefully. He resumed his conversation with Sister Kelly. "And you will have that time, but not till they are moved."

"Of course, we must get them somewhere safe," she agreed.

"How soon till they're all moved?" I asked.

"Tonight. They should have started loading them on the barge by now."

"What should I do now?"

"Go back to the dock, assist Howard, make sure the computers get stowed away safe and out of sight."

"All right. When will you be coming back?"

Dad surveyed the packing operation, "When this is finished."

"I'll ride back with you, Jeb," Sister Kelly said, to Dad she added, "My work is finished here."

Dad shrugged. "Be a few more hours before we clear out of here, got to get those big monitors crated."

We returned to the dock without incident. Sister Kelly was mostly silent on the way back. I did learn the Greens wanted their tithe in computers, and that it had been decided to store the machines in the abandoned government building in Bremerton. That made sense—Bremerton still had electric service due to the naval shipyard, and we could tap it while we conducted salvage operations.

As we got to the dock, we saw army troops.

Spying them, we rode behind a screen of trees, to gauge the situation. They were searching the salvage, dumping scrap bins, looking for something. I nudged Sister Kelly to follow me into the doorway of the nearest building—coincidentally, it was the one I'd been working when all this began. We climbed up a several stories for a better vantage point.

From here I could see Howard apparently arguing with a man in uniform. I recognized him—Major Callahan, Thompson's henchman.

"What do they want?" Sister Kelly said.

"The computers of course. Tipped off I suppose."

A noise from behind caused me to look about. Boomer stood there, surprise etched his face. "So that's it. You found a cache of computer ware."

I was about to query him until I saw the gun aimed at us. In spite of my shock, surprise, and fear, I made one intuitive leap. I stood up and faced him. "You. It was you," I said as I pushed Sister Kelly to one side.

Boomer's eyes and gun followed my shove. "And a witch to check them out. Nice." He redirected his lethal attention on me. "Save us all trouble, Jeb. Just tell me where they are."

Of course Thompson had spies in our work force—how else did he learn about our class "A" discoveries" It was obvious in hindsight. "Where what is?" I asked.

Boomer scowled. "Don't play me, Jeb." He reached in his pocket and pulled something out, an electrical instrument with prongs on the end.

71

"What's that?" I asked, "a radio?"

"You're going–" That was when Sister Kelly whirled into action. She rushed him doing a twirl and her leg came up neatly kicking the gun out of Boomer's hand. It skidded away, hit the wall, and ended up nearest me.

"Get it, Jeb!" Sister Kelly yelled, dancing away as Boomer lunged at her with the thingy held out like a weapon.

I dove for the gun. Boomer, realizing his error, attempted a mid-course correction to retrieve the pistol. Sister Kelly ended that with a kick that sent the air woofing out of him and the whatever-it-is skittering across the floor. She neatly scooped it up in a controlled roll.

All this happened in the time it took me to reach the gun.

"Don't move, Boomer." I said, my voice shaking a bit. Sister Kelly checked the whatsit, clicked a switch, and put it in her robe.

Boomer, on the floor, sucked air and nodded weakly.

"What is that thing?" I asked Sister Kelly.

"Taser." Seeing my blank look she elaborated. "Electric shock gun used to stun a person."

I guess I looked astounded because Boomer gave a desultory laugh. I eyed him and made another intuitive leap. "They wouldn't give just anybody one of those."

"No, they wouldn't." Sister Kelly agreed.

"Who are you?" I asked Boomer.

Boomer looked sullen and said nothing.

Sister Kelly produced the taser again and clicked it on. "We can use this on you, you know."

Boomer sighed. "Fine. My name is Henry Gates; I am a paid watcher for Director Thompson. That's it, that's all."

"And how do you happen to get one of these?" asked Sister Kelly, holding up the taser.

Boomer looked sullen again. "They trust me."

This was getting us nowhere and interrogation could wait. "The real question is, what are we going to do with him?" I asked. "Tie him up?"

"Do you have rope?"

I shook my head, "Nope."

Sister Kelly moved without hesitation and jammed the taser against Boomer. He yelled, and spasmed onto his back thrashing, then she did it again until he went limp. She felt his neck and said: "Good. Still alive."

I felt almost as stunned as Boomer. Until that day I had never seen more violence than a wrestling match between overheated men. I looked from Boomer to Sister Kelly. She regarded me with solemn eyes and said: "I did what I had to. We can't let him loose, you know that, so the question is what to do with him."

I shook my head to clear it. "Take him to Dad. They can tie him up and leave him there."

I saw hesitation in her eyes, then resolve. "OK, I can't be seen at the dock now anyway, but you can. I'll need your horse."

We dragged him down to where the horses were tethered and got him up over the saddle. I tied him on with some wiring waiting pickup. Sister Kelly mounted and said. "I'll take that gun too, Jeb."

Hastily, I pulled it out of my waistband and handed it to her. She checked it, and fixed me with a crooked smile, then flipped a switch on the gun to another position. "Next time always safety your gun before sticking it in your waistband.

Safer that way." I blushed as she rode off with Boomer as baggage.

Howard still attended Major Callahan. Howard's eyes widened seeing me, he made an almost imperceptible negative shake. I made to veer off but Callahan spotted me. "You!" he thundered. "Papers!"

I produced my papers. He studied them and said: "Jeb Carrick. Your father is Evan Carrick. Where is he?"

"At home."

Callahan shot Howard an accusing glare; "You said you hadn't seen him today."

Howard glared back at the Major. "Yes, and I haven't."

Callahan turned his attention back to me. "Why is he at home?"

"He's sick. Cancer."

Callahan digested that while I prayed silently that Dad would lie low till they departed. "Do you know why we are here?" he asked, his voice a menace.

I shook my head. "Clueless."

Callahan reddened; I don't think he liked my answer. Clenching his teeth, he enlightened me. "We have information that you are attempting to smuggle out class 'A' salvage, a charter violation."

I looked at Howard; he looked at me; I shrugged. "I don't know anything about that." I glanced to Howard. "This is it for the Brits, right?"

"Yep," he answered. "As I've already told him."

"Maybe you should tell me who told you this story?"

Callahan reddened; he evidently didn't like answering questions, only asking them. His fingers twitched toward his holstered gun, then suddenly relaxed. He gave me an icy smile. "Fine, we shall just continue our inspection."

I tipped my head toward the office shack. "Fine. We'll be in there, till you're finished."

We left Callahan standing in the yard. Inside the shack I peered back at the Major. He looked sullen and unhappy. Howard dropped into a chair and I followed, giving myself over to a bout of the shakes.

"That was close, Jeb," he whispered.

"It's not over yet," I whispered back. "We need to send a messenger off to tell Dad to stay put."

Howard shook his head. "I radioed him when they showed up. He's staying put."

While we waited, I fired up the camp stove, and made us some tea. I even took a cup out to Callahan. He gruffly accepted it. Perhaps that did the trick, who can say, because an hour later he rapped on the door handed me the cup back and informed us they were finished. He gave both Howard and me the stink-eye as he climbed into his automobile. The soldiers piled into their truck and they left in a roar.

"So where are the computers?" as we watched them go.

Howard glanced around. "In the scrap metal bins, under false bottoms. They tired themselves out before they ever made it to the bottom." Howard turned away and yelled at the dockworkers, "OK you guys let's get that barge loaded."
I watched as the men scrambled into action, and wondered if crime does pay after all.

Promised Land

Matthew Griffiths

Monday

"Gidday. What can I do for you?" Craig Bowen stood in the doorway of his workshop, taking in the new arrivals parked outside.

"The garage seems like it's closed," said the driver through the open window.

"Yeah. The mechanic's away. What's the problem?"

The man looked up at the large, faded wooden sign above the door.

Bowen the Blacksmith: Smithing, Welding and Electrickery.

"Broke something on the way up. Suspension I think. Front left. Someone really needs to fix that road," said the driver.

"You'll be lucky, mate. This is north Queensland, not the main street of wherever you've come from."

"Brisbane."

"Ah. Might be able to fix it, depends what it is. Get you to Townsville or wherever you're going anyway."

Craig eyed the car. A '47 Tesla electric, imported and very expensive. Then he looked at the driver: suit, expensive sunglasses, soft hands. The woman in the passenger seat also wore a suit jacket and matching sunglasses.

"Can you have a look?" the man asked.

Craig looked at his watch. It was almost 5.30pm. Home and dinner were calling. The beef and vegetable stew would be sitting ready to eat on the solar dish. Still, it didn't pay to turn away a customer.

"All right. Pop the lid."

He leaned over the engine compartment and examined the suspension. The man and woman got out and stood beside the car watching. The woman lit up a cigarette.

"The rod is busted. I can probably weld it up enough to get you going again, if you take it slowly and avoid the potholes the rest of the way."

"That's ok. We're planning to stay a few days anyway." said the man.

Craig raised an eyebrow. "It doesn't usually take that long to exhaust the sights round here."

"We'll see." said the man smiling. He held out his hand. "Drew Mitcham."

"Craig Bowen." said Craig shaking it, and then the woman's.

"Karen Burnett."

"Nice to meet you." He turned back to Mitcham. "Leave the car here. I'll take it out in the morning. The hotel is just down the street."

"Ok. Great. Thanks." The man opened the boot, pulled out their luggage, and handed over the keys. "Will it be ready by, say, lunch time tomorrow?"

"Yeah, no worries. Should be enough time for the panels to juice up the batteries for the arc welder. Grid power will cost you extra."

The man nodded, glanced at his companion, then back to Craig.

"I understand there's a Shire Council meeting here tonight. Is that right?"

"Yeah. That's right." Craig looked them up and down again. "You guys really are short on entertainment."

The man smiled. "Come along and find out."

Craig watched them wheel their bags slowly down the main street past the hardware store, the credit union, the council office, and across the road to the hotel. Then he turned, locked the door of the workshop and walked home.

Drew Mitcham stood before the Council. "Government policy is to develop the regions. We might be in a steady state economy but that doesn't mean that we can't increase production in some areas and agriculture is a prime candidate. We are the Sunshine State after all, and we have high rainfall and lots of land, we just need to use it better. Government land, like these underutilised national parks and state lease land, is the perfect place to start. In this shire that includes Black Top Mountain and Lake Sutherland National Parks plus considerable lease land nearby." Mitcham smiled and waved his hand in the direction of the mountain.

The council sat around the large, oval-shaped wooden table, polished to a shine as it had been for nearly one hundred years. It matched the wooden panels on the walls, which recorded the names of the mayors of the shire over the decades. The rest of the room was less appealing. The carpet under the chairs of the councillors was worn and the white of the plaster ceiling had turned a dull cream.

Councillor Martin Thurston-Hawley, his long hair tied in a ponytail, spoke. "It's forty years since the global financial crisis and peak oil. Trying to reinflate that bubble is just a pipe dream. They tried big agricultural development up north decades ago. The companies pocketed the subsidies, ran it for a few years and left behind a big mess."

"Yeah. I heard about that." whispered Craig, sitting in the public seats at the back of the room. "And the rainfall is fine, except in a drought."

Next to him he felt his cousin Alex bristle. "They'll never get away with this. And if they try they'll have a fight on their hands."

Craig grinned. He knew better than to cross Alex. He could still remember her cow pat tricks when they were kids.

"Councillor Crawford?" said the Mayor. She wore a navy blue jacket over a blue knit top, her grey hair cut in a business-like bob. She nodded towards Joe.

"Thank you, Madam Mayor." Joe Crawford paused and turned to the visitors. "Mr Mitcham, Ms Burnett. I am curious as to the status of the agreements and legal protections of the parks you refer to. I was not aware that these had changed."

Karen Burnett stood up. "The new Queensland State Government, through the Department of Sustainable Development, is currently preparing legislation to remove the red tape preventing development of state lands. These properties have been locked up for too long."

Joe Crawford spoke again. "Some of those agreements relate to the relationship of traditional owners with their ancestral lands. How will those relationships be protected under this new legislation?"

Karen Burnett glanced down before answering. "That aspect is still to be fleshed out. It is too early to say exactly what the legislation will contain."

Craig looked at Joe. His face was impassive but it was a fair bet he wasn't happy. He was an elder of the local aboriginal people. They had spent two hundred years trying to protect and then reclaim their lands and traditional use rights. Fishing and animal hunting in the parks provided food and income. He couldn't imagine they would roll over and let them be taken away a second time.

"Councillor Graves." said the Mayor, raising her hand in Paul Graves' direction.

"This should be interesting." Craig murmured under his breath.

"This shire has been dependent on cattle for too long. We are lucky we still have the beef export trade. If not for that we'd be back in the Stone Age. Development of this land for alternative high value crops will be a boost for the local economy as well as Queensland as a whole." Graves stopped for a quick breath. "This shire has been going backwards for too long. It's time to move forward and grab the opportunities that are in front of us."

"Hear, hear." a couple of other voices agreed.

"Just like his father." whispered Craig to Alex.

She nodded. "And grandfather. 'Mr Progress', remember? The old duffer would be spinning in his grave at the idea of refrigerated sailing ships."

"This is not the mayoral election, Graves." someone piped up. "Save your campaign speech for next year."

The Mayor leaned forward in her seat at the head of the room. "Let's keep it seemly, ladies and gentlemen. Everyone gets a fair go around this table."

She shifted her attention to the visitors.

"The lands under consideration are important local and regional resources, as is the groundwater you propose to use for irrigation. The environmental impacts would need to be carefully assessed. Has any such assessment been undertaken yet?"

"Well, certainly only the lower slopes of the mountain would be developed. And the groundwater resources are significant. Subject to specific investigations we believe there is sufficient water for all users. Detailed environmental impact statements will be prepared on a case by case basis."

"What about economic analysis?" asked Martin. "Previous studies into intensive development concluded it was not viable, particularly with the costs of set up and infrastructure."

Mitcham answered smoothly, "Our advice, as consultants to the government, is that the state should provide incentives for development and that the benefits will outweigh the costs over the long term. The government has agreed with this assessment and has allocated funding in the budget. Cutting of timber in the national parks will also contribute significant revenue."

Martin Thurston–Hawley shook his head. *Déjà vu all over again.*

The Mayor looked at her watch. "Well, that seems enough for tonight. Those of us riding home need to do so in what's left of the daylight. I move that council receives the report of the State Government and its consultants on the proposed agricultural development, and requests the chief executive and the council's planner and engineer to report back on this issue in three days. I further move that we hold a special meeting of council three days from now, this Thursday evening, to agree on a response. Do I have a seconder?"

After the council dispersed, Mayor Kaye Bowen convened a short meeting in her office. "Steve," Kaye looked towards the chief executive. "I would like a quick update by the end of tomorrow. I don't think much of their 'consultation.' This smacks of a put up job. We're being rushed to agree to something with too little information. We need to cover off all the angles we can, legal, economic, environmental... anything else you can think of?"

"I'll talk to the other elders. Some of the older ones might remember something about the land agreements," said Joe.

"We'll check the shire records as well," Steve said.

"I'm happy to go through the environmental assessment with the planner," volunteered Martin, "I'm doubtful it really addresses the issues."

Kaye nodded. "Go through the economic report with a fine tooth comb too. We need to know how much the shire will end up having to pay for this scheme. You guys at the Sunshine Co-op farm know more about intensive agriculture than the government or its high paid consultants."

"Maybe. Our style is not monocultures anyway. We use smaller scale multi-copping. A totally different philosophy. It's labour intensive but yields are higher and there are less artificial inputs required." He smiled. "We might be hippies but we work hard."

"They talked about jobs," said Steve, "but it's hard to see many well-paid ones. I heard a rumour that the minimum wage is going to be cut again. I wonder if there's a connection."

Kaye pursed her lips. "You know, if this doesn't come to pass I think the council should look at acquiring some of those leases ourselves, and subdividing. Let families lease smaller lots and encourage the kind of diverse cropping that the co-op does. That will bring more people and useful work to the shire than this scheme... Sorry, that's a digression. Let's meet again late tomorrow afternoon to see what we've learned."

Kaye walked out of the council building and saw Craig and Alex waiting for her. Finding herself mayor of her old home town had been the last thing Kaye Bowen expected. She had left the cattle farm outside the town for university and a high flying career in Brisbane, until the global financial crisis and the oil decline came. She and her husband had survived for years longer than most but eventually the problems had claimed his job, and then hers, and they decided the best option was to return to her family farm to help out and make a new start. Knowing the district and many of the local families helped them settle in and find a way to make a living. Later, after some initial reluctance, she was talked into standing for the council and found that some of her corporate skills came in handy in politics. She hadn't been back to the city once in twenty five years.

"Looks like you have a challenge on your hands, Mum." said Craig.

She smiled and shrugged. "Makes a change from worrying about whether the composting toilets in the main street are working properly. What do you two think about it all?"

"Looks like a beaut plan for some people to make money. Not sure it's good for the town," said Craig. "I got a new customer today though. The consultants' car needs fixing."

"My horse breeding business might be better if more people come," said Alex, "but cutting the trees down in the national park won't do much for the horse trekking sideline. The lake water quality is bound to suffer too, and the fish and the birds." Alex had grown up with the lake and the birds in her backyard, and was fiercely protective of both.

Kaye nodded. "Despite what Graves says, the population of the town has been slowly rising again over the last ten years, with people moving out of the cities and the empty houses are filling up. I'm not sure we want or need this."

Tuesday

"How's it looking?" Drew Mitcham approached the car, this time casually dressed in an open neck shirt, jacket, pants and shiny brown boots. Karen Burnett was similarly dressed. Craig had his head under the hood and the car manual from the glove box in his hand. He glanced at them and took in their new appearance. Was this a corporate *visiting the country* uniform? He shook his head. *Townies.*

He straightened up. "Well, I've welded the rod back together and it seems to work. I took it down the street and back again and it handled all right."

"Good, good."

"Impressive bit of machinery," said Craig.

"Yes, carbon fibre chassis and panels, new battery technology, built in solar PV panels…" Mitcham ran his hand over the roof, "…nice to drive too."

"Where are you off to today?"

"Visiting some of the potential development sites and talking to the owners. We might need a recharge when we get back. Will you have enough power?"

"Enough to keep you going for a few days if you're staying local. Might need a grid charge overnight to get her full for the trip home."

"Ok, that's fine." Drew looked up and pointed above Craig's head. "Sign says you do electrical work too."

"Yeah. I did a diploma in electrical stuff before I apprenticed to old Bill, my predecessor. I had ideas of getting into robotics once, when I was a kid in Brisbane, but the world changed before I got the chance and we ended up here. Decided metal bashing was probably the better option long term. I tinker with solar PV systems and keep old technologies going with whatever spare parts I can get my hands on. Would have been nice to play with stuff like this though." He pushed the bonnet down. "Enjoy your afternoon. There's a thunder storm predicted for later on, so keep an eye out."

"Ok, thanks. Here's my card. We'll fix you up for the bill before we head off on Friday morning." Drew climbed into the car and pushed the start button. Karen climbed in the other side, briefcase at her feet, and waved a hand as they backed out onto the street.

❧

A late afternoon summer storm threw rain against the windows of the dim wood-panelled office and thunder could be heard in the distance. Kaye looked at her chief executive.

"Ok, so the economic and environmental issues are what we expected. Potential benefits and considerable risks."

Steve nodded. "In a nutshell, yes."

"Now, the legal status. Are you telling me that the mountain and the lake and the wetlands around it have been national parks for over one hundred years but there is no record of it?"

"Pretty much. We can't find anything." Steve replied.

"There must be something about it somewhere." pointed out Martin. "Does the library hold any archives that might be useful?"

"Good thinking. I'll get on to Claire at the library in the morning. Anything else, anyone?" Kaye looked around at the group.

"The government office in Townsville might have something." suggested Steve.

"Ok. We can consider that if nothing else turns up."

Wednesday

Councillor Graves knocked on the half-open door of the Mayor's office.

Kaye looked up. "Yes?"

"Could I have a word?" Graves asked, smiling as he leaned against the dark wooden door frame.

"Certainly. What can I do you for you?"

"I think you know what I'm here to discuss." he began.

"I can guess," she replied neutrally. "Have a seat."

He sat in the chair directly across the desk from hers. "I would like to think that we can rely on you to make the right decision. This shire needs development, more jobs, more people, more ratepayers. With a development like this we can put this town back on the map!"

Kaye eyed him cautiously. "That is your opinion, Paul. Not everyone agrees, and there is much more investigation required before we can make an informed decision."

Graves leaned back in his chair, his hands steepled in front of him. "I have talked to some of the other councillors. If you stand in the way of this there will be a lot of people wondering if you are here for the benefit of the shire or just a cushy ratepayer-funded semi-retirement. If you can't bring yourself to support it, at least get out of the way and let the rest of us get on and do it. You can abstain from the vote if you have to. Think carefully." He gave her a thin smile, stood and left the office.

Claire Crawford-Bowen walked in. "What was he so pleased about?"

Kaye looked up at her. "I think I've just been made an offer I shouldn't refuse." She paused to take a deep breath. "Any luck in the archives?"

"No. Just thought I'd pop in and let you know that I couldn't find anything. There seem to be gaps in the records, they may be missing or just misfiled. It's all a bit of a mess. I'll keep looking though. Sorry, that's not much help to you."

"Mmm."

Thursday

The morning dawned rainy and cool. The showers continued as an early morning meeting kicked off in the Mayor's office.

"What options do we have left?" Kaye asked.

Steve looked up from his notes. "We need a more detailed environmental assessment, no doubt about that, and the economics are uncertain. There are risks to the shire as well as pluses. I think it will be hard to stop it with just environmental concerns. It looks like the state government wants to push this one hard. As for the legal background, all I can think of is the government office in Townsville."

Kaye nodded. "Ok. Anyone else got any bright ideas?"

Everyone in the room shook their heads.

"What are our chances of getting something out of Townsville over the phone?" asked Kaye.

Steve shook his head. "With the staff cuts there and who knows what else on their plate I wouldn't expect anything in a hurry unless someone goes there in person."

Kaye sighed. "Crazy. In the old days all this was online. Ok. It looks like I'd better go to Townsville, throw my mayoral weight around a bit, and see what I can find." She glanced at Steve. "The trip will take most of the monthly petrol budget."

"It might be our only chance to stop this thing." said Martin.

"Ok. I'll head off right now. Should be plenty of time for me to get back for the meeting tonight."

Kaye picked up her briefcase, walked briskly out to the council parking lot under the protection of an umbrella and climbed into an old Australian built Holden sedan, one of the last produced before they shut the factories down. It looked like it had seen better days and it had, several decades of them, but the local mechanic kept it on the road with scrounged spare parts, ingenuity and luck. The shire's budget didn't stretch to luxury purchases.

After lunch Drew Mitcham and Karen Burnett came into the blacksmith shop. "We have a last favour to ask. We'd like to see the lake and the swamp land adjacent. It may be suitable for drainage and development. Where is the best access?"

Craig's eyebrows jumped. "You realise that is guaranteed to get the locals up in arms?" He had visions of Alex flipping her lid, never mind Joe.

Mitcham shrugged. "We're just doing our jobs."

Craig scratched his head. "Ok. Umm, my cousin Alex can guide you through the area. She's lived here all her life and knows it like the back of her hand. Let me give her a call."

Mitcham nodded and Craig went into his small office to make the phone call. He came out after a couple of minutes. "She'll meet you at the entrance to her folks' farm. You can take a short cut through there and onto the lake track. She'll be on horseback. You should be fine in the car, just watch out for soft bits. It's not far, I'll draw you a map."

As the car quietly and smoothly rolled out onto the road in the direction of the lake the phone rang in Craig's office.

"Hello. Bowen the Blacksmith."

"Craig darling, this is Mum. I'm on my way back from Townsville and the council car has broken down on me. The mechanic who's looking at it here tells me it's dead as a dodo. Time to send it to salvage."

Craig nodded as he spoke into the phone. "Yeah, well it's nearly forty years old now…….. Ok. I'll get Claire to borrow Dave's car and head on up. I can't leave the workshop for too long. Where are you?……Ok. I'll go and see Dave now." He grabbed his wallet and keys from the office, then hesitated, retraced his steps, and made one more phone call before heading out the door.

On his way back to the workshop he saw Paul Graves leave the council building and saunter across the road to the hotel bar. His company ute was parked outside. *Celebrating his victory already? Or perhaps waiting for a meeting with the consultants to get his story straight?* Craig opened up the workshop and finished off a welding job as another rain shower began to fall.

Two hours later he heard horse hooves crunching on the gravel outside the door. He looked out and saw Mitcham and Burnett on the back of Alex's horse. She was holding the reins and an umbrella as they dismounted. Karen shook out her wet, bedraggled hair.

Drew Mitcham was very wet and very annoyed. "Damn thing died on us. It's been playing up the last couple of days. Maybe the battery has gone. I bet that flash new technology is not as great as it's made out to be. Only three years old too. Half the cost of the car is in the battery you know. Then it started sinking into the swamp." He shook his head. "I took some photos for the insurance. I doubt it's worth hauling out except for scrap."

Craig listened sympathetically. "I can arrange that. It's not the first vehicle to get stuck in there. We can organise some transport for you back home tomorrow as well, no problem."

"Thanks. We'd better fix you up now. What's the bill for the welding and recharging the last few days?"

"Well…" said Craig. "If you're prepared to leave the car with me, how about we call it even?"

Drew Mitcham considered the offer for a few moments. "Ok. Thanks." Then he turned and nodded towards the hotel and he and Karen Burnett walked slowly down the street holding matching umbrellas. Craig watched them go silently.

Alex came and stood beside him frowning. "It just conked out. It wasn't the bog I took them through, that was just the icing on the cake." Then she smiled. "You should have seen their faces when it started sinking in."

Craig looked at her sheepishly. "Should be able to get it going again, according to the manual, it's waterproof." He pulled a small plastic box with electrical ports from his jacket pocket. "It might have had something to do with this. I, umm, forgot to put it back in when I was charging it the other day, and I also made another slight modification." He shrugged. "The council needs a new car. The old one has done its dash."

"You!" Alex punched him on the arm. "…are unbelievable."

࿐

Several Councillors around the table looked at their watches and turned to their neighbours. *Where is the Mayor?*

The Deputy Mayor circled the room talking to the councillors to gauge support for starting the meeting without her. Word of the government's proposal had got around the shire quickly and there was a crowd of onlookers in the back of the room gossiping amongst themselves.

Kaye burst through the doors and walked quickly to the head of the council table. Claire came in behind her, sat down beside Craig and gave him a peck on the cheek. "Where are the kids?" she asked.

"At the neighbours." said Craig. "I didn't want to miss this."

The Mayor deposited a pile of papers on the table in front of her, took a deep breath and began to speak.

"Thank you all for coming here this evening at short notice to discuss this important matter. Apologies for the slightly late start. I had some transport difficulties; horses are more reliable these days than old council vehicles." She smiled and a few onlookers laughed.

"We are here to discuss the proposed large scale agriculture development on the national parks and state owned lease land in this shire..."

Kaye Bowen continued and was then followed by the chief executive as he gave his summary of the economic and environment assessments. Debate ensued and opinion around the council table was divided.

Finally the Mayor called an end to the discussion.

"It is time to put it to a vote. I move that the council," she began, looking around the table, "support the proposed legislation to enable development of these lands in the shire, subject to more rigorous site specific environmental and economic evaluation, and prepare a submission to that effect."

Joe Crawford and Martin Thurston-Hawley looked at her, stunned. One of Martin's eyebrows rose in a sure sign he didn't agree. Craig recognised that from long ago when he was a student in Mr T.'s class at the local school. Both Joe and Martin moved to speak but Kaye raised her hand to silence them.

"Do I have seconder?"

Paul Graves raised his hand, smiling broadly.

"Ah. Councillor Graves." She paused. "Councillor, government records show that the Graves Pastoral Corporation, of which you are an executive, along with your father, has recently purchased the leases to land within the proposed development area."

She waved some of the papers in the air.

"You therefore have a conflict of interest which you have failed to advise the council of, as required under the official meeting rules. I would ask you to stand down during this vote. We will deal with the transgression later."

Graves flushed red and looked around the table before slowly getting up and retreating to the back of the room.

"That should knock him out of the mayoral contest for another term or two." Alex whispered.

"Couldn't happen to a nicer guy," agreed Craig, "but what's Mum up to with this vote?"

Alex frowned and bit her lip.

"I have a seconder. Thank you Councillor Tan." said the Mayor, turning to the secretary to make sure she had recorded it.

"All those in favour please raise your hand." She gave a faint nod toward Joe and Martin. They exchanged glances as they reluctantly raised their hands, along with the majority.

"Those against?" A small number of hands were raised.

"Thank you. The motion passes."

94

Drew Mitcham and Karen Burnett nodded to each other, smiling.

The Mayor continued, looking at them. "There is one further thing Mr Mitcham, Ms Burnett. As part of our submission we will make the state government aware of the North Queensland Parks Acquisition Amendment Act of 1923, which is the legislation governing the land currently included in the Black Top Mountain and Lake Sutherland National Parks. It mandates that if the use of the lands should cease to be as national parks then those same lands shall return to the control of the shire and traditional owners respectively." She waved a piece of paper in her hand.

Mitcham and Burnett cast each other confused glances.

"And the shire, and the traditional owners' corporation I'm sure," she nodded towards Joe, "will fight any attempt to negate those protections to the highest courts in the land if necessary. We would welcome the government's move to return the land to local control, if it should choose to proceed with the legislation, however it should be noted that we, as owners, may well choose not to participate in the agricultural development scheme."

She paused and looked around the room with a small smile of satisfaction.

"I have a further proposal for council to consider. As an alternative to large scale monoculture development I propose that council investigate acquiring state lease land close the town with a view to sub-leasing small plots to families and other groups to develop intensive multi-crop orchards and gardens. Such a style of development would promote employment, agricultural production and the rejuvenation of the shire without the environmental risks. We already have some local examples." She nodded towards Martin.

"And perhaps the Graves Corporation may wish to divest one of its recently acquired holdings since insider trading is frowned upon around here."

She stared directly at Paul Graves. He looked down at the floor to avoid her gaze.

"Do I have seconder?"

Martin raised his hand, smiling.

"Thank you. The motion is open for discussion."

Story Material

Rachel White

Melanie entered her hallway, leaving a trail of garden dirt on the tile floor. Squatting so her arms could reach the tiny brass handle, she pulled open the lowest left hand drawer. Her wrinkled fingers reinforced the folds of the makeshift envelope containing leftover carrot seeds, then shoved it back in with the other envelopes. Before shutting the drawer, Melanie paused for several moments, her mind whirling backwards in time.

She remembered her scrawny nine-year-old self trotting several blocks to the library and how she had often pulled open a drawer such as she had just now. Then, however, it had been used for the purpose it was manufactured for—full of book titles, authors, subjects, and call numbers instead of seeds and sewing supplies. Melanie recalled the excitement she'd felt when discovering the location of books and subjects that interested her. Whether her curiosity on a particular day had been about Aborigine myths or amphibians of the northeastern United States, sign language or origami, she loved the feeling of independence as she walked to an aisle to find what she was looking for, sometimes stumbling across an unexpected book she couldn't resist picking up along the way.

She'd leave the shelves with a tall stack in her arms and wander over to one of the maroon, soft-cushioned armchairs in the reading nook. In the comforting quiet, oblivious to the cars and fast-paced life abuzz outside, Melanie lost herself for hours in worlds beyond the library until her hunger made her realize it was well past lunch time and she had better hurry home. That love of books and the miraculous way the varied arrangements of letters and images on pages could transport her to a myriad of other worlds were what had led her to become a librarian.

She sighed, unable to let go of the nostalgia. Much had changed in seventy years. Cailyn and Fiona, despite being almost eight and ten, had never had that experience. She didn't care that they hadn't had other experiences like she had had—flying in an airplane to far-off places like California or New Zealand, going on road trips to the amusement park, or walking through a shopping mall with its glittery onslaught of consumerism—but their lack of knowing the richness of a library full of books pained her. Before the girls were born, when Melanie lived with her nephew Aidan—Cailyn and Fiona's father—their study's walls were covered with books. It was a much smaller collection than any libraries of her youth, but sizeable enough to have interested a curious youngster for days. But that house had burned down in the Fire of 2048, which had destroyed numerous neighborhoods during the Six Years Drought, when the underfunded, ill-equipped fire department had been unable to respond like it used to in the old days; and the water pipes running dry had not helped matters.

Sure, Cailyn and Fiona still found books to read. Despite their family's meager income, Melanie had managed to acquire a few books in recent years. More often though, they borrowed neighbors' books, particularly from the Davidson family, one of few families nearby who valued reading. The Davidsons welcomed them to browse their two bookcases and borrow anything they wanted. While the Davidsons' bookshelves contained a small fraction of the choices that a library or bookstore would have had, most of the books Cailyn and Fiona read came from there. Although Melanie had wished their collection offered higher quality children's books than the late 2020 cult series *The Adventures of Princess Claudia the Invincible* and *Auto-saurus Action*, she did admit it was interesting to analyze how cars had still prevailed in popular media then, even as they were becoming less prevalent in real life.

Melanie told the girls many stories too: stories patched together from fragmentary memories of books she had once read, folk tales from around the world she had learned from her storytelling days as a librarian, true stories from her own life, and stories entirely made up on the spot. In a way, she tried to remind herself, the girls were born into a imagination-rich home, for despite having almost no newly manufactured toys or books, whenever they came asking for a story, Melanie had no shortage to tell. Perhaps what they couldn't access bothered her more than it bothered them: they were growing up in a world that was simply normal for them, whereas she had a visceral knowledge of what had once existed.

Yet she couldn't deny the many specific books to which she wished she could introduce them: *The Blessing Cup* or *Roll of Thunder, Hear My Cry*, or *The Ruffled Edges of Time*, which only came out in e-book format in 2021. She wasn't sure if she'd ever find them. There were particular interests the girls had—ocean life, Helen Keller, and secret codes—and she'd been unable to find books about them, either. Many bookstores had closed long ago after struggling to compete with the digital medium. The ones she heard still existed were too far to visit and lacked their former broad selection. It wasn't only Internet access that had disappeared in many areas; book publishing had waned too. Unreliable electricity, fuel shortages, and rising costs of materials had severely curtailed production processes such as typesetting, printing, and distribution, which had been thoroughly computerized and depended on global trade. She knew of a few used bookstores in the region, but her family generally had too little extra money to afford even used books.

The times when a mere click of the mouse on Amazon.com resulted in books delivered at one's doorstep within a few days were long gone. The normalcy of just-in-time shipping, the highly intricate global network of specialized businesses, finance and employment had unraveled. She remembered how forty years ago she could easily obtain out-of-print books simply by going online. Now her grandnieces asked her questions about what "online" meant—to them it was as much of a foreign concept as "card catalogs" were to the children who used to come to her library.

She hoped someone somewhere was holding onto each of the many books that had deeply touched her and shaped her identity, because she doubted most of them were currently in print.

Melanie decisively pushed the drawer closed, as if in an attempt to shut away the memories and desires that kept creeping back in, and she stood up. She stared at the entire card catalog in front of her, its *Library Bureau Sole Makers* metal tag still attached to its solid oak wood. Despite a few scratches, it had survived well through its century-plus existence. It certainly outlasted the computer catalogs that had had to be replaced every few years at great cost and exhibited regular glitches that distracted her from other library work she had wanted to do. With no Internet access in most areas and erratic electricity, she laughed and wondered who would now want a computer, and thought about how much harder it was for the average person to repurpose such a device than a card catalog. She figured millions of computers like those had been dumped during her lifetime.

Melanie recalled when she first saw the card catalog. On spring break during her senior year in college, she'd attended an antique auction with her mother. Someone had almost bought it for fifty dollars, but on the spur of the moment, her mother pledged ten dollars more, and won the bid.

"Why do you want a card catalog?" she'd asked her mother as she reluctantly helped her load it into their car. Melanie was incredulous. Her mother had never completely adapted to the changing times, and held steadfast onto relics of a bygone era: manual typewriters, her high school slide rule, a treadle sewing machine, a washboard, manual pencil sharpeners that were discarded from Melanie's elementary school—machines that many people now would cherish, she admitted.

"Melanie dear, don't worry. You know I always find uses for things."

And her mother had, using it to store her wide array of sewing supplies, stamps, and other odds and ends. Her mother had bequeathed it to Melanie's niece Genevieve and when Melanie inherited it after Genevieve's death, many of her mother's spools of thread, needles, and buttons were still in its upper drawers. She had left them there but chosen to use the other drawers to store garden seeds for the next season.

As she swept her hand across the oak wood to brush off some dust, a feeling of sorrow washed up like waves lapping at the shore. There was grief about her desire to be a lifelong librarian and what had come of it, and anger not only about all the wrong choices made at her workplace, but the certainty they had been the right and inevitable ones. Somehow the knowledge of the seeds contained therein gave her a small bit of consolation. Once planted they would grow into an edible rainbow of kohlrabi, carrots, squash, watermelon, tomatoes, kale, peppers, eggplant, and okra. They couldn't grow libraries, but still she felt that within the absence there was possibility.

&

By the trellis made of a discarded bed frame, Melanie finished planting the snap peas and patted down the dirt. After putting her well-used garden tools to rest in the shed and throwing a bowlful of kitchen scraps to the chickens, she hastened inside. Since she was going into town, she changed into fresh clothes, put on her knitted cardigan, and slipped her feet into sandals fashioned from old tires. Then she filled her water bottle, packed some day-old bread with homemade quince jam and two hard-boiled eggs into her bag, and left the house.

It was Fiona and Cailyn who usually fetched the mail. Full of youthful energy, they enjoyed the adventure of traveling the four miles to the post office and back in one day. But they were away with Lisa, their mother, in a nearby town. Lisa's friend, pregnant with twins, had asked Lisa to come help. The closest hospital was too far for the expectant mother to travel to, sorely lacking in supplies, and a delivery there would have cost the family a half year's savings. Lisa, a skilled midwife, felt obliged to assist. Melanie expected the girls' return within the week, but it had been over a month since the mail had been picked up, and her anticipation was too great to wait any longer. Had what she'd been waiting for arrived?

It would be a long walk, but she could likely stay the night in town with her friend Deena, easing the concern of whether she had the strength to return that day. If she left before noon, she'd likely arrive well before darkness. Because of broken street lights, potholes and even sinkholes, and as she was unfamiliar with who lived on certain stretches, Melanie avoided traveling in dark whenever possible.

She knew the route well. Walking along the edge of Brentwood Street, she carefully watched her footing to avoid the bumps and holes while leaving the neighborhood. In her younger years, the neighborhood would have been prime real estate for well-to-do young families, with its two-car garages, decent-sized homes, well-funded public schools, and playgrounds every few blocks. Now many of the houses were dilapidated and abandoned, covered with graffiti, any useful remains salvaged by others. Those who continued to live here struggled to make a living; none regularly commuted to high-paying jobs as they used to. Gardens filled the lots of those who chose to stay. In contrast to the deterioration, the sight of towels and clothes on clotheslines rustling in the wind filled her with joy, as she remembered the absurdity of the middle-class neighborhood ordinances that had banned them during her early life. It was comforting to see small signs of improvement from the old days.

Children's cries of exhilaration became louder as she turned the corner and glanced at the playground. The fun they were having seemed no different than the fun children had had on the brightly colored, regularly refurbished playgrounds of her youth. Three young boys and one girl ran around, playing tag on the rusty and broken playground equipment. The metal swing set still stood there, absent the swings. A solitary rusting chain hung from the horizontal pole; one boy ran and swung from it. The jagged edges of a broken plastic window of a climbing structure glistened from the midday sun. In their chase, children scrambled over a slide collapsed on its side. As she heard shrieks of laughter and glee again, she briefly closed her eyes. Despite appearances, some things never change, she assured herself.

As Melanie took a shortcut through a grassy parking lot of rusty, abandoned cars, she thought of the mail that might await her in town. She wondered if she might receive a letter from her nephew Trevor, who was away many months of the year at work for a company that salvaged scrap metal from big city office buildings. But what she most anticipated was receiving her first Valley Haven annual newsletter, presumably sent out last month, which should have arrived by now. She hungered to learn more about their work.

In the autumn she'd met Daryl, a traveling monk, during a potluck dinner at her neighbor's backyard across the street. She'd heard from someone that he would stay one night in the area on his way east. Then she overheard him briefly mention to that he was trying to obtain certain books. Eventually, she struck up conversation with him, intent on asking which books he sought. He gave some answers, but a quiet, humble air characterized his nature. He asked her many questions but said little about himself. She found herself pouring out many heartfelt stories from her days as a librarian and about all the books she wished she could find, stories she hadn't shared for a while. He listened sympathetically. Then, as the evening drew to a close and she paused in her storytelling, he finally shared that in addition to being a monk, he too was a librarian. Her curiosity peaked. Suddenly, she had a flurry of questions. However, it was late and he needed to sleep before early travel the next day. Before leaving that night, he'd written down her mailing address and assured her he would keep her updated on his work by sending her a Valley Haven annual newsletter next March. There she could learn further details.

When she had returned home, she felt as if she needed to say something more to him before he departed. Despite her sparse book collection, his warmth and willingness to listen that evening had inspired her to give him a few books he was interested in. Carrying them in a crocheted bag, she had walked in the dark over to the doorstep of the house where he was staying. Hoping he'd find them as he left the house the next morning, she had placed them there, along with a brief note:

Daryl, it was a pleasure to meet you this evening. It meant so much to me that when I came home and saw these books on my shelf, I knew they should go with you. I look forward to reading your next newsletter. Best wishes, Melanie

Ever since their conversation the previous year, memories of her abandoned library career regularly resurfaced, like apples pushed deep down into the rinse basin that always rose back up, waiting to be pressed. It troubled her. She had hopes within her that she had boxed up for too long.

As Melanie left the lot and walked along a path beside the stream that eventually meandered into the town center, her mind wandered back a few decades. She could almost hear the unwavering, monotone voice of the library board president as he discussed renovation and modernization plans at a staff-wide meeting.

"...We will not stay stuck in the past; we will march forward and reinvent the library to meet the needs of the 21st century with 21st century technology. Despite what some say, the library is not an obsolete institution; it is needed as ever in this age. We must change our architecture and shift our services to remain popular and to progress with the times. It is now my pleasure to let our architectural team show you some pictures of what our fabulous new library will look like."

One of the architects came forward and began his PowerPoint presentation outlining the $180 million Library Plan 2017. The staff stared at his many slides of how different parts of the library would look. He mentioned the 3-D printers, a greatly expanded digital section filled with latest models of computers and other devices, video game consoles for all ages, a high-tech makerspace, an e-career start-up lab, and even a tech "petting zoo" where patrons could test out new technology. He hardly mentioned books.

After the applause, when it was time for questions, Melanie had raised her hand.

"Where will all our current books fit with all these new additions? I'm a bit concerned—" she asked as innocently as she could, before being cut off.

"Don't worry, there will be something for everyone in this new library."

Three years later, she had entered the finished new library for the first time. It was a hideous monstrosity, encased in glass walls that had replaced the old sturdy brick structure. Entering the children's section, she was accosted by screens everywhere—the animation of Early Literacy computer stations, video game consoles, tablets available for check-out, and a giant iPad-like structure as the area's centerpiece. Trendy fluorescent plastic furniture filled the spacious room. Only a few small aisles of books inhabited the section, inconveniently located in the farthest corner. When she had later criticized the invasion of screens into the book area— suggesting, for example, that they reconsider the addition of animated computer games for preschoolers, so that books would remain the primary focus—she had been accused of advocating censorship.

Melanie vividly remembered how overwhelmed she had felt that first morning at the new library. Lacking words to communicate the turmoil inside her, she hadn't said much, her disillusionment only compounded by the head librarian's cheery remarks at the ribbon-cutting ceremony. While sitting at the reference desk in the afternoon, she suddenly told a co-worker that she needed to use the restroom and would return soon. She rushed into the restroom, sparkling clean with lemon cleaner scent, and burst into tears. Melanie wasn't someone who cried too often, but walking into the new library had made her feel as though a beloved friend had died. The lack of acknowledgement of that death made the tears flow even more profusely. *Why can't one quiet haven, a place to reflect and explore great literature away from the onslaught of screens, continue to exist? What am I to do?* She knew she should return to the reference desk before her co-workers started to worry. Trying to calm down, she wiped away the tears as much as she could.

Library jobs were hard to get these days, her friends had reminded her; they had told her she should be grateful that she had a job. As the days went on she tried to ignore all that had debased the library, instead highlighting to patrons the few quality books left in their diminishing collection. During story times she continued to tell stories from her heart; the collection of stories inside her never dwindled. But still she had felt overpowered, like a small fish trying to swim against a tide.

Within the year after the new library had opened, the fracking bubble popped, triggering a more severe financial crisis than the 2008 one. Despite the shiny new library that it was, with shrinking budgets and declining tax revenue it suddenly didn't have enough funds to maintain the lengthy hours. A third of the staff were laid off. She had still held onto her job, but with the library open only four days a week, her salary had been reduced.

಄

Melanie carefully avoided a dangerously deep sinkhole bordering the road. She believed it had formed during Hurricane Nina, which ravaged the state five years ago. Although the area had been far from the highest winds, the flooding had damaged much infrastructure. She had heard rumors that the county intended to repair that area of the road, but she doubted it would do that anytime soon. She left the road, instead following a meandering path around an empty car dealership. Passing by its parking lot with overgrown bushes and weeds, Melanie increased her gait as memories from her library career cut short continued to flood back.

What especially bothered her, painfully so now, was that all the proposed changes to the library had been presented as if they were an embracement of an inevitable age coming, not as a choice to be made or not. Although there was no doubt that older libraries, consisting mainly of rooms densely filled with books, had worked well for her and so many other children, to continue such a tradition was seen not as a virtue but rather as something backward and obstructive to efforts to appeal to then popular whims.

Within months after the library had closed, her younger sister Heather died of pneumonia. With no one else to care for Heather's three children, Melanie hadn't hesitated to take them into her care. She tried hard to raise her two nephews and niece so that they had a decent and nurtured childhood, despite the War, high unemployment, fuel shortages, and riots over food prices. Life was tough, downright exhausting much of the time; her concerns had shifted to day-to-day survival. While she collected books once in a while and tried to share a love of reading when possible, her librarian identity fell away like wilted petals of a flower that had once bloomed, she unaware of the flower's perennial nature. Having sufficient food on the table, clean water to drink, and a safe home for the kids became her utmost priority.

She thought back again to the last decade her library had been open. It wasn't a sudden event that shuttered hers and many other libraries, but rather a gradual degradation of funds and infrastructure, interspersed with some major crises, and compounded by poor decisions, that ultimately led them into the dark. During the twilight of the library's existence, they had to figure out how to cope with smaller budgets each year. She remembered the heated and unresolved arguments at library board and city council meetings, trying to determine how to slash the budget in the least painful way. All full-time positions were eventually eliminated; certain branches closed; hours cut more and more. Although the city had a sizeable population who used the library, she remembered the day the entrance sign had been changed to advertise brand new hours: open only Tuesdays 10-2, and Thursdays 2-5. Even those paltry hours hardly indicated the sober reality. In the last several years of its existence, the library repeatedly had to close even when it was supposed to be open. The electricity often went out for days, once even for three months before it was restored, only to go out again a week later.

Once at a staff meeting discussing their many troubles, she dared to interject.

"More often than not we are closed because we have no electricity. Wouldn't it be sensible for us to try to adapt our library services so that we can continue to serve the public with or without electricity?" From her studies she knew of libraries that had thrived long before electricity; she didn't see why theirs couldn't as well.

"For instance, even though patrons couldn't use the computers, we could still find a way to allow the public to check books in and out, and instead of job training classes for mostly non-existent jobs, we could find more useful ways to support people struggling to survive in these hard economic times. And we could continue to have story times for the children, outside under the sycamore tree if needed…"

Perhaps her suggestions were wishful thinking. By that time, physical books occupied less than three percent of the current library's space; only 3,000 volumes at most remained in the entire city library system. Two decades prior, the library system had contained 700,000 books. The situation, of course, was not quite as dire as some of the all-digital paperless libraries around the country that had been lauded by futurists. Although much of the library wasn't books anymore, she acknowledged to herself, maybe it wasn't too late to reverse that trend.

Visibly annoyed, the Library Director stared at her. "I see no reason to take on a defeatist attitude. The mayor informs us these troubles are only temporary, and I'm confident that our library's brightest days are just around the corner. Let us remind ourselves, American Libraries for the 21st Century honored us with the Building the Future Award several summers ago for our cutting-edge technology in our services.

We have to stay true to that vision. I'm confident in what we've done so far and the future that awaits us."

Even when the electricity had been working, problems overran the library. No funds were available to fix or replace computers that malfunctioned; the Internet connection was spotty at best. Despite being broken, the 3-D printer remained, collecting dust in the tech makerspace. During one long drought, they had no water. In the summertime when they had no air conditioning, it was often too hot to remain open according to the library's temperature policy. The building architecture was like a greenhouse, retaining too much heat. Of the few books they had, many went missing and could not be replaced.

One winter after the city had gone bankrupt, city officials unilaterally voted to close the library after the end of the fiscal year. Melanie momentarily thought about possibly trying to continue the library as a volunteer-run operation, but so little of the current library consisted of materials not dependent on electricity. Therefore it seemed like it would have been a wasted effort, and other more pressing concerns had been on her mind that she had to deal with—the water that the city was cutting off to her portion of the neighborhood, for example. Melanie continued to arrive at work those last two months, muddling though the technological disarray she rarely could solve, here and there talking to a patron about a great book that usually wasn't available.

ॐ

As she picked her way around a rusting carcass of an abandoned car, she vividly remembered one of her last mornings at work. The lights had been working when she arrived, so she prepared for a scheduled story time, feeling spirited as a few children and their parents staggered in. Ten minutes before it was supposed to start, the lights flickered out. She knew that the library would immediately close. But feeling extra vitality that morning, she turned to the group that had gathered.

"If you don't mind the darkness, I intend to tell stories as planned." She knew the Library Director would disapprove. But she had nothing left to lose because she was losing her job within the week anyhow. "Please follow me into our story room."

A few children trotted in, excited by the darkness, and found places to sit. She felt compelled to tell some timeless stories, ones passed down through many generations. Lighting a candle which had been stashed away in her purse, she began, the faint glow illuminating the faces of both storyteller and listeners. She told her favorite Tibetan folk tale, followed by a Coyote the Trickster tale. To end the morning she chose a Jewish story that always filled her with hope and possibility, even when all the evidence around her spoke otherwise.

"Once upon a time there was a poor tailor. Even though his house was full of beautiful cloth, he could not buy material to make himself a coat. One day he realized if he could save scraps of material left over from clothes he made, he could make a coat."

The children looked at her, wide-eyed, wondering what she was going to say next.

"He got out his scissors and worked day and night cutting and sewing himself a gorgeous coat." She acted out the cutting and sewing.

"He loved that coat. He wore it in the spring and the summer and the autumn and the winter until one day it was all worn out. He was about to throw it away, when he decided he could make a jacket with it, which he wore until it had fallen apart..."

"From the scraps he sewed a vest. When his vest wore out, he sewed himself a hat." She patted her head as if putting on a hat.

"...But the hat eventually unraveled. He cut his hat into usable scraps and made some buttons which he wore until he grew old. And one day the buttons wore out."

Suddenly the flame of her candle fluttered out, and all was darkness. The children, captivated by the story, did not budge. She continued.

"And he used the material to make a story."

Melanie's own life was like a garment sewn together from many scraps of material, then worn out, cut up and sewn together again into new purposes, only to unravel again and again, each time recrafted into new meaning. As she neared the end of her time on earth, it sometimes felt like the worn-out buttons in the story, nothing left to be made from it. But despite many losses and struggles, she liked to think that her life was worth it, and there was some story left yet to make from it all.

Her legs grew tired, but she was determined to trudge forward, knowing that she was almost in town. The superhighway loomed in the distance, completely quiet. Although she occasionally heard an old vehicle clunking through the streets, no one used the highway anymore. The bridge it led to had collapsed; the route had become a dead end. She had heard of many other bridge collapses too. People now used boats to cross the river when it was necessary. Life went on.

As her feet touched the quiet earth under the highway, a billboard that must have been put up decades ago loomed above her. Despite being torn and faded, she could still make out the caption of a bank's retirement plan ad in big print: *1 in 3 babies born today will live to 100. Are we prepared?* She almost laughed at the incongruity of that affirmation with the reality of her own family members' life spans. She was quite lucky to have lived past seventy, longer than most others had in her family. Her sister Heather had died years ago; before that, Heather's husband had committed suicide a year after he lost his six-figure salary when the banking industry imploded. Melanie's niece Genevieve died during childbirth; Melanie's nephew Aidan and Genevieve's husband were both presumed dead in the war; Trevor's partner died from a bullet wound. Her grandnephew Arthur died from an unidentified disease at age two. But Cailyn and Fiona were sprightful, healthy youngsters. She had devoted much of her energy to nurturing their learning and curiosity, in hopes their childhood could be as magical as hers had been.

೨

She recalled their delight at the simplest surprises. On their most recent birthdays, celebrated together since they occurred less than one week apart, she had given them each a present.

Fiona opened up the first one, a book! *Anne of Green Gables.* Fiona cried with delight. The paperback was worn, once waterlogged, and missing a few pages, the type of damage that—if it had been in Melanie's library—would have landed it in the trash. But it was a book for her very own. Fiona, red-headed and independent like Anne, was the kind of girl who would appreciate Anne's adventures.

Fiona immediately hugged her. "Thank you! How did you know I had wanted a new book for my birthday?"

Cailyn then opened her gift, also a book, but in better condition. *The Cow-Tail Switch and Other West African Stories.* The 398.2 call number tag was still taped to its plastic library binding, with a discard stamp visible on the inside cover. Because of its good condition, Melanie figured it probably was one of those books that back in the day hadn't circulated in two years, meeting its fate in the discard bin. She imagined all the library books weeded over the years, wishing they could be seeds of a new library that would sprout up after a long, barren winter.

"Wow…" was all Cailyn said, grinning with joy. She loved to hear stories from faraway lands, most of which Melanie told from memory.

"There are some stories in there that I've never told you."

Turning the corner where a mobile phone shop had once thrived, she walked down the main street. It was remarkably empty of activity, except for a few people on horseback in the distance, and a man urinating in the ditch across the street, something that she would never have seen back in the town's posh days. After passing the shoe repair shop, one of few thriving businesses in town, she entered the post office.

"Why, good day, Ms. Melanie. It's been a while since you've stopped by. Where are your girls?" Henry always greeted her with friendly words.

"Oh, they are traveling with Lisa. But they won't be gone much longer, I suspect."

"Let me see..." he said, turning and looking for the appropriate box. "I do believe there's some mail for you." Melanie grew excited.

"Thank you so much," she said as he handed over her mail.

She walked outside to a bench to rest her tired legs and see what she had received. There were three pieces. The first envelope had a foreign stamp—from the country of California—and had been postmarked five months ago. She immediately knew it was from her friend, a dedicated letter writer, whom she hadn't seen since half a lifetime ago. She decided to save it to open at home.

The next envelope was addressed to Lisa, from an association of midwives she belonged to. Melanie would give it to her when she returned.

Her heart sank as she looked at the third piece, having just a handwritten address of her P.O. box, with no return address. It didn't look official enough to be what she was hoping for.

Just in case, she tore it open and unfolded the several papers it contained. There on the letterhead she saw a small woodcut drawing. It looked like a valley, with a row of books filling the lowest part of it. Underneath the logo, in fancy letter print, were the words: *Valley Haven Library, Established 2026*. Her heart leapt with joy.

As she read through every word of the newsletter, Melanie was astonished to discover that such a library existed, and that this was where Daryl, whom she had met that one evening, lived and worked. She read through a paragraph summarizing its history, getting a better idea of its mission. Apparently it had been started as a small project in the 20s by a few forward-thinking librarians, interfaith clergy, and farmers. That was only a few years after her library had been renovated, yet it had been unknown to her all these years!

Concerned with the long-term consequences of current trends in library services at the time, they had started a modest library, while exploring non-digital preservation techniques that didn't rely on electricity and unsustainable technology. Thirty-some years later, they worked in an old brick factory building converted into a library, full of 57,000 books, with a thriving farm adjacent to it, located in a mostly forested rural valley several mountain ranges away. Although their focus was cultural preservation, they did have a smaller lending library for their supporting members. One could only get to Valley Haven Library and Farm by an overgrown dirt road. Their mailing address was a P.O. box in a town miles away. She got the sense that they didn't want to publicize themselves too much. Maybe that was why Daryl hadn't disclosed too many details, which made her feel more blessed to have earned his trust enough to be sent the newsletter.

She turned to the next page, entitled, "Some New Books at Valley Haven Library." Looking through the list, she recognized some of the titles: *Hope in Hard Times: Stories of Struggle and Renewal After the 2019 Financial Crisis* by Karen C. Patterson, *Encyclopedia Americana* (all volumes except #4, #25, & #29 of the 30-volume 1982 edition), *Land of the Long White Cloud: Maori Myths and Legends* by Kiri Te Kanawa, *Amidst the Cracks: Wells of Emerging Stories* (the original unabridged 2028 edition) by Joanne Moynihan, *Extraordinary Popular Delusions and the Madness of Crowds* by Charles McKay, *I Had Trouble in Getting to Solla Sollew* by Dr. Seuss, *A Time to Break Silence: The Essential Works of Martin Luther King, Jr.*, and *Basic*

Ecology by Ralph and Mildred Bushbaum. Most of these she hadn't seen around for years!

The remaining pages explored their library's projects and news in more depth. One of their librarians examined the pros and cons of various preservation techniques and some of the risks they needed to think through. Another article discussed their plans to start a small publishing enterprise, with an apprenticeship program to train others in letterpress printing, inkmaking, and bookbinding. On the following page was a heartfelt commentary on some of their challenges of the past decade, most especially the damage caused by the Flood of 2054, the unexpected deaths of two long-term librarians, and concerns about looters and invaders, despite Valley Haven's humble presence. Another writer relayed news about what was growing on the farm, mentioning the new raspberry patch and the goat kids born last summer. They were also interested in how they might assist more librarians elsewhere with starting or sustaining libraries. One article mentioned that they had recently started two sister libraries, since warehousing books in only one location made themselves more vulnerable in an unpredictable future.

On the second to last page, there was a notice and request for feedback from members:

> After much lively discussion, we at Valley Haven Library have decided that somewhere on our land we want to make a memorial to honor books and other cultural materials that are or will be lost forever (of course, we may never be sure of the specific items that fall into this category). This may sound strange, because much of our work revolves around preserving heritage for future generations and minimizing loss of important materials. But, as our work is largely in response to the aftermath of a society's failure to recognize limits, we

too have to recognize our own limitations, which is as important as recognizing our capabilities and allows us to do the work we do. Although we have done great work, we are small, and every passing year, we cannot deny our work becomes more difficult as certain books are harder to find and preserve. We realize that many exquisitely brilliant books, articles, musical pieces, movies, scientific documents, and other works will be lost in the years to come, never to be known to anyone ever again, and we cannot help but grieve over this. Even when only absence and the unknown are left, they too can be a source of knowledge and stories. We hope to design something simple yet meaningful, and we welcome ideas on what it should be. Please don't hesitate to send us your ideas.

Melanie shed a tear reading this; it reminded her in some way of the story she told during her library's last story time.

The last page, a handwritten message to her, elevated her spirits immensely:

Melanie,

We can't thank you enough for your donation of The Robot and the Cobbler *(I didn't realize that a few non-digital copies had been made when it was published in 2024!). Thank you so much also for* Winesburg, Ohio *...and the half dozen other books you gave us; we did not currently have those in our collection!! Utmost attention will be put to making sure they are preserved and possibly even reprinted if deemed necessary. Daryl greatly enjoyed hearing some of your stories from your days as a librarian, and we sincerely hope you can find ways to continue to honor that passion. Even though Daryl's meeting with you was brief, the richness of your character comes across to us in a deep way.*

As a small token of our appreciation, if you can arrange a way of traveling here, we invite you to visit the Library so you can have a better sense of our work. We are also open to your insight and interested in other ways you might be able to contribute to our mission. Our accommodations are modest, but we can provide basic meals and a loft to sleep in during the week you wish to come. Just reply and send us the dates you expect to come. We will then send you more information on how to get to our exact location and other important details.

With gratitude,
Thomas Blevins
Valley Haven Library

P.S. According to Daryl, you mentioned The Blessing Cup. *We just acquired a copy! A beautiful story about finding hope and blessings in challenging times.*
P.P.S. I forgot to mention, the two girls can come too!

Without hesitation, Melanie took out a piece of paper and pencil stub and started writing a letter back to Valley Haven Library. She hadn't figured out how she and the two girls would travel the 100-some miles to get there, but knew they'd figure out a way. The late afternoon sun peeked through the clouds, lighting up the world around her—the potholes and the dandelions blooming from the cracks of old pavement, the decaying storefronts and the cobbler's new sign, and in the distance, the crumbling highway and a sailboat crossing the river. She felt blessed to be alive.

Al-kimiya

Tony f. whelKs

Christina Rose looked cross when I finally entered the glasshouse, or at least she made the face of it. I had kept her waiting and the air was hot, thick with the scent of orange blossom and wafting pollen. Beneath the new tendrils of the kiwi vines, speckled shade was dotted with the cheerful citrus hues of marigolds. Hoverflies trembled the still air as they danced between the limnanthes, the flowers spilling across the beds like heaped platters of poached eggs.

"You took your time, Michael," in a not-quite-chiding tone.

"Distillation is a finicky business, Chris. My apprentice is doing well, but I can't leave her alone with it yet."

"Distilling?" A raised eyebrow, more inquisitive than inquisitorial.

"Peppermint," I began.

"It's a bit early in the year for that, isn't it?"

"The crop was ready. Mint doesn't understand the calendar, only the weather."

Chris gave a wry half-laugh. "I'm glad someone understands it. I certainly don't anymore."

"No," I sighed, "And the lavender won't be long either."

A dark shadow appeared to cross her face, a misgiving, maybe. "I know it's a busy time for you, Michael, but I need you to do something for me, for the farm."

She paused.

"A candidate. Check him out."

☙

New Alchemy Farm—my home, workplace, refuge, call it what you will—is a closed community, nominally a cooperative, but one in which all its members invariably defer to Christina Rose. We have a written constitution and democratic forms, but that's mostly honoured in the breach. Christina decides, we agree. It works for us.

We don't take new members lightly; after all, there's only so much land. Any new candidates have to bring something to the table. It's hard, but it's a hard world now. Refugees get a meal, shelter for the night and a speedy farewell, and that's a meal and a rest more than they get anywhere else. Unless they can bring something to the table, of course, in which case we'll extend the welcome for a week or so. We don't tell them they are candidates, but if we—that is, Christina—are happy, then they're invited to stay. Candidates usually come to us, which is why I was so surprised at Christina's request. It had been decades since I last went into the city and I must admit I felt some trepidation at the prospect.

☙

The travelling party was small. Myself, of course; Jake, the laconic Scot who had served in some never-specified regiment during an equally unspecified war; and Yusuf, a

124

recent refugee who'd arrived one day with a haunted look and an unusual facility for weaving and tailoring which we appreciated enough to let him stay.

Jake is a wily old coot, and if you ever need anyone watching your back, then Jake's your man. That's why he was with us. Going into the city these days, it's good to have someone to watch your back. Yusuf was wearing more than one hat, though. His well-muscled six-foot frame and steely gaze were deterrent enough for the sort of miscreant the road might offer, but more importantly, he was our introduction to the candidate. For all that I was wearing a few items of his handiwork, I still didn't really know Yusuf by then, he tends to the quiet side, but there's nothing like a journey to get to know someone. Jake I've known for years, almost since he was first stranded south of the border during the troubles that followed the dissolution of the Union.

It's only seven miles to the city but we gathered as the sun rose over the rolling fields. In my youth I could walk there in a couple of hours. In my youth I didn't need to, though, because buses still ran and then later I could drive. Now only military vehicles could be seen on the road, though rarely this far from London, and it was never good to let them see you.

"You've decided on a route?" Jake asked as I locked up the workshop.

"I was thinking of the old railway line, then the old A50, as we may as well stop off at Dr. John's and deliver this." I held up the rucksack full of supplies. Jake looked dubious.

"That's under. I prefer over."

"It all depends, Jake. You told me yourself that the Squire's men have been patrolling recently. No one's been robbed down there for months."

Yusuf was looking confused. "Under or over what?"

"The motorway," I explained. "We have to cross the M1 somewhere between here and the city. It's a choice between who's lurking in the shadows or a detour of a few miles. You'll be carrying the rucksack, Yusuf, seeing as Jake is going to be scouting ahead, and I'm too old."

"Fine, fine, but I don't like it," Jake grumbled.

In the event, it was fine as we passed from the dappled sunlight of the overgrown track into the cool, damp shade beneath the motorway bridge. Blackened scorch marks and smoke trails obscured some of the decades old graffiti on the concrete and a ring of boulders marked a fire pit. Whoever left it there hadn't cleared up after them, and I couldn't help wondering if I'd been overconfident after all. The enclosed space beneath the silent highway echoed with distant memories from my childhood.

Once the potential trouble spot was cleared, Jake forged ahead on the path, senses alert for any danger. I turned to Yusuf, wanting to break the silence that had fallen over me in the bridge's chilly underbelly.

"I remember when that motorway was newly built," I said, pointing back with my thumb. "I saw the last train on this track before it was ripped up and made into a footpath. I was only a toddler, but I saw it."

"You are a local man, then?" Yusuf replied, politely.

"Oh, yes. This used to be my playground as a boy. That bridge was my limit. My parents always said I should never go any further from home than there."

"And you obeyed?"

"Did I heck! The best blackberry picking was always on the far side of the bridge," I laughed. "What about you, Yusuf? Where did you grow up?"

"My parents came over from Pakistan, but I was born in Leicester. They would be about your age, I guess."

"Would?" I asked, tentatively.

"They were on the Last Hajj."

"I'm sorry." I didn't know what else to say. What can you say?

"We weren't close," he added. "They disowned me."

"Even so..."

"They said Allah hates gays," Yusuf continued, the revelations coming thick and fast, I thought. "Otherwise I would have been with them. On the Hajj, I mean."

"You miss them, though, surely?" It felt trite, even as I spoke.

"They put me out of their hearts. I returned the favour. I got used to being alone." There was a vehemence to his voice, as though he was trying to convince himself, too.

"So that's why you wound up at New Alchemy?"

"Yes. At first the community just shunned me when they found out I was gay, but after ... *that* ... I couldn't go to the mosque any more. How could I pray when I literally had to face what had happened, what my fellow Muslims had done? I helped protect our neighbourhood from the nationalist thugs and then the rioters, but it was my own neighbours who burnt my house and chased me out. So here I am. A lonely, gay, apostate outcast. I feel like I'm everyone's scapegoat some days."

The last ten years or so haven't been easy for anyone, but I could understand how difficult it had been for Yusuf.

"Well, there'll be none of that at the farm," I said.

"No. I'm glad of that. It feels like a bubble of sanity in a sea of crazy."

"We've had our share of crazy, too, but it seems to be calming down again now." At least, as long as Christina stays on the right side of the Squire, I thought to myself. I'm still not quite sure what sort of a deal she's done, but he's someone we need inside the tent, as they say, and he has brought back some sense of order around the villages. Not exactly law, but order at least. That's a start.

We paced side by side for a few minutes in silence, then bumped up against Jake crouching beneath the cascading foliage overhanging the path. He gestured for us to be quiet and edged forward, pulling out his treasured binoculars. Jake spent a couple of minutes scanning the surrounding area, then, satisfied, he waved us on once more. We broke cover on to the street of what used to be a quiet country town. A boarded up pub, opposing rows of once-desirable houses, then on the bend in the road, the irony of a petrol station, forlorn and silent.

This had once been a good neighbourhood, with the misfortune of lying too close to a bad one. We would be skirting the bad neighbourhood for a while after we made it to the A50, but that had become just as depopulated as this town. The area had suffered disproportionately during the second wave of fuel protests. I'd heard the stories, but I hadn't seen it with my own eyes. In the year 2000 the truckers' blockades had come close to toppling the government, but in the second wave a few years ago they didn't stop the protests after three days. The government had learnt from previous experience, though, and troops hit the streets once the riots began.

Yusuf barely batted an eyelid at the damage. He'd been in the city at the time, and had seen much worse, he told me. Luckily we'd been reasonably isolated on the farm, except that it was about this time the Squire started making a name for himself; he was strictly poacher then, his conversion to gamekeeper still ahead of him.

Jake had us through the burnt out street in next to no time, and the wide avenue of the A50 opened out before us. Up ahead a small band of travellers were also on their way towards the city, clearly traders heading for the market. Thursday had been market day since Domesday, a thousand-year tradition persisting through all the tumults and disruptions of English history, and persisting still, regardless of any central authority to uphold the ancient Royal Charter. There had been a market on the Thursday before Richard III marched his army out of the city towards Bosworth Field, and again on the Thursday after his naked and broken corpse returned, draped across a horse's saddle. Neither Cromwell nor the Luftwaffe had broken the rhythm of commerce, but the fuel protesters had come close. People still trudged to the city with their wares, and we trudged along with our own. The land rose steeply here, and Yusuf groaned quietly and shucked the rucksack on his shoulders until it sat more comfortably.

"Cheer up, laddie," Jake called. "The doc's just ahead now." Seeing the other travellers on the road had cheered the

Scottish veteran somewhat, further indication that the recent banditry had been suppressed, for a while at least.

৵

The cluster of low, squat buildings where Dr. John Jackson runs his clinic still glories in the title of hospital, although most of the abandoned buildings were mothballed in the austerity years, whilst others fell into disuse more chaotically as the services became impossible given the constrained resources available more recently. What began under the guise of regionalisation, the concentration of services into 'centres of excellence,' amounted to little more than the withdrawal of the legions and an off-hand note that us provincials should 'look to our own defences' as the centre, that is to say London, looked out for itself. A generation of medics raised and trained in the high-tech NHS of the early 21st century found their skills too abstract and specialised to cope. Front-line healthcare fell to an ever-ageing cadre of GPs with memories and training from a less sophisticated time, and they struggle on, training the few driven acolytes willing to relearn medical basics and adapt to a new reality. Dr. John was at least ten years my senior, any prospect of retirement long gone, erased by the need to pass on the torch before it sputtered out.

We halted at the gate to the grounds, and a guard with all the looks of another veteran peered through the chain link at the three of us.

"Morning, gentlemen," he growled, wary eyes looking us up and down. "State your business, please."

"Supplies for Dr. Jackson," I told him, but he still eyed Yusuf suspiciously, the bulging backpack evidently causing him some concern.

"He's in surgery. Got an appointment?"

We hadn't, so I gave the guard my name.

"Step back from the gate, gentlemen." A quick whistle summoned a boy from the shade of the ramshackle shed that stood nearby, and the guard spoke a few words into his ear before the youngster scampered off towards a curve in the path and disappeared between the overgrown rhododendrons that grew in patches throughout the grounds.

We sat on the verge and passed around the water bottle as we waited. We didn't speak much, Yusuf just muttered a comment about being everyone's scapegoat once again, and Jake quietly surveyed the small groups of people passing along the road to the weekly market. Occasionally guards passed us as they patrolled inside the hospital fence, each casting a wary eye over us and exchanging meaningful glances with the gate keeper. Resounding footsteps heralded the return of the message boy and we were admitted.

"Michael, so good to see you in person. How are you keeping? What have you got for us today?" Dr. John's greeting was effusive, and the man had a nervous energy, almost birdlike with his thin frame and flapping voluminous white coat. He had come into his waiting room to meet us. Before leading us through to the dispensary he had a quick, reassuring word with the next waiting patient. The young woman sported a ragged mass of bandages on her forearm, and she nodded as Dr. John explained that his assistant, Martyna, would redress her burns shortly.

The dispensary was a large room edged with cupboards, the walls lined with shelves above the work surfaces. Although the hospital could still generate a trickle of

131

electricity, there was only enough for a few lights. Old, yellowed power sockets clustered redundantly around the work spaces, and all the equipment was manual. Where once digital scales had stood, a glass-cased apothecary balance with brass weights held pride of place. Beside it, a polished tablet press, a rack of ointment spatulas and marble mixing slabs. Mortars nestled in a stack like Russian dolls. An ancient autoclave sat atop a gas burner, fed by a rubber tube which snaked its way from a hole hacked into the wall and crudely resealed with plaster of Paris.

The shelves would once have held phalanxes of cardboard boxes, their bright colours and commercial logos lined up in a parade of proprietary synonyms and intellectual property rights. Now, nearly all the blister-packed petrochemical by-products were gone, replaced by the hand-labelled bottles and jars of dried herbs. The few staple medicines that occasionally found their way out of London filled no more than two or three shelves.

Jake found himself a chair and promptly nodded off to sleep, as old soldiers are wont to do when they can. Yusuf gratefully shed the burden of his backpack, and under Dr. John Jackson's eager eyes, decanted the containers inside on to a clear patch of the bench.

Dr. John instantly eyed the dark brown glass bottle. "Iodine?"

"Yes, alcoholic tincture. You mentioned in your last letter that antiseptics were getting scarce."

"I did, I did, thank you! But how...?"

"Not easy. We had to trade for this. We could make it ourselves, but we can't haul enough kelp so far inland, and then you still need sulphuric acid. Anyway, that's going to cost you some silver."

"Not a problem, Michael. It's worth its weight in gold and not a moment too soon. Did you get a whiff of that bandage when you came through?"

Two clear glass bottles containing distilled alcohol were next, and Dr. John nodded eagerly, already seeing uses for the new materials.

"These are our own," I said as Yusuf placed out the smaller bottles containing essential oils. "Peppermint, lavender, eucalyptus and wintergreen. You will need to assay them to sort out doses," I cautioned. We do what we can to standardise the products, but variations in the weather and individual plants can make a lot of difference. Precision was one more of the luxuries that went away with the failure of industrial pharmaceutics.

Next followed the salves and ointments in screw-top jars. "Arnica, calendula, echinacea," I announced each tub as Yusuf reached into the pack. "There's also some echinacea extract," I added.

By now there were only the paper wraps of dried herbs left.

"We've got something new for you this time." I beamed. "For your insomniacs, neurotics and worriers. Valerian root. We managed to acquire some seed a couple of years ago and have finally gone into production. Treat it as a mid-range sedative. More potent than chamomile, and saves your opium for pain-relief."

"I'll file it under 'Valium,' then," the aged medic laughed. "There's not been much to replace the benzodiazepines to date."

133

The backpack was nearly empty by now, and Yusuf placed the final bags of herbs on the counter top. Dr. John read off the labels. "Chamomile, good. Digitalis, feverfew, willow bark, excellent. And these?" He held up the last two small bags, which were unlabelled.

I spoke quietly. "You mentioned some... ah, delicate... requirements when you wrote last."

Dr. John nodded gravely as he peered into each bag and sniffed at the contents. The bitter tang of rue and the aromatic pungency of pennyroyal assailed his nostrils and he slipped the herbs into a nearby drawer, which he locked with a small, brass key. Regardless of the need, given the moral climate, some things are best left unspoken.

The medic was as good as his word and handed over the silver coins. I woke Jake and he stashed the payment in an inside pocket.

"Is there anything else you need, John?" I asked.

"Apart from everything?" he replied ruefully. "We really need quinine, but there's none to be had. The malaria is spreading northwards, you know. I don't know if quinine is even still being imported or if it's something else they're hoarding in London."

"There's nothing we can do for that, I'm afraid. We can produce citronella for mosquito repellent, but nothing more."

"No, I guessed as much. It's getting harder every day, Michael," he confided. "Some days I feel like the little Dutch boy with my finger in the dike, holding back the tide of diseases we thought we'd defeated. A lot of the time palliative care is the best we can offer. Sometimes I find myself wishing for the old days, when the surgery was filled with the worried well, when everyone wanted antibiotics for their colds and sniffles."

"So what do you give them now? Rose-hip syrup?" I asked.

"Exactly, but there's not many who come in with colds nowadays. They save their silver for the children. Since we've had no vaccines, childhood illnesses are back in force. So many of my younger colleagues had never seen them before. We are all learning forgotten lessons all over again. Let's face it, we're almost back to Culpeper, Michael. We've just dropped the astrology in favour of germ theory."

We took our leave of the medic and he hurried back to Martyna in the surgery, clutching the iodine tincture almost as a talisman. Back on the road, the market traffic was steady and I could see a donkey cart ahead of us, heaped with new potatoes standing proud above the scattered walkers with their packs. Clearly some groups had travelled together for mutual protection, but the huddles were loosening somewhat now the city was in sight. As we crested the hill we could see out across the rooftops, hazy with the wood smoke which settled in the valley. We had made good time after all, and it was not yet noon.

Yusuf, free of his burden, had more of a spring in his step, but Jake was more guarded with his own burden of a pocketful of silver. We walked on towards our next meeting. There were a few stationary figures posted at intervals along the road. Hard looking men squinted in the sunlight, a preponderance of red showing in their clothing. Most sported lengths of polished wood that could serve as clubs or staves, some of which resembled, and probably were, old police truncheons.

Jake caught my sidelong gaze as we passed one group. "The Mayor's men," he hissed. I felt no more comfortable for their reassuring presence than I had felt driving past the speed camera vans that had used to lurk on the verge. Yusuf, I noticed, was gazing intently at his feet as we passed the watchmen.

Occasionally we saw small children sitting on a garden wall, bucket and shovel to hand, ready to dive out and retrieve anything the few horses or other draught animals may deposit on the ancient, pot-holed tarmac. In an isolated island struggling to feed itself, every scrap of fertility is valuable, either for the family garden or to exchange for food with others.

The changes in the city, the destruction and dereliction, were shocking to me, but then so were some of the things that had survived the troubles of the past decade. Between the highway and the slum estate, the large allotment gardens still produced, barricaded behind rusted wire and unruly hawthorn hedges, busier now with gardeners than ever I saw in my youth.

As we crossed the first of the bridges that marked the ancient boundary of the city, I was reminded of Dr. John's revelation. The water was turbid and mud showed along the edges, the Soar's flow reduced dramatically. Sure enough, there amongst the silted islands and willow regrowth, stagnant water pooled, lying in wait for mosquitoes and malaria.

Beyond the bridge, on the island formed between the river's natural course and the canalised, navigable route, lay what used to be a vibrant light industrial zone. I can just about remember it being vibrant, anyway, but the fires in vacant factories had started long before the last recession, when it was still possible to insure the buildings. After that it went through a twilight phase of car-washes on vacant lots, a half-hearted redevelopment scheme that embarrassed a few city councillors and saw a few more incarcerated, and finally it had become a haven for urban wildlife, largely ignored as the windblown buddleias had worked their roots into powdery mortar. The shuffling figures I could see amongst the debris and rubble were being watched over by more of the hard-faced men in red. Picks and hammers worked at the stone and brick, whilst carts trundled in empty, and out again laden with beams, girders and carefully sorted masonry. As I peered through the fence I could see the ropes hobbling the workers and binding them into teams. They clearly were not there voluntarily.

I was roused from my musings by a shout from one of the watchmen on the bridge. "Keep moving there!" Jake pulled at my arm, and I stumbled after him.

"Don't draw attention," he whispered. "They'll think we're planning a breakout."

We moved on quickly, until we reached the second bridge where the mayor's salvage wagons and the market traffic combined to form a snarling bottleneck in the narrow carriageway. Once we had cleared the crush, it was time for us to part from the crowd, as our route wouldn't be taking us to the market.

"OK, Yusuf, which way now?" I asked

"The Muslim enclave. When we get there, please, let me do the talking."

Christina hadn't told me much about the candidate, just that she was very keen he should join us. I'd asked her why, but she'd just said 'You'll see.' I had pressed her on how she could be so sure about someone she'd not even met. She couldn't, she had admitted, but she did trust my judgement, a rare honour indeed.

The enclave was a neighbourhood of two-up two-down terraces, and as we approached, I could see barricades across the narrow street. Yusuf walked ahead, Jake and I following close behind.

"*Salaam elaikum*," he called out. At first there was no answer, then an upstairs window opened just beyond the barrier, and a brief exchange in Urdu followed.

"We must wait, my grandfather is coming," Yusuf explained.

~

Hafiz, the grandfather, the candidate although he didn't know it yet, led us through the silent street to his home. Yusuf was looking nervous, as well he might entering a neighbourhood that had once turned against him. For my part, I was dismayed. Hafiz must have been older even than Dr. John, and less sprightly, too. Had Christina realised his age? My intention to be back at the farm by nightfall was beginning to look impractical, to say the least. Even Jake raised a querying eyebrow at me. I couldn't see this working out well, any way I looked at it. We were going to have to hire a cart, and staying overnight would mean we'd miss the market traders heading out of town.

The small, terraced house was cool inside, a relief from the sun that was finally burning through the haze outside.

"So, Yusuf, you have come back to us."

"Not to stay, grandfather."

"You can if you want. Why not?"

"You know why not. For the same reason I had to leave in the first place."

The grandfather looked wistful. "Things have changed. In the community, I mean, a lot can be forgiven. We need young men, Yusuf, you belong with other Muslims."

"There are no Muslims, grandfather!" Yusuf almost shouted. "It's over. How can you still believe after..."

"He was my son!" Hafiz snapped back. "You think I don't feel it, too?"

"I'm sorry. I didn't come here to argue. You're all the family I have left, we should stick together, not fight."

"So why are you here? You and your friends."

"I, we, want you to join us," Yusuf began. "It's not safe for you here. We have a farm, outside the city. Your experience would be valued, more than it is here."

"I'm safe enough here, Yusuf," the older man countered. "You've been gone two years. It's safer now."

Yusuf snorted. "Hnnn! Safer? Why are the barricades still standing? Why else do you need young men?"

"It's years since the last riots," Hafiz said. "It's true, the nationalists still cause some trouble, but we can protect ourselves. I'm too old for farm work now, anyway."

"We need you as a teacher, not a labourer. Teach me. Let me look after you."

At this, Hafiz turned to me, scepticism clear in his voice. "So what is this farm my grandson is talking about? What use is an old man like me?"

I was beginning to wonder about that myself, and suddenly found myself in the spotlight. "Well, as Yusuf said, it's outside the city. We've been running over twenty-five years now, ever since the big recession. A few of us were out of work, so we got together and tried to make a living growing food, but the fuel crisis made us rethink things quite a bit."

Hafiz nodded. "Everyone had to rethink things then. I had just moved to England to be with my family. It was not a good time to be a Muslim here, not when the Saudis stopped exporting their oil. Everybody blamed us! We were the evil Muslims keeping all the oil."

"Aye, you and the Scots alike," interjected Jake.

"I should have stayed on my own farm," continued Hafiz. "Life was simpler, even when the Taliban were trying to tell us what we can and can't grow. But when my wife died, Yusuf's father insisted I come here to live with them. Then there was the so-called Saudi Spring, he went off on Hajj all excited about the new republic and never came back. All I have now is this godless grandson who never comes to see me."

At first the world had cheered on the Saudi Spring; the al-Saud regime was toppled but the 'democratic revolution' turned to bitter, sectarian civil war and thousands of pilgrims were trapped. Outside forces were rumoured to be at play, as they always are. Which faction, or nation, deployed the weapon that caused the ultimate atrocity can never be known for sure, but the destruction of Mecca and the Last Hajj plunged the Islamic world into crisis. The faith of millions was shattered and the world reeled. Yusuf and his grandfather had found themselves on opposite sides of a great divide. Yusuf's faith was blasted and his god destroyed; Hafiz's faith tested beyond bearing, but unbroken.

"I can't put everything right, grandfather, but there's a place on our farm for you, if only you'll come," tried Yusuf once more. "And I promise, I'll see you every day so you can pass on your knowledge."

Hafiz blinked away what seemed to be a tear and asked, "What's so different about this farm that it would feed a man too old to work?"

I continued with my short history of the farm. "After the fuel crisis, transport became difficult and getting bulky crops to market was a struggle and barely worth it. So we decided to grow food only for ourselves and I returned to my roots, as it were. Before, I had been a pharmacist, so I knew what a world oil shortage would do to the pharmaceutical industry. We converted as much land as we could to medicinal crops and collected all the herbs we could find to build up a seed bank. Maintaining the genetic stock is vital, but the collection is far from complete."

Suddenly, Hafiz's expression changed. He beamed a wide smile at Yusuf. "Now, I understand. All right, Yusuf, I'll teach you everything I know. I thought the tradition would die with me; your father never approved, you know."

Jake and I were both surprised at the suddenness of the reconciliation, but Hafiz turned to me and said "Come, come. You must see my garden, then you'll understand the gift Yusuf has offered me."

As I stepped out into the narrow back yard, realisation dawned on me, too. To one side of the path a host of shimmering poppies, on the other an unmistakeable mass of serrated, fingered leaves, fragrant in the heat of the day.

"Swat Valley's finest!" Hafiz exclaimed, with pride in his voice.

Christina had known all along I would accept the new candidate. Hafiz's knowledge, and his seed stock, would be invaluable to the farm.

"This farm of yours," Hafiz asked, "What is it called?"

Yusuf spoke before I could open my mouth. "New Alchemy Farm, grandfather."

"Ah, yes. *Al-kimiya*. That's a good Islamic word."

Crown Prerogative

Martin Hensher

They had made good time from the end of the railway line. The weather was cool and the horses were pleased to be off the clanking, jolting train, with its hot clouds of wood-pellet smoke and steam; and the going was easy along the old highway. The bush was growing in thick either side of the road, but the asphalt was still mainly intact, the white lines fading slowly away as the road surface took on a grey-purple tinge. Donaldson could hear his grandfather's voice saying "what do you expect, boy, that cost good taxpayer's money." Now it was a road to nowhere, speeding ahead towards nothing but the blackened ruins of half a dozen country towns that hadn't survived the Big Fire. Neither the men nor the horses liked passing through them. Brick hearths and chimneys stood out from the rich green scrub like some ancient monster's teeth, while here and there stood untouched but long-abandoned buildings, grinning at them like enchanted houses from some nightmare fairy tale. He could see the men's grip on their carbines tighten as they entered each village and loosen as they left. But this was not where they were going to find trouble, he reminded himself.

It was as they left the last of the burned-out towns that they met the Palawa, sitting quietly on the river bank. Unlike the highway itself, the big road bridge ahead of them was now little more than rusty beams and the empty air between them, yet next to it sat a yellow sandstone bridge that had probably been built by convicts soon after Settlement; its arches and cobbles patiently sitting out the centuries and waiting for the clatter of horseshoes to return. There were three Palawa; two very young men, and a much older man. All three wore sealskin cloaks and boots, and carried bags and pouches slung over their shoulders alongside long, powerful-looking bows. They left their spears at their feet as they rose to greet the approaching party. Donaldson paused for a second before he dismounted, wrestling away a sudden fear that he was about to make some terrible yet unknowable mistake. He dropped to the ground and passed his reins to Trooper Jackson, then motioned Mackay, the aboriginal policeman, to join him. The two of them scrambled down from the road to the river bank to join the Palawa men. Mackay stepped ahead of Donaldson, opening his hands in greeting.

"Ya pulingina," he said, nodding to each of the Palawa in turn.

"Ya pulingina milaythina mana mapali tu," replied the older of the three men, nodding back to Mackay and Donaldson. His face broke into a broad smile, radiating out from a thousand creases and wrinkles. He laughed out loud and turned to Donaldson. "Don't worry, son. I still speak the King's English. Even these boys here do if you twist their

144

arm." Donaldson looked to the two younger men, who smiled in embarrassment.

"You are welcome in our land," said the shorter of the two, in a songlike accent unlike any Donaldson had ever heard before. His companion just smiled again, and spread his hands in the same gesture Mackay had used.

"My name's Mikey Daniels," said the old man. "I took a clan name when we come out here, but it never really stuck. Never knew it was me they was talking to when someone called me. So I went back to what me old mum named us."

Donaldson's mind raced as he took that in. This was one of the original Treaty reclaimers? That must make him eighty years old if he was a day. But then he could have been anything between fifty and a hundred, this skinny old geezer with sinews like metal hawsers under a skin like an elephant's hide.

"These lads here are Maulboyheener and Rolepa", Mikey stated, gesturing first at the shorter man and then to the taller.

"G'day" said Donaldson, perhaps rather deliberately. "I'm James Donaldson. Tasmanian Light Horse. It's an honour to meet you. This is Police Sergeant Geoff Mackay."

The old man nodded. He turned to look at the troops waiting up on the road, and Donaldson saw his eye rest long on the mule train carrying their two pack howitzers and the machine gun tripods. He turned back slowly, the smile no longer filling the folds of his face.

❧

They had called him to the barracks first. Jacobs, the Army Commandant for Hobart, had been apologetic—"Sorry to call you in so soon before harvest, James, but you're the best bloke for this job." Not the first time his plans had been screwed up by a mobilisation, after all—and at least this time Ellie wasn't about to have a baby. But rather than receiving his travel warrant and beginning another long journey north to the mainland and beyond to some desultory tropical stand-off, this time he found himself being driven across town with Jacobs in his staff car. Seeing the passing trolleys and trams from the car window was quite a novelty for Donaldson; he savoured the feeling as if he were a little boy once more, and that sensation in turn filled him with an unaccountable longing. Not something he could explain to Jacobs, who in any case was fully absorbed in his efforts to flick some intruding substance visible only to himself from the brim of his slouch hat. Jacobs raised his eyes as the car drew through the gates of Government House and looked at Donaldson. "Ready?" was all he said, before an orderly opened his car door and he stepped out onto the gravel, putting his hat back on with precision and evident satisfaction that it now met his standard for cleanliness. Ready for what, though, Donaldson at that stage had no idea whatsoever.

They were led onto a verandah where they waited long enough to be served morning tea by another white-jacketed orderly. Donaldson stared out over the sparkling waters of the Derwent, the morning sun already burning white in the sky, although the air was still fresh. A bulk windjammer under Chilean flag was being towed carefully under the bridge by a tug to load up at the zinc works, her four masts seeming to reach nearly as high as the great arc of concrete itself. Further downriver, three graceful white pinisiq were putting in to Macquarie Wharf, crews furling their sails as their reserve motors manoeuvred to the dockside, ready to unload their cargoes of coffee and spices before returning to

Sumatra with new loads of grain and wool. In the foreground, a train puffed and wheezed its way out of the port railyards and along the riverside, wagons swaying along the track as it passed the botanical gardens. He looked around as a door opened, and a secretary requested that they follow her inside.

They were shown into a large room, where a group of men were seated round an imposing table. Donaldson had collected himself sufficiently from his earlier reverie to salute the Governor on entering the room, who was seated at the head of the group. The Governor waved them to seats at the table, as Donaldson took in with some surprise those other members of the group he could recognise. "Captain Donaldson", said the Governor, "You know the Premier? The Solicitor General, and the Police Commissioner?" He nodded, somewhat stupidly—he didn't really know them, although he had once declared his ardent passion for the Premier's younger sister at a grade ten combined social. She had not been impressed.

The Premier had started the meeting, staring intently at the two soldiers through the thick lenses of his wire-framed glasses. "We have a problem in the Treaty territory," he had begun, "and we need to resolve it promptly and decisively.

"We and the Palawa have always respected the terms of the Treaty very carefully, as you know," he continued. "Once the land grant was made, and the Reclaiming clans returned to their lands there, it was agreed that there would be no further contact between the Palawa and the outside world unless it was explicitly initiated by the Palawa. While there has been a certain amount of—shall we say—traffic between the Reclaimers and the majority of Aboriginal people who chose to remain among us, we have turned a blind eye."

Donaldson saw the Commissioner of Police suppress a chuckle. "Our only formal contact has been an annual visit by an immunisation team, to give them some chance against pandemics. And they have never asked us for any other help before.

"But this year, the immunisation team came back with a message from the Palawa leaders. They had been attacked by armed white men and several of their young men killed. They are invoking the terms of the Treaty to seek the Crown's protection from this threat. And that, Captain Donaldson, is where you come in."

The Governor sat forward in his chair at this point. "I have spoken with Canberra about this at length, as you would expect." He looked down into his coffee cup reflectively, as if inspiration lay in its dregs. "We agree that upholding the terms of the treaty is paramount. And the Australian Government believes that this is a job for the Army, not just the state police. And both Governments therefore accept that this may have consequences in terms of the level of force that may be used in this operation. Michael here will be able to advise you further, won't you?" he said, looking at the Solicitor-General.

"Yes, Governor. It's pretty simple. Any reasonable and necessary force may be used by the Crown to ensure the sovereignty and integrity of the Palawa people and the Treaty lands. The Crown in the Commonwealth of Australia and the State of Tasmania is their ultimate protector, and the Treaty voids the rights of any non-Palawa Australian citizen who enters the Palawa Treaty lands. Whoever attacked them—if they are still there—has no rights under Australian law.

148

Which allows you significant discretion as to how best to execute your mission, Captain."

They looked at him meaningfully, but Donaldson struggled to answer. He was grateful when Jacobs intervened.

"Can we tell James any more about who we might be dealing with here, Sir?"

This question was passed to the Police Commissioner, who pulled up his substantial frame to sit erect in his chair before answering gruffly, "Not a lot. No more for sure than what the Palawa told the nurses—seven or eight white fellas with rifles who attacked a hunting party and killed five of their hunters unprovoked. By now I expect the Palawa know more about who and where they are. I wouldn't put it past them to have dealt with them themselves. We don't know any more than that yet. But we have made an arrangement," he said as a smile flickered over his face in pleasure at his cleverness. "You'll rendezvous with some Palawa guides who will track them for you."

The Commissioner spread his hands on the blotter in front of him. "Look, they could be anything. Illegal miners, illegal loggers, Deep Greenie head cases trying to be more authentic hunter-gatherers than the First Australians. We've seen all of them on the mainland. All we really know is that they were armed, they're trespassing, and they shot a bunch of black fellas who were out hunting kangaroos. So they're not good neighbours."

The Governor stared once more into his coffee cup, as if calculating precisely how long it would be until it was refilled. He looked up as the Premier spoke. "Two and half centuries ago, we all but exterminated the Palawa's ancestors. The Treaty was signed to go some way to right that wrong. And the Palawa have honoured their obligations to us. If white blood has to be shed to honour our obligations to them, so be it."

The Governor leaned forward. "We will not tolerate anarchy here, James. The Crown will uphold the Treaty. You will see to that." And with that he rose from the table, as an orderly pulled open the patio doors for lunch.

⌇

With Mikey and his two companions leading them, it didn't take the party long to locate the intruders; they marched for a day and half, sometimes through bush but often through open, almost park-like grasslands. The Palawa men weren't tracking; they clearly knew exactly where they were going ahead of time, and Donaldson was not inclined to query their knowledge. For their part, the aborigines kept themselves separate from the soldiers and their officers, staying ahead and conferring quietly in Palawa-Kani from time to time – usually mindful of whether Mackay was nearby before they spoke. On the afternoon of the second day, Mikey explained that they were drawing close, and they should halt this side of an imposing ridge. Donaldson and his men drew the horses into the trees and set up their patrol harbour. The Palawa men went off hunting, and returned some hours later very pleased with their haul of wallaby meat and duck eggs. The soldiers were less entranced by their tinned rations, but, as Squadron Sergeant Major Franklin-Tsang reminded them, dinner was a parade, not a gastronomic event. They tried to get a decent sleep, for they all knew the next few nights would be busy.

In the morning, Donaldson had Mikey and his men guide his initial commanders' recce. He took Anderson and Cohen, his own troop commanders, Duckworth, the artillery troop commander from Launceston, and Sergeant van Wijk, the machine gun section commander. Mikey led them up the big ridge on foot until they were just below its crest. He stopped them there to explain. "Other side of this ridge, you'll see 'em. A little way off, but it's clear from here. They don't have any look-outs this side, only other side."

The men moved forward at the crouch until they crested the ridge and crawled forward into some bush from which they could see the ground in front of them. Before them, a broad valley opened out to the sea beyond. The valley was deep rainforest, filled with trees that had stood long before the French had first sailed up the sparkling coast that lay beyond, the first European eyes to take in this land. A river flowed down the valley, opening out in the coastal plain into a series of great lagoons behind sand spits, traversed by a bridge, which was the only visible sign of a road which seemed to have been consumed by the growing forest around it. But it took all of them only seconds before their eyes were drawn further upriver. The green of the rainforest canopy gave way at one point along the river to a broad swathe of brown and grey mud. Felled trees lay beside the river on both sides, while the river itself seemed to turn from sparkling silver to shimmering black just beyond that opening in the forest. As they looked more closely, bringing binoculars up to their eyes in silence, they could make out plumes of smoke and structures of some kind—small, but many of them. And tiny figures, on the river bank and in the water itself. Donaldson counted at least thirty on his first attempt. He put down his binoculars and turned to Mikey.

"What are they doing?"

"You'll see, soon enough," the old man replied. "They don't come up this way much," he continued. "They go down to the sea when the ship comes for 'em."

"When does the ship come?" asked Donaldson.

"Every couple of months, we reckon," said Mikey. "Probably soon."

So they stayed on top of the ridge for a couple of hours, discussing how best to recce the camp below, how to work their way around unseen, and how to block off any exit to the sea. Donaldson did not wish to rush into anything here. This was a mission he knew he did not yet understand, and much as he wanted to get home, he knew that this was no time for laziness.

In the end, Donaldson had them spend five days recceing and observing the encampment they had seen from the ridge. The weather turned to rain and cold winds, and the soldiers cursed and swore as they stumbled in the mud and on the slippery roots in the great rainforest, and shivered in misery under their oilskins. But the weather protected them from their targets, who huddled on their river bank, apparently unaware they were being watched. And a picture began to emerge as the patrols came and went to be debriefed and to hand over their drawings and notes. They were miners, or prospectors, at least. They had quarries near the river, muddy holes in the ground they were working with pick axes and crowbars. They had dammed off ponds in the river; next to them were stone kilns on the bank, which they fed with charcoal they were burning themselves. The ponds were blue and black, and the river ran black downstream of them. And they had women and children there, families living in lean-tos and ragged tents of branches and old sails. The men broke and hauled the rocks, while the women fed the kilns and charcoal mounds, and the children paddled in the noxious tailing ponds, faces down searching for whatever lode all this revolved around. A kilometer downriver, closer to the bridge, they had another furnace. This was surrounded by mounds of discarded insulation, and they appeared to be melting down cables and scrap they had gathered from the burned out town that lay beside the lagoon. They went out at times to hunt kangaroos with rifles and dogs, but no other weaponry seemed to be in evidence. One day, a ship arrived off the lagoon, a single masted cutter, and a large portion of this community busied itself unloading stores from two whaling boats and reloading them with panniers which the patrol assumed contained metal ingots or processed ore.

After a few days, the officers were able to estimate that there were perhaps a hundred people down there in this camp, men, women and children. Which, of course, raised the very awkward question of what to do with them all.

As their intelligence formed itself more clearly, Donaldson spent some time reflecting on the true nature of his task. For all their apparent eagerness to despatch those who had killed the Palawa with force, he was confident that the Government would not thank him for causing a massacre of women and children. Well, he wasn't entirely confident—but he had no desire to cause one, and it was a helpful rationalisation. Yet he was even more confident that—whoever these people were—they would be unlikely to welcome the opportunity to be escorted to Hobart or Launceston. Their most likely option there would be convict labour on the farms or the railway, with their children almost certain to be removed from them. Given that they had already chosen to bring their families into a deserted wilderness to scratch in the mud they had themselves contaminated, he had little expectation they would come willingly into the embrace of the authorities.

Donaldson had been careful to communicate only minimal information to Hobart in his nightly radio checks. He had kept his messages short, as the signallers cranked the charger handle on the big HF radio. His brevity was aided by the fact that most evenings their skywave signal could only reliably manage Morse transmission. He had reasoned to himself that Hobart had little to offer him by way of help, and only really offered the prospect of interfering to order him to do something regrettable. He had been left to his own devices in a number of foreign jungles in the past, after all. It was all a long way from his grandfather and the old infantryman's stories of drones and satellite links and computer displays in his helmet. Not that they had really seemed to help make anything clearer, if you had listened closely to what the old boy was saying. Now that his plan was forming more clearly, Donaldson realised that he would need to provide more detail—and a very clear request for help with how to remove these people—but that he needed to do so only at the point where Hobart could have no option but to comply.

Which just left the Palawa.

The Palawa men had chosen to camp outside the Light Horse perimeter. After some discussion, they had agreed to tuck themselves down in a dip, so they would at least be in dead ground and out of their field of fire in the event of an attack. As the days passed, Donaldson came to see why Mikey had been so dismissive of the likelihood of such a thing occurring. As a result, they had had little contact except when they accompanied recce patrols, retiring to their shelter as soon as they returned.

Donaldson made his way past the horses, bored and wet as they waited to be taken to forage in the grasslands below, and followed the track plan out to the sentry post. He paused to speak to Trooper Chingarai, the sniper, who was doing his turn on stag.

"I'm going to speak to the Palawa," Donaldson explained.

"Are you sure, Sir? Watch out for what they're up to in that hut of theirs," replied Chingarai, his eyes opening wide in his broad black face in an equal parody of concern and lewdness.

"Really, Chingarai, we've only been out here a week," he opined in mock disapproval, stepping past the sentry hide.

"Righto, Sir, but try not to bend over," chuckled Chingarai, returning himself to the warmest position he could find while still able to see out of the pit.

Donaldson approached the Palawa's shelter, a temporary structure of branches and sealskins with a small fire burning within. He paused in the doorway to say "May I come in?"

Maulboyheener pulled back a skin covering the doorway and motioned him to enter. "Please,' he said, "Come in" and gestured for him to sit. "Mikey is sleeping." Rolepa looked up from some complicated work he was doing, which appeared to be making laces or straps from skins.

The old man was indeed lying on the floor of the warm shelter, wrapped in kangaroo skins. But his eyes flipped open immediately, and he sat up.

"Captain. You've come to talk."

"Yes, Mikey. I need your advice—and your agreement."

"You're happy for these boys to listen?"

"Of course."

"That's good. I'm old now. They need to know what happens next, and how and why. Our people need to know how this goes."

"Look, these people attacked you. My job is to make sure they are removed from your lands. And I will do that. But I don't want to kill them if I can possibly avoid it. And I really don't want to kill women and children. I think I know how to do this; but I need to understand what you and your people really need here from us."

Mikey turned away for a while, as if looking through the walls of the hut at something far away. As he waited, it occurred to Donaldson that the distance the old man's gaze traversed might perhaps be better measured in centuries rather than meters.

The Palawa man nodded to himself at last, and turned back to face Donaldson.

"Before the white man came here to Trowunna, there were maybe ten thousand of my ancestors here on this island. It only took thirty years for there to be more white fellas here than Palawa—and just a few more for them to have killed off almost all of my people. A hundred and fifty years after that there were half a million souls in old Tasmania. Growing, building, expanding always.

"Our elders had fought for recognition, and for restitution, for decades before I was born. And it had come, in some ways, with land rights, and apologies and even a little bit of power here and there. But let's not bullshit ourselves, Donaldson. We're only here now, in our own land, living by the old ways, because so many people died back then. Disease, the droughts, the fires. After the Big Fire, the old Government came and asked us if we wanted this land back—not us asking them. They knew they couldn't rebuild that time. Couldn't afford it—had to "conserve resources for the core," they said. So a dream of an idea started to be born among us, my parents, my uncles and aunties. And they seized on it too, the Government and their scientists and that. You know what the Treaty really was? Not just restitution—although we give thanks every day for that, for there was repentance there too, among your grandfathers. But really, it was an insurance policy for the human race, you understand?

Donaldson listened and waited, tasting the smoke from the fire in the back of his mouth. The old man continued.

"Back then, people were starting to think that white man's civilisation couldn't last. It felt like an ending. And there was all this space the fire had created, all this land emptied of its inhabitants. And there was us Palawa, who had been busy reclaiming our culture and our knowledge, wrestling ourselves back from the brink of extinction. And we got to thinking maybe we didn't need anything much of the little they still had. Just needed the land and the shore and the sea. And they thought to themselves, those clever Government fellas, 'they might just survive even if we can't—let's give'em a chance.' So they offered us a one way ticket. A ticket back into history to have another chance.

That's how it felt that day we stepped off the boat onto the shore, like we was walking along a beach back three hundred years and our ancestors was about to jump up out of the bush and embrace us, and we'd tell them of a nightmare we'd just woken from, filled with white spirits of the dead. No offence, mate." He chuckled and paused, his eyes narrowing for a few seconds.

"I'll tell you what we learned, and then I'll tell you what we need from you, Captain Donaldson of the Tasmanian Light Horse. We learned that we could live the old way. A lot of us died trying, but we have rekindled the secrets of the time before, along with some new ones we learned from you. We learned that ownership of the land is everything for us, just as it is for you. And we also learned that the white man's time wasn't up yet either. You're still here, like you always were—just fewer, weaker and poorer than before. We don't bear those people down there in that valley any grudge. They're poor and desperate, poisoning their children even as they believe they are providing for them. But we can't let them be in our lands, because our history and yours shows that they will never be satisfied until they own it all again, never stop until they have taken every centimeter of it from us."

"When I was a young man, like these boys here"—he gestured to Rolepa and Maulboyheener, whose eyes were fixed on the elder, "the old King came to Hobart on the day they promulgated the Treaty. He looked us square in the eye and told us 'these lands will never again be taken from you.' That's all we need from you, Captain. Enforcement. Making good on a solemn promise. No backsliding."

158

Donaldson blinked repeatedly. The smoke was almost overpowering now, but the burning in his eyes came not from any physical irritation but from the rising sense of horror at what history seemed to be demanding of him.

Then Rolepa spoke quietly to the old man in Palawa Kani. It was the first time Donaldson had heard him speak. His words sounded like a river running over stones, repeating words and phrases more like an incantation than a conversation. Mikey nodded slowly after a while, as if in assent.

Rolepa turned to Donaldson and stared intently at him. "Our land asks for no more blood. It is still soaked with the blood of our ancestors—and yours. It needs no more," he said, his voice still like a softly flowing river, even in unfamiliar English. "But my grandfather is right. They cannot stay. And no others can ever come in their place. He says you have the power to kill them all if you choose. But can you give us what we need without killing them?"

Donaldson breathed deeply, and looked each of the three Palawa men in the eye before speaking. "Yes."

But when he left the Palawa hut, he turned away from the patrol base and walked further into the forest, where he knelt, resting his face on the muzzle of his carbine, and prayed to the Lord.

⁊

Three mornings later, they were ready. Hobart had agreed with his plan, and he had busied the men with preparation and rehearsals. Half his force had set out before dawn, to establish their cordon and stop groups well before the rest revealed themselves to the prospectors. The fire support group followed them, to hide themselves in the high ground above the miners' encampment—although Donaldson wanted them to make themselves and their heavy weapons very visible to the people below at the right moment. That left Donaldson and another twenty men, with the Palawa. They began their descent towards the mining encampment at about eight a.m. Initially they moved through the forest, staying hidden for a while. Further down, they joined a track that they knew would lead them down to the camp. After about half an hour, the forest either side of the track opened out, where he guessed the miners had been logging for their charcoal kilns. At the start of this clearing, two wooden frames had been hammered into the ground, one either side of the track. Each frame contained a sodden animal pelt, stretched out and threaded tight with twine through the battens.

"Kullener," said Rolepa, angrily.

Mackay edged his horse closer to one of the frames. "Thylacines." He said. "Look at them. This one on the right is a reintroduced clone—see, the darker fur comes from the Tassie Devil DNA they used to culture it. This lighter one on the left is natural. I've never seen both side by side before. That's something."

Mikey replied, "Yes, they live together here now. Maybe even breed together by now. You know it's funny. They went to all that effort to recreate old kullener—all that science and genetics and all – when all they really needed to do was take the people away and he just quietly came down out of those mountains where he was hiding all along."

"But why kill them and string them up here?" asked Donaldson.

160

Rolepa looked up at him sharply and said, "To make a sign. To make a sign that they have taken this land back from nature and from us."

Donaldson nodded and sighed to himself. These people liked making themselves difficult to sympathise with, he thought.

Further down the track, they finally came upon a look-out. He was a boy, no more than ten years old. They saw him stand up in surprise as they rounded a bend. He stood stock still for a few moments, his mouth open, and they had time to take in the rags he was dressed in before he turned and flew through the bush, his bare feet carrying him soundlessly from root to root. A couple of minutes later they heard his shouts as he neared the camp.

Donaldson turned to face the party. "Ready, gentlemen?" he asked, before kicking his horse forward gently.

಄

As the track left the forest and joined the river bank and the miners' camp, Donaldson was relieved to look up and see the fire support party up above them on the hillside, very deliberately setting up the howitzers and heavy machine guns in full view of the valley below. They slowly walked their horses along the path leading into the middle of the riverside clearing, as women and children poked their heads out of shelters and men and women came running from the kilns and pits. Donaldson and his men stopped in a more open space where some of the people were already congregating, careful to keep out of the line of fire from the hill above. They waited.

The growing crowd was quiet, with little more than whispering to be heard. Some of the more observant among them were looking around to see what else was happening, and they soon spotted the support weapons trained on their settlement from above, which caused a murmur of concern to run through the group. A handful of men and women who had recently arrived were allowed to push their way to the front of the crowd. The way the others parted for them made it clear that these were leaders of some kind. All faces were turned to Donaldson in expectant silence; many looked anxious, a few were hostile, but none seemed especially surprised. All the faces were gaunt; the children were thin and dirty.

When he judged that all were present, Donaldson began.

"You know why we are here. These are Palawa lands. They are closed to all but the Palawa nation. You are trespassing, and some of you have killed Palawa men. I have come to remove you by the authority of the Crown. You will never come back here. And others will know what will happen to them if they try to come here. Here is what I can offer you.

"At 3.00 this afternoon, transport ships will arrive to take you to Hobart. By 12.00, you will have packed everything you wish to take with you, and you will assemble here to be escorted to the beach. You can take anything you can carry; we won't ask any questions. When you reach Hobart, you will receive a rail or sea ticket to anywhere you wish to travel to in Australia. Again, no questions asked."

A man at the front of the crowd, with a face like raw meat and a grey beard that reached down to his waist, stepped forward. "Thanks, cobber," he sneered. "That's generous. But I don't think so. What'll you do to make us?"

"Anyone still here after 12.00 will be arrested. You will all be interrogated until the people who murdered the Palawa are found and punished. The rest will be charged with being illegal aliens; by the look of what you've been up to here, there'll be no shortage of other charges. Your children will be taken into the care of the State. Any attempt to resist arrest by anyone will cause me to use those weapons up there to finish this. And the Palawa here will find anyone who tries to go bush. They have all the time in the world to come after you. The Navy will make sure that your friends with the boat don't pay you any more visits either."

Donaldson looked out at the faces staring at him. He saw anger in some, but in others he saw resignation and weariness. Good, he thought to himself.

Then a woman stepped out of the crowd and turned side on, as if to address everyone present. Her skin was deep brown from the sun, her cheeks were sunken and her face lined. She looked as if the beauty of her youth was still visible in outline, but its substance had been leached out of her by whatever poisons they had filled their tailing ponds with. Her voice was clear and articulate as she spoke, as incongruous and unexpected to Donaldson as a drunken pub brawler pausing to declaim Shakespeare.

"We know why you are here, yes. But do you know why we are here?" she asked, looking Donaldson clear in the eye. She turned back to the crowd. "Because we have nothing anywhere else. Because there is nothing for us. Because you and your government can give us nothing except pain and contempt. You can give us a ticket to anywhere you like— but that's where we already left from. You people—you have the land and the water and the houses and the food. But we

163

can't survive on the crumbs off your table. And now, when we try to do something for ourselves, make some honest value for ourselves out of this land of Australia, along comes His Majesty's finest to kick us to our knees again."

The crowd was murmuring its support, and Donaldson could see the woman was warming up nicely.

"Why do you keep us out of these lands? To indulge these people in their role playing?" She pointed at the Palawa men. "How dare you lock up all the wealth of this land, how dare you lock up the copper, the gold, the timber, when we have nothing? How can you waste all these resources which we can extract and turn into value, to grow a new future for ourselves? How can you protect these people above us? They don't want to achieve anything, they just want to hunt kangaroo and seals and live like they did forty thousand years ago. How can you side with them when we want progress? When we—the poor and the dispossessed—want nothing more than to use the hard work of our own hands to extract the wealth from this land, just like our forefathers have done these hundreds of years? To build back what we have lost? Why don't our traditions count? We are a mining people. Why do aborigines and landowners get a monopoly on tradition?"

She had the crowd on her side now. Donaldson could see defeat beginning to spark into defiance in the faces of the adults. But then it happened. Out of the corner of his eye he saw movement. Before he could even register what it was, he heard the crack and thump of a rifle round pass by him, always redolent of countless days in the butts, and the moving object changed direction and resolved into the shape of a man arcing away from him under the impact of

Chingarai's sniper round, a shotgun tumbling from his hand as he flew backwards.

The woman screamed, all oratory gone. "Davey! No!" Even as the words ripped out of her throat, Donaldson could see the man's face, a younger version of his mother, fire and passion turning to bewilderment as the kinetic energy of the metal impacting his body took control of his destiny. She started running towards her son, the indignation of seconds before transformed into naked horror. Mackay wheeled his horse towards her, and planted the butt of his carbine square into her cheek. As she reeled backwards, the policeman slid down from his horse on top of her, pinning her to the muddy grass. It was Franklin-Tsang who saved the rest, his Sergeant Major's roar of "Lie Down!" hitting the crowd at the very instant of their indecision. "Lie down, or you will all be killed," he reinforced. And they did, some meekly, some angrily. In the silence that followed, Donaldson gave thanks that van Wijk and the machine gunners on the hill above kept their fingers from their triggers.

Donaldson swallowed. "Nguyen! Treat the casualty," he ordered, and the medic dropped from his horse and ran to the young man. To the rest of the men, he said, "Dismount and search these people for weapons, one at a time. Move them over by that hut once they are cleared." The men moved forwards, organising themselves, weapons trained on the by now cowering crowd, who no longer needed Franklin-Tsang's encouragement to keep low. One by one the adults were pulled up from the ground and searched unceremoniously.

Donaldson moved across to the wounded man, just as Nguyen snapped the wrapper on the trauma pack ampoules.

165

He watched in fascination as the bright blue nano gel swarmed into the gunshot wound in the man's shoulder, forming itself to the contours of his body and visibly sealing the exit wound in his back as Nguyen rolled him to check.

The medic moved quickly to insert a line into his other arm, pushing volume expanders and targeted coagulants into his veins. He sat back on his feet and inspected his patient. "Zimbo's a good shot, Sir. He'll be right," he opined to Donaldson, "long as we get him back to Hobart before any infection sets in." Donaldson looked over to the young man's mother, whom Mackay had now released, but who knelt on all fours, tears, blood and snot running down her face. He walked to her and knelt.

"He'll live," he said to her. "But we need to get him out of here as soon as we can—on the ship."

"You bastard," she replied. "Please save him." She raised herself up on to her knees and surveyed her people in their indignity. "Will they really let us go?" she asked him.

"They have told me they will," he replied. She looked deep into his eyes, and he felt for a second that the hatred with which she had first fixed him seemed to give way to longing.

"They just want to feed their families as free men and women."

"I know," he answered. "But not here. This is not your land or my land anymore." And he turned away from her and walked back to his horse.

రా

The ships arrived on time, coming into sight as the soldiers marched the bedraggled miners and their families down to the sand spit. Two clippers under full sail, chartered for the occasion, and an old and battered-looking destroyer whose smoke-stack occasionally belched a black cloud of diesel fumes. They set anchor beyond the surf, dropping cutters and whaling boats, their crews rowing smartly towards the shore. The miners were slowly transferred to the ships over a couple of hours, until all were aboard.

Once they were alone on the beach, Donaldson had the men prepare for their return march to the railhead. They were eager to oblige, and as they repacked stores and weapons, he came and sat with the three Palawa men, who had been observing for some time.

"I hope you can tell your people that we did what was needed," he said to them.

Mikey regarded him carefully for a few seconds, before answering "Yes, we can tell them that. And we give you our thanks. You upheld the Treaty and the promises that were made to us. And you did it without any more killing."

The old man sighed. "Once I would have liked to see them who killed our boys brought to justice. But now I'm simply happy you got rid of them. Thank you."

Rolepa rose to his feet. "We must go now, Captain Donaldson," he said. "nentegga menyawa gondalyerroo, gondalyerroo nentegga menyawa."

Maulboyheener also rose and smiled as Donaldson looked at him quizzically. "It means 'yesterday was tomorrow, tomorrow will be yesterday'. We wish you a safe journey home, Captain."

Donaldson watched the Palawa walk away down the beach for a long while. They did not look back towards the soldiers.

Eventually, he turned back to the men and found them all watching him. It was Chingarai who broke the silence.
"Can we go home now, Sir?"

The Big Quiet

Diana Haugh

Cathy idly watched her frosty breath condense on the tarp covering her dugout and snuggled deeper into the huddle of blankets. Vastly pleased with herself, she wriggled in comfort.

I don't have to do nothing, she thought. Nothing to do but lay here and daydream. No farm work. No worry and no being robbed and shot. It seemed an ideal situation. In the little log and dirt dugout she had hastily built were neatly stacked boxes of her home canned vegetables, three bushel baskets of apples and potatoes and cabbage and a sack of shell beans. There was room for a toilet bucket and a demijohn of water. She had everything she needed and there was nothing to do but enjoy herself thinking.

She tried to pinpoint when it had all started. Not with the bank holiday; things still held pretty good back then. It was most likely when Leo Grundlach, the township supervisor, came walking up the state road as she waited by the mailbox. She could see the Wallers, down the road near the bend, waiting, too. Mail had come every Monday for three weeks now and if there was to be any, she didn't want to miss it. She was a little antsy with Leo coming up because she was also trying to listen back to the house, to hear if the power came on. Generally they didn't have it on more than an hour or two, and she didn't want to miss even a minute, there was so much to do.

"Hey, Leo," she said politely.

"How do," he said with a look on his face like this was going to be something she didn't want to hear.

She liked Leo. A polite and respectful man, he was quick to promise anything you needed even though you'd never see it. A consummate crook and politician, he lent distinction to their little hamlet.

"Waiting for the mail, I see."

"Umm hmm." Cathy was never one to waste words and besides, she could see he wanted to talk.

"We're going to have to make a change with the taxes, Cathy. Until they get the bank thing straightened out, the township is going to take taxes in kind. A cord of wood from every household, deliverable by the end of the month."

"Leo, that's not fair. You know you commandeered my gasoline two weeks ago for the snow plow. What am I to run the chainsaw on?"

"I know, I know. I don't expect a woman your age to go at it with an ax. We'll make an exception for you and let you pay in potatoes. I remember you saying back at the end of summer you had a bumper crop. I'll send Paul and Johnny over to pick 'em up this afternoon."

Cathy thought quick and bit her lip. The township didn't hesitate to condemn and take any property with unpaid taxes.

And with Conyngham's over across the way growing only hay and field corn, which you can't really eat, hers was the only farm in the township growing real food. Other than her farm and Conyngham's, and a scattering of houses, it was just miles of forest and the abandoned coal mine. So they'd seize her property for the food in a hot minute if they could find any excuse.

"That's fine, Leo. When are we going to get any gasoline in? I can't run my tractor on air and there's a crop to put in come spring."

Leo nodded his head. "That's true. I put in a request over to the county seat last week. You'll get your gasoline back when it comes in and we'll be getting another shipment of emergency food relief. We don't expect you to feed us all on what you grow. Why, you wouldn't have any left for your farm stand, would you?"

Cathy gave up on the mail and walked slowly back the lane, paused at the house and veered over to the barn. The barn cats, skinnier than ever, came out crying. It had been a long time since she had any cat food for them, but at least they kept the barn polished free of mice. She pulled back the tarp covering her potatoes; 7 bushel left, not counting the seed potatoes for spring planting. She had understood clearly what Leo didn't say. He didn't expect to get any food relief, there wouldn't be any gasoline and he expected her to feed them all.

Time for action. She moved half of the potatoes and the apples to the old root cellar by the spring. Somebody would remember the root cellar before long, and they'd come for it, but not just yet. They'd be happy with what they got today for as long as it lasted. What would Leo being doing with the potatoes? Certainly not passing them out to the neighbors. No, he'd be feeding his family and Paul his son, the constable and Johnny his son-in-law, the code officer. His power base would have to be fed and four bushels of potatoes wouldn't last long. They'd be back for more.

But that wasn't the day things went haywire. No, things still seemed normal, just every day a little worse than the day before, the way it had been going for years. It must have been late in January when she heard shouting across the way. She pulled back the curtain to watch and listen. It was Larry Bonsell, the other township supervisor, along with four, maybe five of the fire department boys. Larry was fire chief and he was shouting at Leo. Paul came running up quick, his hand on his holster. Johnny came out of Leo's house, followed by Suzy, Leo's daughter and the kids.

Fire department hasn't been getting their share of the goods, looks like, Cathy thought.

There was pushing and cursing and then Paul ran the fire department boys off at gunpoint. 'Well, at least they got gasoline,' she said meditatively, as the fire truck pulled away, screeching. It wasn't no hour till it came roaring back and the boys jumped off the truck, every one with a hunting rifle cocked and loaded and without stopping they shot Paul and Leo. Leo went down, surprised like, blood oozing from the side of his head. Paul just crumpled. Suzy started screaming and Larry swiveled and trained his gun on her. Johnny quick threw his hands up as the kids started to cry. Everything seemed to stand still for an instant, Leo's dapper body on the ground and the firemen and family staring in disbelief. Then Larry barked an order and the boys marched Johnny and the rest of Leo's family off down the road. And from then on

172

things weren't normal any more.

That's when I knew, Cathy thought. That's when I came up here on the mountain to build the dugout. She had always had a way of knowing, seemed like, more than other people. It wasn't something to be talked about, but it was there. Was it something she noticed first the summer she had told Carl, her husband, that she wanted raspberries planted along the fence at the bottom of the property?

"No, raspberries are a world of work, you have to order the canes and get them in by fall and even if they take, there's thorns," he said, protesting.

Then winter set in and a long, cold one it was, and pneumonia that spring. By May, when she was out and about, here there was a row of raspberries growing fine and fancy along the lower fence with young raspberries big as thimbles. She ran to hug Carl but he didn't know anything about it. He was as surprised as she was to see them.

'But that wasn't necessarily anything extraordinary, was it? That could just have been the work of birds, dropping raspberry seeds as they perched on the fence. That's the natural rewards you reap from being in harmony with nature, right? Let the birds eat your spilled grain, and they'll do for you? But how to explain the oak tree? Last year she suddenly knew the oak tree was coming down, and she got Carl to move the tractor quick and it wasn't a half hour till CRACK and then BOOM and the old monster came crashing down. That could have a scientific explanation too, couldn't it? Like maybe subsonic cracking noises she had picked up on? She was always real good to listen and pay attention the way most people never do. That's how she knew the day before Carl had his heart attack. Tiny details of listening. Of course, by then the ambulance service had gone out of business so there wasn't nothing could be done.

"I wish I could have taken physics in high school," she said aloud. If she could only understand time. Time kept nagging at her. The thin wisps, the whisperings of the future that sometimes drifted across her vision. What was that? "I'm not stupid; I ought to be able to figure it out if I just think it through." Somebody said once, somebody like Lao Tse, that from two facts or from three the whole universe can be deduced. Just marshal the facts. Think it through. She whistled and whirls of her frosty breath drifted across the dugout.

Everything has an explanation. What seems supernatural is very natural if you just understand the science behind it. So what was time? What does time do? It scours away the past, for one thing. Her evil stepfather, no trace of him or his evil remained. Fifty years ago the good and beautiful forest roundabout was a barren moonscape of black coal waste and stripping holes. How quickly the earth healed itself once the mining was abandoned. The good, the permanent is polished by time. Is time a cleansing agent? Does it exist to right the universe? And what about her time sense? It couldn't just be her; other people had to have it too. Maybe they just don't pay attention to it.

Or maybe they do, she thought, and just can't bear it. Do they sense the Big Quiet coming? Does it unnerve them? Maybe they have known all along. Maybe like a spool of thread unwinding, the last bit of thread leaving the spool with nothing to follow, they feel their unconnectedness to the future? That would mean they are sensing their own death. That would explain the drugs and the frenetic attachment to devices, music, tv, anything to blot out the sensing. Cathy could certainly feel the Big Quiet coming, She had sensed it coming for a long time now. Last time she was in town, the noise, the traffic, the commotion of people all seemed as wispy and unreal as an afterimage. It was the Big Quiet that kept bearing down on her. But I don't feel unconnected, she thought. I don't feel my death coming. Strange. What did it mean?

And now Leo and Paul were gone, and the young fire department guys were trying to run things. But guts and a gun don't give you the skill to govern, to get people to do what you want, to keep them in line. Other people had guns too and were hungry. Cathy could hear gunfire now and then from the comfort of her dugout, bursts of shots ricocheting across the valley, followed by other bursts. Some days it was just a single shot, a more ominous sound, like an execution. Was this how the Big Quiet was coming? Shot by shot until they were all gone? Every man's hand against his brother? Or was something more to follow?

She would have been content to lay there and work it all out but she heard a faint voice yelling in the distance.

"Mom! Mom! Where are you?"

Reluctantly, Cathy wiggled out of the dugout and trudged down the mountain. Her daughter kept calling but she didn't answer till she was in sight of the back field. She didn't want to give her dugout away.

"There you are! Mom, you're a mess! Where have you been? What's going on?"

Sandy, her elegant city daughter, was a mess too. Beside Clyde, her husband, she had brought friends, Benny and Anita and their two children. They'd had enough gas to get a

175

hundred miles on the road, and had walked the last thirty. They were hungry, and after hugs Cathy went to work cooking onions and apples, fried potatoes and cabbage. While they ate, Cathy heated water and they all had a good wash. Gathering around the woodstove, they brought each other up to date.

Sandy said things were terrible in the city. Cathy said the same was true, here, too. She told them she had been hiding in the woods.

"We'll be getting a knock on the door soon. They'll see the smoke from the chimney and know I'm back in my house. I'm the only one has any food except for anybody who's gotten a deer. But I imagine they've been too busy shooting each other to do much hunting. None of you has any guns, do you? Good. That will save our lives."

The knock came right then and Cathy politely let Tim Miller and the Peters boy in. Both had rifles and looked angry and scared.

"How's your mother, Timmy? You remember Sandy from school? This is her husband and friends come to help me farm. Without gasoline for my tractor I'm going to need all the hands I can get. Care to come in for a bite? We don't have much but you're welcome to share. Pull up a chair."

The young men looked at each other doubtfully. Hunger won out and they sat down and ravenously piled into the potatoes. The children stood in silence, staring at the guns propped up against their chairs. Time ticked slow until they were done eating. The Peters boy spoke first. He wiped his mouth on his hand and said, "We got to search for weapons. All firearms are confiscated."

"Sure, help yourself." Cathy showed them through the

house and asked if they'd like to search the barn. They said yes and went on out.

"That was scary," said Sandy.

"It's not over yet. They're going to argue about coming back in and demanding food. Tim will wind up shooting the other boy. Or maybe the other way around. We'll have to bury the body."

"How do you know that?" Benny asked in amazement.

"My mother just knows these things. Keep the kids away from the windows." Sandy angled herself so she could see out but be out of the direct line of fire.

A shot rang out. Another minute and Tim knocked on the door. "I got two little kids and they don't have nothing to eat." He was red faced and apologetic. "I'm sorry, but Ronnie Peters wanted to kill you and take your food."

"Yes, I know, Timmy. You're welcome to everything we have. Of course the children have to eat. It will be lean times for us all till we can get the seed in the ground next month." Cathy urged the basket of potatoes into his hands. "Thanks for looking out for us, Timmy. Who ever thought it would come to this?"

Tim agreed and left.

"So that's what passes for order these days? That kid is running things now?" Clyde seemed dumbfounded.

"For the next day or two until somebody takes him out. Listen, you can control interactions with people if you initiate it and set the tone like I just did, so remember and jump in quick to start down the track you want. Or let me do it. Main thing is, we'll be safe now. And they know they need us at least until we get the crop in. But there's something else we need to talk about. There's a big change coming. Can you

177

feel it?"

Sandy nodded. "You've been telling us for years. And it's here now."

"No, not this. Something more. This is ending, something new is about to begin."

"I felt it since the end of October." Clyde shivered. "Something about death, death everywhere."

"Everybody feels that in October," said Anita. "That's most likely our genetic memory of the last die-off. El Dia de los Muertos. The Day of the Dead. There's a reason why the whole world commemorates last of October, first of November. A watery cataclysm that swept an ancient civilization away. It's in the folk stories of people all around the world." She nodded solemnly.

Cathy agreed. "This is like that. We're on the cusp of it. And here's what we have to do. There are laws of the universe, laws as unyielding as gravity. Stay in harmony with the laws. Don't resort to violence, to threat, to anger. Stay peaceful, work the land. Stay connected, in harmony. Listen carefully. Listen and obey. Our salvation will come from waiting quietly in our place. We will all get through this."

Sandy said, "My mother has a way of being right about these things."

"Well, what choice do we have, anyway?" Clyde looked to Benny and then Anita for agreement.

And then as if to make a liar out of Cathy, the next day the old world struck back. Three trucks pulled up in front of Leo's old house, now Tim Miller's headquarters, and a bunch of National Guard jumped out. A lieutenant went on in to talk to Tim and when they came out the lieutenant got on a loudspeaker and called for everyone to report for duty in fifteen minutes.

"We're here to collect your state and federal taxes. All taxes have been transmuted to labor hours at a uniform flat rate. Go get your shovels and report to the Allen mine within one hour. You will receive your labor assignments there. Dismissed."

"Tim, they want us to work digging coal? Will they be feeding us? Joe is as weak as a kitten and I'm not much better." Betty Waller had gotten rail thin and Joe looked like he could barely stand up let alone work.

Tim shrugged. "Orders is orders. Who's to tell them no?" He nodded towards the heavily armed men. He went into the garage and came out with a shovel.

"Women and kids, too." The Lieutenant ordered him back into the house to fetch his family. Tim looked like he'd like to say something but didn't dare.

"Let's go." Cathy led her family back to the barn to collect the tools. "Tell you the truth, I didn't see this coming and I don't know why. Just when you figure it's over, it gets another little gasp of life. But don't resist the evil day. Yield and let it roll over you."

There were only about twenty people left to make the walk back the old dirt road to the mine. Half were kids. They were put to work breaking the scattered boulders of coal strewn about and shoveling the bits onto the trucks. By nightfall they were all staggering and were sent home with orders to report at daybreak. Exhausted and filthy, Cathy trudged up the mountain to her secret stash to fetch some food. When she reached the dugout, wispy filaments began drifting across her vision, whispering, whispering. There was something about the stillness of the place, perhaps the magneticity of the rocks that made this spot a special place where the future leached through like light seeping under a closed door. She listened until it dissipated in the moonlight.

She came back to the house with a sack of shell beans and a grim face. The others cooked while she cleaned up. After they ate she softly said, "Leave everything. We're going to wait till the moon sets and then we're going to file out of here, quietly, quietly, one by one and head up the mountain. I have a hideout up there."

Clyde looked up, worried. "They said they'd shoot anybody who didn't report tomorrow. I believe them. We can't hide forever. There's only one more truck to fill and then they'll be gone."

Cathy shook her head. "We have to hide tomorrow. The rock face is going to fall. Not a soul is going to make it out of there alive. I don't know how. I don't know if they're going to try to dynamite or if it's just a fault in the rock face. But nobody who goes there tomorrow is coming back."

Terrified and with sore and aching muscles, Cathy led them up the mountain, stumbling over roots and through briars in frigid darkness until they reached the dugout.

"Ah, Mom, it's just a hole in the mud," Sandy cried with dismay.

"It is, but it will keep us safe and warm. Now squeeze down through that hole. You first. We'll all have to sit, there isn't room to lie down." And after they were all in, with the branches pulled back into place to cover the opening, she began to talk quietly.

"The way I figure it, at least what I always heard, was that time is a property of the universe. Which means that when the universe was formed, so was time. All of it. I know,

I know, it keeps on expanding. But the future exists no less than the present. Think of the universe as a house and the future as a room that you haven't gone into yet. You know it's there, the structure is there, but you're not in it yet. You can't see what's in that room. And what you will do in that room hasn't been decided; it's up to you. But you can figure out a lot about the room even before you've gone in by looking and listening. So listen. Listen with your whole mind. Listen now in the dark with no distractions. Prepare for what you will face when you walk through that door."

The kids had nodded off to sleep and Anita was yawning when Benny said, "Something's coming. I feel it. It's dark and falling."

Clyde said maybe.

"Is that the rock fall? All I feel is silence." Sandy was a doer, not a worrier, not a listener.

"The silence I call the Big Quiet. I hear it too. Can you feel the subharmonics of that rock shear? The rock is groaning. You can feel it through the ground beneath us."

"So that's not the future, just the ground?"

"It's both. The one is the other. The future sends out foregleams just like you can see foregleams of light before dawn. It's a sort of a shock wave, but it's a low frequency wave. Something you feel more than you actually technically hear. Only now, just at this moment, do I understand how we'll deal with natural disasters in this new life. We'll feel them, hear them coming before they get here, in the peaceful Big Quiet. It's something that can be learned. And there will be no racket, no distractions. Did you hear that? It's getting louder. Listen!" And indeed, the crackles of the rock face were almost audible. They didn't actually hear them with their ears, but someplace deep in their heads.

They went to sleep one by one after that and worn out, slept late into the morning in cozy dark of the hole. Getting on towards noon, they were awakened by a roar and a long rumble and then the ground around them shook.

"Now," said Cathy, "We can all go home."

A Fish Tale

David Trammel

He floated on a warm bed of salt water, the Sun shining down, and all around him the life force of the ocean vibrated through him like a musical tune barely heard. A dolphin surfaced and swam beneath his outstretched hand, his fingers touching its skin and its fin sliding beneath his palm.

Then the alarm went off.

Ben rolled over and shut it off. 5am Monday came awful early. He had never been to an ocean, but his mother Elisabeth had told all him about it. She'd grown up onboard the French ship her great grandfather had used to explore the world's oceans, making documentaries and doing research. That was before carbon had collapsed the ocean's ecology.

"Get up, sleepyhead," his mother said with a chuckle. "You have school today."

Saint Louis was just about as far from an ocean as you could come in America. Ben lay there for a few more moments, then picked up the alarm and quickly wound it before putting it away. His mother had opened the shutters on the room's one window, letting in the dawn light. Climate change had made the weather wacky, there could be a few inches of snow or 80 degrees outside in March. They never knew so they insulated and made d0.

She was sitting next to their little rocket stove, a big pot of something cooking, watching a thermometer dipped in the pot. Satisfied with the results, she pulled the pot off and set it in the nearby haybox. No hay in that box, just rags and pieces of cloth from outfits Ben had outgrown. Still they insulated the pot just as well as hay would have. Supper would be waiting for them when they got home.

"What's for dinner?" he asked.

"Mushroom chowder."

He groaned at the thought of more mushrooms.

His mother chuckled. The basement grow center was a booming success and their weekly share as members of the Co-Op always included a big box of them.

The official name was the Broadway and Tyler Street Co-Operative Living and Business Center, but everyone just called it American Brake, after the company who built it back in 1901. Their name was in stone letters on the front of the building. Ben loved it because unlike a lot of old buildings, this one had huge windows on all the floors. It was never dark and stuffy. First floor was used for the businesses the Co-Op ran, while the two above were housing. The roof had the gardens and a small park.

Ben swung his legs off the upper bunk of his bed and dropped lightly to the floor. Turning, he folded both their beds into the wall. That made the room a bit more open. No one would call their squat spacious, at eight feet by ten; still, it wasn't an abandoned car or derelict building, and they had slept in both of those when Ben was younger. He'd been born in 2025, and growing up had been on the road, always headed east, just the two of them.

She never spoke of his dad.

He was fifteen years old now, they had been here at American Brake for over two years. The fear of someone attacking them in their sleep was almost forgotten but his mother still locked the door when they went to sleep with three locks.

"Be right back," he muttered.

There were just two people ahead of him in line for the communal toiletss: ladies to the north, gents to the south. At least a semi-reliable water supply was high on the St Louis Government's list. The cholera outbreak in '28 had opened their eyes to the importance of sanitation.

Electricity wasn't. They got a few hours in the late evening when the business load on the sowntown grid went soft, and the Co-Op used that to charge a big bank of salvaged batteries in the basement. A spider web of old wiring fed ta few 12 volt lights hanging from the ceiling here and there so you didn't have to go stumbling around in the dark.

Half a dozen early risers sat at the tables in the common area; coffee was being served up from the communal kitchen. Patriot News was doing their top of the hour reporting on the radio, talking about recent Rebel bombings in Atlanta. They would turn the room's one television on at 6, for the local news. The days of dozens of channels was long gone. Patriot News was all that was broadcast now.

The Party saw to that.

The personal rooms formed a center core in each of the larger bays on the second and third floors. There was an open communal space between that core and the outside walls that everyone called the Patio. You could put stuff out in front of your squat and people would leave it alone. Moses had insisted that there be a lot of public space on the housing floors.

"No damned anthill," he always said at the monthly meetings. "People need to live like people."

Ben and his mother had a bunch of recycled planters with various vegetables, recently seeded and just coming up, along with a couple of old plastic lawn chairs, and a garden gnome they had lugged from Kansas City. Sometimes they would sit out there and read, or just watch the sunset. It was all a hodgepodge of scavenged materials.

When he came back his mother offered him a hot bowl of oatmeal flavored with a little honey from the rooftop hives as breakfast. As he put his school clothes on, he ate.

"I need you to work some this week after school," she said. "We could really use the credits."

Ben nodded. There was a time bank, where you could trade labor for credits to purchase things at the Co-Op or pay your rent. Everyone contributed. Something always needed to be done.

"I'll ask Moses if I can help out in the garden." He ran a finger around the rim of his bowl, licking it clean. "It always needs weeding."

"I'll be home late," his mother said. "We've run across a good section and Harron will want to work until the light gives out."

The Co-Op was involved in a lot of things but its major business was scavenging and salvage. If you knew what to look for, the many abandoned buildings around them yielded treasures you could resell. Right now they had a big contract with the St Louis government to harvest chain link fencing. Crews from the Co-Op were working their way through the old suburbs a few miles north, up Broadway and onto Grand, then Hall, slowly stripping the abandoned homes and industrial lots of their chain link fences. His mother was working on one of the crews.

Rumor had it they meant to fence in the downtown core so the Burbies weren't a bother anymore. Riots and mobs disrupted $20 cups of latte.

He set his empty bowl in the bucket they had. They would wash up later this evening after dinner.

"Here," his mother held out a cloth wrapped bundle. "Happy birthday."

The wrappings were an old blanket he'd last seen on his mother's bed. There were two things inside, a shirt and a small belt pouch.

"I know Patriot's Day Dance is coming up and I wanted you to look good for Debbie," she smiled.

Ben blushed. The shirt was nice, very stylish, in red, white and blue, Patriot's Day fashion. It was the belt pouch that really caught his eye, though.

"It's a Koop and Rima," he said when he opened it. "Wow, it must have cost a ton."

The pouch held a digital multimeter. He touched the On button to be rewarded with a soft glow and numbers. It had a small solar panel at the top of the case but also the pouch had a secondary charger, a themoelectric panel you wore inside your pants against your skin that turned body heat to electricity.

The last two years in school, Ben had taken a variety of hands-on courses. The one that interested him most was on electronics. The flow and ebb of the electrons, the way the circuits fit together, made sense to him, and it was a skill that was worth much now. Salvaging the derelict buildings meant you came across plenty of old tech, and it mattered a lot if you could tell whether it worked. Good electricians were sought-after members of crews but they were only as good as their tools.

He stood up and hugged his mother. All the long hours, the nights she had come home exhausted to climbdirectly into bed made sense now. Ben didn't know what to say.

"You and me against the world," he whispered in her ear as he hugged her. It was their private motto.

"You and me," she whispered back.

There was a loud whistle from the ground floor.

"That's Harron, I have to go," she said, wiping at her eyes. "Don't forget to feed the fish."

They both laughed.

His mother's birthday was twelve days after Ben's. Last year's gift from him had been a five gallon aquarium tank. He'd found it when he and few friends had been out exploring the buildings around the Co-op. A feral cat had been using it as a place to sleep. His friends hadn't recognized what a treasure it was, but he had, sspecially since all the glass was still in good condition.

Surprising her with it was worth the work. Ben had traded for a few old *National Geographic* magazines and cut out the pictures of the fish, so the aquarium had residents.

A Fish Tale

There were a dozen or so of various sizes, held up on slivers of wood so they looked like they were floating in water.

"Feed the fish" was their promise of hope that they would one day have a home.

❧

"Hey, Mudfoot!"

"Hey, Stumpie!" Ben replied.

Kenny Nine Fingers laughed. Ben and he had a friendly game of insults going.

The 11th Street Warlords lieutenant was sitting on the steps of the building plucking at his old guitar. It was missing two strings so he had to improvise his tune. His girlfriend "Just Mary" was softly singing to the beat while cleaning her fingernails with an icepick. She was a member of the Sisterhood of Death, an all-girl gang off 9th Street. The Co-Op was at the border of the two gang's territories and neutral ground, and hired them both as security.

If tales were true, it was Just Mary who had bitten Kenny's little finger off in a fight between the gangs several years back. Even given his lack of strings and digit Kenny was very good, and Just Mary, who was a dark and scary little bit of a Goth girl, had a voice everyone thought amazing.

Ben ran down the steps and grabbed his bike.

❧

There were a lot of bicycles on the streets now that gasoline was above $50 a gallon: bicycles, and not a few horse-drawn wagons. Still, the occasional car weaved in and out of the slow traffic, downtowners about their business in their electrical vehicles.

189

St Louis had one of the micro nuclear reactors that had been touted as a way to solve the energy crunch a decade ago, bought by the Enclave, a billionaire hedge fund which owned a couple of dozen city blocks and the skyscrapers on them. The Summer of Rage in '24 and the riots in '25 and '26, had made the Percenters scared. They abandoned their mansions in Ladue and Wildwood for the towers of downtown. There they bought security and safety.

Some nights Ben and his friends would lay on the roof of the Co-Op and gaze at the lit up wonderland of Downtown. Out here in the Burbs it was total dark.

He meet up with Barry as he was going out the front gate of the Co-Op. Barry was a schoolmate and friend. School was just a few blocks away, across the Madison Street overpass.

&

The Oxes had a check point up.

The St. Louis Police Auxiliary Patrol—everyone called them the Oxes—were a nuisance at times and a real bother at others: local toughs and petty criminals who had official sanction to steal. Their row of little electric scooters stood side by side. The Oxes were the police in the Burbs, since the government no longer had the money to spend enforcing the law beyond of the Core.

This checkpoint was more serious than most. A vehicle marked "Homeland Security" was among the scooters. There were officials in long brown trench coats, carrying Pads, standing like the scarecrows the kids of the Co-Op made to protect the corn on the roof. They had a bus stopped and were searching it, comparing the faces of the men with something on their Pads. Clearly they were looking for someone.

A micro drone hovered above the checkpoint, making slow passes across the scene. Homeland was there to protect them, Ben's mother told him. Loyal patriots have nothing to fear from them. Always answer their questions honestly and stay out of trouble. They weren't stopping women or children so Ben and Barry peddled quickly by.

∾

"So, the corrupt Congress bought by special interests let the debt crisis of 2024 again stop the government.." Mrs. Cesaria, their teacher said, continuing her history lecture. "In a show of purely partisan politics they forced a default on our national debt, thinking this would win them the election. The crisis caused the collapse of the banking giant L,G & F. The financial markets froze and..."

She pointed to one of Ben's classmates.

"No one would lend?" the girl said hesitantly.

"Correct." She nodded. "When businesses could no longer carry lines of credits, national capital stopped. That meant nothing moved. Not material, not goods, not food. And what do people without food do?" she asked.

"Fight back!" everyone in class shouted.

"Yes, it was then that the riots started," she continued. "But then the corrupt government reacted, and deployed troops."

"Then Cleveland," Willy Peters volunteered.

"Yes, Cleveland." Mrs. Cesaria said. "Where police fired on unarmed peaceful patriotic protesters, killing many."

She turned to the portrait on the wall next to the American flag.

"That was when General Arnold and his men decided they had to protect the Constitution and this great land. They rounded up the corrupt politicians and the President..."

The lunch time buzzer rang out. Everyone gathered their books and bags up, heading for the door.

"Remember," Mrs. Cesaria called out. "Your reports on the General Arnold and what you learned from his actions in the Patriot's Day Coup are due no later than Friday."

&

"So you thought of a birthday present for your mom yet?" Willy asked.

Willy Peters, Barry and Ben sat on one of the tables in the school yard, eating lunch. They hung together between classes.

"Maybe," Ben said, around the sandwich his mother had packed.

Willy had a bowl of something pasta with fish, an old plastic bowl with lid. Always fish for Willy. His father ran an aquaponics store off 33rd, in a three story building they were squatting in.

Barry was just nibbling a protein bar, one of the things you got cheap from the cafeteria off the School Lunch Program. It stilled the hunger but never filed you up. Barry's dad was out of work and his mother only part timing it.

Ben took the little bag of Co-Op cookies his mother had packed in his lunch and tossed them on the table.

"Try these," he said.

Barry reached out and took them, a look of gratitude in his eyes.

Willy after a moment, slid his half eaten bowl of pasta over too.

"I'm full," he said.

His mother's birthday was soon but he still had time to find something. With her gift of the multimeter it had to be really special.

❧

"Frackin' pipes!"

A jet of water arched up almost to the ceiling.

"Kill it," Horace Peters yelled.

Willy's dad rose from behind the large barrels filled with fish and water, wiping his face with a handkerchief. Much of that jet had hit him.

"We're gonna need a whole new seal on that one," he said to Penny, his wife, who had been at the circuit breaker box.

"Fish, fish, fish!" he yelled, throwing the handkerchief to the side. "God, what I'd give for a good well done steak dinner sometime."

His wife, who was used to his outbursts, laughed.

The first floor of the building was filled with interconnecting 55 gallon plastic drums. Ben was familiar with the set up. Mr. Peters had been one of his instructors while he was doing his 10th year hands-on, and he had almost decided on aquaculture as a specialty. The water was pumped up to the third floor where the garden was, so the plants could filter the fish waste and recycle it as fertilizer.

"Hi, Ben," Mr. Peters said, noticing him. "What's up?"

"Can we talk, Mr. Peters?" Ben asked.

❧

Alongside his aquaponics business, Mr. Peters was one of the few exotic fish dealers in St. Louis. His second floor office was wall to wall aquariums filled with brightly colored species.

Ben slowly walked along the rows looking at the fish. One in particular caught his eye.

"That's a Queen Angelfish," Mr. Peters said. "Gorgeous blue and yellow, isn't it? Just got it from a breeder in Nashville."

"It's beautiful," Ben whispered.

"And expensive," Horace said. "What's on your mind?"

Ben told him.

"That's gonna cost you," he said. "You'll need a tank, pump, chemicals, supplies, that won't come cheap."

Ben nodded.

"I got a 5 gallon tank and I can get the pump," he replied. "I can pay for some of it with cash, but you said you'd really like a steak..." He grinned.

"We trading, then?" Horace asked.

∽

Next day after class, Ben grabbed Barry.

"Your uncle still work at that restaurant?"

Barry nodded.

∽

"So I want to ask her to marry me, but it has to be very special."

Barry's uncle Kevin was on the rooftop of Longhorn, the upscale restaurant where he was head chef, not far from downtown. Its specialty was Canadian beef. Climate change had made the Canadian heartland a lush prairie of grass and Canadian beef was some of the best, and some of the most expensive. The owner, Rico Angeleros, came from a family that owned thousands of acres of Canadian prairie; he stood next to Kevin, and both men looked over the container garden on the roof of the restaurant. The produce went into the meals served to Percenters and wannabes who dined there.

"She's got this whole fantasy after seeing *Heavy Weapon—Reloaded*. Roses, a band, some woman singing..." Kevin sighed. "Where am I getting roses?"

Rico chuckled. "You're screwed, son," he said.

❧

"You set that up and we have a deal," Kevin said to Ben. Ben nodded.

❧

"Ben, whatever are you doing here?" Mrs. Cesaria said, answering the door.

"I wanted to get my report to you," he said.

"You could have waited til school."

Mrs. Cesaria lived in one of the Collectives, groups of single homes that banded together in the After. Many older people resisted joining a Co-op, clinging to their single homes.

After giving his teacher his report, he paused. "Is there anything I can help out with?" he asked. "Mom says I should help my elders."

Mrs. Cesaria was clearly touched. "There is one thing..." She led him out to the backyard, where a small side building stood. "I need this cleared out."

"What happened to the tenant?" Ben asked, because it was clear that she had been renting it out.

Mrs. Cesaria blushed. "Homeland Security came and arrested him," she stammered. "I answered their questions. I told them I only rent to loyal members of the Patriot Party. He seemed harmless..."

The small building was perhaps fifteen feet by twenty, an old garage turned residence. The only thing that set it apart was the thick hedgeof roses growing on the side.

"They searched the room and took things," she said. "Still, there is a lot of stuff that I just need cleaned out."

"I think I can do that for you," Ben said. "If you'll let me pick a few flowers..."

❧

It took Ben two days of work after school to clean out the room. A lot of the stuff wasn't worth trading—clothing, personal items, a few books. He put those on the curb so the Pickers could come and gather it up for recycling. Still, Ben did collect a box full of old electronics and a few books he thought he could use for trade.

He also got permission to come back for some roses. After he told her what they were for, Mrs. Cesaria had positively glowed.

"You take as many as you want," she had said.

Ben almost like her then.

❧

The door had a bell on it, so it rang when you entered.

"Hello in the shop," Ben called out. It was Saturday and almost noon.

Mr. Henry's shop, a two-story squat on 27th, was a treasure trove of old electronics. It was the time he'd spent there that had convinced Ben he wanted to be an electrician. Pat mentored a couple of dozen students. He was a veteran of the Venezuelan War, missing both legs below the knees. He had some prosties he'd made with a second hand 3D printer, for when he had to go out, but in the shop he usually stayed in his wheelchair.

He was not alone.

"Hi, Ben," Pat said.

The visitor was black, short and muscular. He watched as Ben put his box of electronics on the counter, not speaking.

"Got some trade," Ben said.

"And you need?" Pat asked.

"Water pump, solar panel and battery backup."

"In the shelves." he said. "See what I've got."

Ben nodded.

&

"Adams said she has the tubes blown and finished, last time I talked to her." Pat said. "We just have to go get them."

Ben was back among the rows of shelves in the store. Mr. Henry had a huge inventory of spares and stuff but hunting for things was always an adventure. From where Ben was looking, he could see both of them at the counter. The stranger was clearly agitated.

"The kid?" the stranger asked.

"He knows how to keep his mouth shut," Pat replied.

"Branson went dark last month," the stranger said. "And it wasn't equipment malfunction. They had four ham operators and they all went off the air the same day."

The shelves in back were full of large plastic trays, which were probably more valuable than what was in them; plastic, like the oil it was made from, was expensive now. There was a box in the tray Ben was looking through marked Wurm Pumps but it held a couple of 40 amp circuit breakers instead.

"You don't think Homeland is going after the HamNet, do you?" Pat asked. "Hancock's a bit of a hothead down there but..."

He let the statement trail off as he pulled the box Ben had brought off the counter and onto his lap.

"We're just about the last uncensored way people can get news any more," the stranger replied. "If the noise on the HamNet is true, some of the changes the New Constitutional Congress is proposing are flat out scary, but you don't hear anything about that from the official news."

Ben stepped to the next tray full of boxes.

"Let me give Sammie a call," Pat said.

He had a cell phone he used for business. The days when you could surf the Internet on your phone were long gone. Now phones just called people.

A quick glance at the next two trays yielded no pump for Ben either.

"This is not good," Pat said putting his phone away.

"Not home?" the stranger asked.

"I got her voicemail. Sammie used the go word 'Daffodils' in her message. Somehow Homeland knows you're here."

"I still have to get those tubes," the stranger said firmly. "Kansas City and Wichita are both down to one radio, and Tulsa went dark a week ago from equipment failure. You have just about the last tube witch in the Midwest here. We all depend on what comes out of St. Louis to stay on the air."

Pat opened the box Ben had brought over. When he got a good look what was inside he called out to Ben.

"Where did you get this?" Pat asked.

He came out from the shelves and told his instructor about cleaning out the room for his teacher.

Pat held a copy of an old book clenched in his hands. It had something written across the front in marker. Clearly it meant something.

"Homeland got Hamilton," he said to the stranger. "This is serious. You have to get out of here."

"How can you be sure?"

"This is an autographed copy of Greer's final book." Pat held it up. "It was the gem in Hamilton's bookcase."

"Not without the tubes."

Ben saw an opening.

"I could get them for you..."

❧

The stranger, who introduced himself as Washington, seemed open to the idea. Ben's instructor, though, was fighting tooth and nail against it. They had been arguing now for ten minutes straight.

"I have to get home sometime," Ben finally said.

The two men looked at each other and seemed to come to a decision.

"You know what I want is contraband?" Washington asked. "Homeland catches it on you, you'll be headed to a Re-Ed camp tomorrow."

Pat was clearly not happy.

Ben smiled. "Everyone out here in the Burbs runs something illegal from time to time." He shrugged. "I've done my share of it for people. No one looks at teenagers on bikes."

Washington chuckled.

"Ok," he said. "And what's it gonna cost me?"

Ben told him.

"That's robbery!" Washington exclaimed.

"And the water pump," Ben said. "I need that too."

Washington glared at Ben for a long minute, then finally nodded.

Ben was on his bicycle outside the shop. Pat had put his prosties on and walked outside to see him off.

"First sign of trouble, you be safe," his teacher said firmly. "Get rid of the tubes. No heroics."

Ben nodded and rode off.

It took him over an hour to get there. The house was in a really rundown part of the Burbs. There was an old skeleton of an auto on the street out front that had caught fire and burned out. Maybe one in ten houses was occupied. Most were slowly crumbling in on themselves. Ben rode past once, ignoring the house, then did a quick around the block to come back. He parked his bike in the alley between the houses and slid slowly forward toward the back door of the house watching his surroundings. He was two steps from knocking on the door when the unmistakable sound of a shotgun slide clacking froze him in his tracks.

"Looks like rat is on the menu tonight," a woman's voice said behind him.

"No leaky boats on the Delaware." he said the words Washington told him to say.

"Hope the General doesn't get his feet wet," she replied.

Mrs. Adams turned out to be a grey headed tiny old woman with a grin and a shotgun almost as big as she was. She led him inside through a side door of the garage, then into the main house. Ben followed her down the stairs to her basement. There was equipment everywhere. Beakers, tools, all sorts of things young inexperienced minds didn't recognize.

"First time?" she asked.

Ben nodded.

"You in it for the money or the principle?" she asked.

Ben felt a bit confused at the question but admitted.

"The money, Mrs. Adams."

She sighed, sitting down across the big workbench from him.

"You know, son, democracy used to mean something. We held our elected officials accountable and when they weren't, we kicked them out. Not like now, where the Party nominates one lone representative and you just get to sign on the dotted line." She started to work herself up on the subject. "Damned Arnold and his cronies, it's been 17 years since the last election. This State of Emergency bull is getting kind of thin. If I had my way, I'd march every last one of those bastards up against the wall."

It seemed an old argument to her, and Ben, wise in the ways of talkative elders, just kept nodding as she spoke.

"People just stand meekly by and let Homeland Gestapo take their liberties from them. When are they going to learn that freedom has to be fought for..."

She seemed to catch him ignoring her rant and chuckled. She shook her head.

"And its Sammie to my friends, not Mrs. Adams, got it?"

Ben nodded.

"Okay, be careful with the package, it's breakable."

It was about the size of a thick book. She turned and grabbed something. "Gotta couple of 'Get Out Of Jail' cards for you too."

Ben's confusion at the reference must have shown on his face.

"Monopoly?" she asked.

Ben shrugged. Games about capitalism were no longer played, on the Party's orders.

The old woman just shook her head.

"Okay, red and green." Sammie put two small tin cans on the workbench. One had a splash of red paint, one green. "These will give you some distraction if you need it. Both will put out a big cloud of smoke." She pushed them across the workbench. "Red goes off quick, 10 to 15 seconds once you pop the tab. Green is slow, maybe 4 to 5 minutes. Don't use them unless you have to."

Ben put them and the package in his backpack

"These tubes are important," she said. "Don't frack this up boy."

He finally put it all together. "You're Rebels!"

Mrs. Adams slowly reached for the shotgun. It had never been far.

"Hey," Ben said softly, feeling the tension in the room shoot up. "I got a deal worked out, so I only care about getting it done."

Sammie gave him a long look, her hand on the shotgun barrel. Patriot News always ran stories about how bloodthirsty the Rebels were with those who got on their wrong side. If she decided against this, Ben didn't think he could get up the stairs fast enough to not get shot in the back.

Her phone buzzed. "Hello honey," she answered. "You ordered pizza from a new store, which was risky of you."

She listened to what the other said.

"I was going to give him a big tip but I'm not sure he's right for his job. I was about to call his boss and get him fired."

She listened some more.

"Ok, if that's what you think, I'll ask him for a coupon for his next visit."

Sammie closed her cell, ending the call.

"Ride safe," she said, taking her hand from the shotgun.

∾

"Anything else you need?" she asked as she let him out the garage door.

"Don't happen to have a few guitar strings, do you?" Ben asked.

"What do you need with guitar strings?"

Ben told her.

"Oh my," she laughed. "Mother Gaia has a sense of humor, doesn't She."

Ben was confused.

"Is your musician any good?"

Ben nodded.

Sammie turned looking around the old garage. It was filled with boxes and stuff.

"Ok, now where did I put that?"

∾

It took the old woman almost twenty minutes to find what she wanted. Ben at first humored her, but the gravity of what he was doing, transporting contraband for the Rebels, got him nervous. He was about the just beg off and get out of

203

there when Sammie gave a whoop of joy. She tossed a couple of boxes to the side, then dug out a beat up guitar case.

"I won a scholarship to Juilliard Academy when I was about your age," she said.

Opened, it revealed a gorgeous old acoustic guitar.

"Can I have the strings?"

She laughed.

"Hell kid, you can have the guitar."

Ben's eyes lit up.

৵

"Watch out for checkpoints," Sammie said.

She had helped him strap the guitar case to the back of his bike. It was unwieldy but it wouldn't fall off.

"No worries," Ben said, taking off.

৵

Ben was worried.

He was half a mile for the electronics shop and thought he was home free, when he had blundered into a checkpoint. He had come racing around the corner and couldn't turn around before the Oxes stopped him. Now he stood in line while they checked the IDs of those before him. A few they were searching. Homeland was there too, an agent checking the faces of men against some image on his Pad.

Ben was standing next to two open trash cans at the curb, piled high. Maybe if he dropped one of Mrs. Adam's grenades in it, he could get away in the confusion. He slid his backpack off his shoulder slowly.

"What's ya got there, Burbie?"

The Ox was a big guy, and fat. He had walked up behind Ben and was eyeing the case on his bike.

"My guitar," Ben ad libbed. "I'm taking lessons."

"Worth anything?"

"What are you doing?" said another voice, with a sharp crack to it.

Ben and the Ox turned. The Homeland agent was a hard looking man, razor sharp in his brown trench coat.

The Ox stammered something.

"We're not here to indulge your petty larceny," the Homeland agent said. He gave a sigh of disgust. "Did you at least ask him if he'd seen the suspect before trying to rob him?"

The Ox blushed.

The Homeland agent flipped his Pad around so Ben could see it.

"Have you seen this man?"

The image was one he recognized. It was the man he had meet today at the shop, the man who called himself Washington. Ben's mind raced. He remembered his mother's word, always cooperate with Homeland Security, they were there to protect them.

And the Rebels, they were criminals. What did Ben owe them?

"Is there a reward?" he asked.

"Could be," the agent said. "If it leads to an arrest. This man is very dangerous."

Ben looked at the image again. A big reward could help Ben and his mother out a lot.

"Yeah, I think I know where you can find him."

❧

Everyone in the Longhorn was clapping.

Ben was standing at the back of the crowded restaurant, Mr. Angeleros next to him. Kevin was still on his knee, while his new fiancée kept kissing him, her arms full of roses and tears of joy streaming down her face at his marriage proposal.

Behind her, Kenny Nine Fingers and Just Mary were smiling. Kenny holding his new guitar. Part of their deal. Just Mary had cleaned up rather well, and was actually in a dress. Black of course. Her singing as she and Kenny had come out on cue, had stopped the conversations of the diners in their tracks.

"You did good, kid," Mr. Angeleros said.

Ben blushed.

"Those two aren't half bad either," he continued. "Might just have to get them here on weekends singing to the clients."

Ben grinned.

"I think that can be arranged," he said.

"Ok, Mister Wheeler-dealer," Mr. Angeleros asked. "Who gets this steak dinner you bargained for?"

Ben dug out one of Mr. Peter's Aquarium business cards.

"Fish," Mr. Angeleros nodded. "You know we were thinking about offering Greenland lobsters. Might have to talk to him about the tanks."

≈

"My dad can't stop talking about that dinner. Mom and him went there last night," Willy said two days later at school. He opened his lunch at the table. "Yuck! Fish..."

Ben laughed

"Dad said we can come over and set up the tank whenever you want."

"Me and Mom are going to take the horse trolley down to the Arch tomorrow and make a day of it for her birthday,"

Ben said. "I'll talk to Co-Op security and they can let you both in."

Willy nodded.

❧

"Those were good hot dogs," Ben said.

"Nothing compared to a Woofies," his mother replied, as she took off her shoes, tossing them into the corner of their squat. "They could do a chili cheese dog you would sell your soul for."

It had been a good day, the sun out and the temperature warm but not too hot. Saturday and the Riverfront had been crowded with people out enjoying the Spring.

"It's a shame you never had one before they closed."

Ben had noticed the birthday present as soon as they had entered. His mother, though, had seen what she had seen a hundred times before and glanced right past it.

He had been wound up tight all day. Not knowing if Willy and his father had been able to get in and set the aquarium up. So many things that could have gone wrong. His mother yawned, as she took off her light jacket. She pulled down her bed and sat. Still she didn't notice the new aquarium.

"Maybe I should feed the fish," he finally said, fit to burst with excitement.

She turned, looking at the tank and gave a soft gasp!

"Oh Ben!" she staggered forward to the small table the tank was on, kneeling down to look. "They're beautiful."

His original deal with Willy's dad had been for a dozen or so of his cheaper fish, but floating in the center of the aquarium was the Queen Angelfish, alight in yellow strips and blues. It slowly swam back and forth, almost as if it

207

knew it was the prize of all times. Around it floated at least two dozen lesser fish, all brightly colored.

"Happy birthday, Mom," Ben whispered.

Her fingers on the glass, his mother softly cried her happiness that the aquarium said they finally had a place to call a real home.

There was a knock at their door.

❧

"This came for you," Moses said.

He held out a small package. They were on the roof in the garden. A runner had knocked on the door of their squat and told Ben that Moses needed to speak with him. Ben, like all the kids at the Co-Op, knew the old black man. Most of the times a kindly white-haired grandfather figure, he seemed to radiate seriousness today.

"Been running with a dangerous crowd, have you?" he asked.

Ben shrugged. He opened the paper wrapped package. Inside it was three things.

The first thing was an envelope. It contained the three hundred dollars Washington had agreed to pay Ben for his going to get the tubes. The second was a short handwritten note from his mentor Pat.

"Thanks for everything. Our friend got out of town safely with his items and is on his way to Kansas City. We couldn't have done it without you."

Ben had lied to the Homeland agent, telling him he had seen Washington at a restaurant a block back. They had shut down the checkpoint and raced to catch the dangerous Rebel before he had a chance to escape. Ben had given the agent a false name and address when he had asked for the reward.

208

A Fish Tale

Thirty minutes later Ben and his package were safely at Mr. Henry's electronics store.

Washington had laughed at what Ben had done.

"Kid, you're a natural," he'd just said.

The last thing in the package was a book.

"*The Private Life of the Late Benjamin Franklin.*" he read the title out loud. "I've heard of him. He was one of the Founding Fathers, wasn't he?"

Moses nodded.

"You can learn a lot from that book," he said. "And from that Ben."

The old man seemed to consider him for a long moment.

"No leaky boats on the Delaware," he finally said.

Ben's eyes lit up in surprise.

"Hope the General doesn't get his feet wet," he replied.

Moses chuckled and walked away. Ben would have to think on the revelation that Moses was a Rebel. And now, for better or worse, Ben was too. Well, he thought, tomorrow would bring what tomorrow would bring.

For now, he had fish to feed.

A Break with the Past

Joseph Nemeth

Mark tried to recall exactly when worry had given way to panic. He knew he'd been running for a while, his mind blank. He'd lost any sense of time. Two minutes or twenty: he had no idea. Then he'd felt his feet tangle in something, and struck the ground with force enough to drive the air from his heaving lungs. He'd passed out, struggling to draw breath.

He was calm now. He'd somehow managed to roll over on his back, and his breathing was slow and steady. His face felt numb, like he'd slept on it, but with a suggestion of pain just beneath the surface—he'd probably landed on it, and would soon have a fat lip and two swollen black eyes. But his eyes had not swollen shut, and he could see a small patch of gray sky through the trees. Gray—not black. So he hadn't been unconscious long.

Panic started to rise in his chest again, but he fought it back. He needed to *think*. That's what they said. Don't panic. Never panic. *Think*.

What did that even *mean*?

As quickly as the panic had filled him, it receded, and self-pity flowed into the vacuum. Tears leaked from his eyes, and ran down the sides of his face.

The temperature was dropping quickly, and he was starting to shiver. As if cued by his misery, a slow drizzle began to fall and painted his face and clothing with moisture. He was at least an hour from the city, assuming he had any idea what direction to walk, and there couldn't be that much daylight left. No one knew he was out here, except Danny and Lovo, and they wouldn't tell anyone: there'd be Hell to pay if the city guard found out they'd been outside city limits. If the other two made it back before curfew, they'd lay low and keep quiet, and assume he was doing the same. He wouldn't be missed for days.

He was well and truly fracked.

He tried to remember anything he'd learned in school about surviving in the wilderness, but all he could remember was something about making fire with two sticks. That's how the primitive savages made fire.

At least if he got up and started moving, it would warm him up. He rolled over and stood up.

As he put weight on his left foot, pain spiked through his leg and he collapsed with a shriek.

᧰

Danny wore the grin he always had when the three of them were about to make mischief. Lovo was his usual inert, grumpy self. Mark took a quick, reflexive look around, to see who might be watching. But they were alone.

"Packed for the day?" Danny asked.

Mark shook his knapsack in answer. "Let's see this fabulous map, boob."

Danny bent and pulled a much-folded map from his own knapsack, which sat on the ground propped against his skinny legs. He unfolded it carefully. This was real paper, old-style paper, yellowed around the edges. The colored rectangle that filled one side was an unnatural old-style shade of pale green that went with the paper.

"Here's the edge of the city," Danny said, running his finger along the edge of a white area full of complicated lines. His finger stopped moving, and he said, "We're right here." He pointed to another spot halfway across the page. "There's where we're going."

Mark tried to make sense of the image. They'd done a section on maps in the very class he was ditching at the moment, but it had never made any sense to him. No one except the mercs ever left the city, and they took a transport or one of the rails. There were routes. You had to know the routes. That made sense. But trying to figure out the wastelands in between the stops? Who cared about *that*?

Now, with a thrill of excitement, he wished he'd paid more attention.

"What's out there?" Lovo asked.

"An old mine," Danny answered.

"Metal salvage," Lovo said, his eyes suddenly bright.

"Maybe even some tech," Danny said with a nod.

Mark scowled. "How far is that from the city?"

Danny made walking motions with his fingers on the map.

"'Bout two hours, I figure," he said.

"You boob! That close, it's been picked clean ages ago."

Danny scowled back. "Quit calling me boob, tube. 'Sides, it might still be there. There's no road for the transports, just this teensy little trail. Crews wouldn't go out there."

"Picked clean," Mark insisted.

"Fine," Danny snapped, and folded the map. "Go on back to class. Lapdog."

Mark thought about it. Yes, the mine would be picked clean for sure, but he had a sandwich in his pack and his sturdy shoes on. At least it wasn't school.

"Nah, I want to see the look on your face, boob. Three chits says there's nothing there."

"Frack you, tube. You're on."

They shouldered their packs and followed the line of the old electric fence, long powerless, that surrounded the city, until they found a place where the creepers had torn it down. A moment later, they were in the cool green light of the forest that surrounded the city.

Danny eventually found the path. It was heavily overgrown, but in the distant past it had been marked with concrete posts, and where those had crumbled, tall piles of stones stood. Posts and stones alike were covered with a thick patina of moss that made them hard to see in the dense growth.

After a little more than an hour, they reached their objective, a black hole bored into the side of a small hill. A few fragments of rotted wood that protruded from the hillside suggested there had once been some kind of wooden structure covering the hole, but there was no trace of it now.

"Three chits," said Mark. He held out his hand.

"You just wait," Danny growled. "We haven't looked around yet."

But a careful search turned up nothing of value. They found a concrete pad that might have been a foundation for a well pump, but the concrete had been split and the metal pipe pulled up out of the ground. All that remained were rust stains on the concrete. Not even a rusty nail remained. Danny eventually dug into his pocket and slapped three wooden disks into Mark's hand.

They sat and ate their lunches, and chucked stones into the black maw and listened to the hollow echo of stone on stone.

"Maybe there's something inside," said Lovo. He'd not had a sandwich, but only half a processed rat, as they called the high-protein ration issued by the city government to the poorest citizens. He stood up.

"Don't go in there, Lovo," Mark said.

"I ain't scared o' no Earth 'vengers," he replied. "They're fairy tales." But his swarthy face was an unhealthy shade of yellow.

Mark felt a chill run up his spine. He'd grown up with the stories of violated earth spitting up creatures that lived far underground, to wreak havoc on the surface-dwellers who had done such damage to the world. It was just a story, but the Prophets of Doom believed they were real, and told gruesome tales of what happened when an Avenger got hold of a human. Mark put on a sneer to hide his reaction.

"Yeah, dumb-boob, but an old mine isn't *safe*," he said. "They prop up the roof with wood, and wood rots. I'll bet if we threw some bigger rocks, this whole thing would cave in."

Danny had that look in his eye. "Yeah, or maybe it would stir up the 'vengers, and they'd drag us all down to the bottom of the world. I say we go find some bigger rocks and stir 'em up."

Mark wasn't comfortable with this idea at all, and Lovo looked like he wanted to be sick, but neither of them could back down in front of Danny. So they helped him find a big rock, maybe a hundred pounds, and they wrestled it to the door and heaved it as hard as they could into the darkness. The ground inside the mine entrance sloped downward, and they could hear the rock roll and pick up speed. Then it must have fallen into the main shaft, because there was a moment of silence, followed by hard cracking sounds as the stone struck the walls on its way down.

That's when the eerie howl started to issue from the black hole in the hillside, growing louder by the moment. A second howl joined it. All three boys froze.

And then, they were running.

Within moments, they'd gotten separated, and by the time Mark stopped running, breathless, the others were long out of sight or hearing. The hairs on his neck still crawled as he forced himself to walk away, not run, from the old mine. It took another quarter-hour for him to calm down enough to realize he was lost.

Mark was pretty sure he'd headed in the right general direction when he'd started running. But there'd been no pretense of trying to follow the path back home, and he'd been entirely absorbed in replaying horrific Earth Avenger stories in his imagination. He could have walked right into one of the concrete posts without noticing. Now, he had no idea where he was, or which way to go. The sky had clouded over, and the forest was dim. Every direction looked exactly the same.

Worry set in. He decided to try to backtrack, even all the way to the mine if he had to, since he knew the path ended there. After all, there were no such things as Earth Avengers. It had been some wild animal. Nothing to be afraid of. He turned around, but could see no sign of his own passage. He switched directions several times, trying to pick up his own back trail, but the undergrowth swallowed his footsteps like water. Within moments he had no idea which direction the mine lay.

Worry flowered into panic, and then he was running through the forest, his mind as blank as the gray sky that could be seen in patches above.

Mark lay on the ground where he had collapsed. His ankle was gripped in a relentless vice of pain. He slowly sat up—every movement brought new peaks of agony – and pulled up his pant leg. The sight of his ankle made him throw up. He retched until his stomach was empty.

It was no sprain—he could see the unnatural angle of the shinbone right above the ankle, even through the swelling. It was a break, and a bad one. He tried to unlace the boot, but the effort ripped another scream from his throat. There was no way he was going to be able to pull off the boot, even if he got it unlaced. Nor could he walk. He tried to roll over to crawl, but shrieked as his leg changed angle and twisted the foot.

He realized then that he was going to die out here. Maybe tonight, if it got cold enough. Maybe in a day or two, from thirst. Maybe sooner, if a wild animal found him. Or whatever had risen from the mine.

As if on cue, he heard crackling in the undergrowth, moving toward him. He scrabbled around for a stick or a rock to defend himself with, but the motion shifted his foot, and he screamed again. The crackling stopped.

"S-stay away from me!" Mark shouted, teeth chattering. "G-go away! Shoo!"

Something moved closer.

"N-no! G-go away!"

A shape appeared in the dim twilight, tall and sinister and two-legged.

"Do you insist?" it asked.

Mark gaped.

"Do you insist?" the figure repeated. "I do not wish to intrude on your privacy. But it seems you need some assistance."

"Oh, G-god, y-yes," Mark stammered, racked with shudders. "H-help! P-please...."

The forest was growing unaccountably dark, a darkness that crept in from the edges of Mark's vision. He saw the figure move forward swiftly, and kneel beside him. When it spoke, the voice held concern.

"You are going into shock. You must lie down. Focus on my voice."

Mark felt hands on his chest and the back of his neck, urging him to lie down, and a moment later, something was shoved under his good leg to elevate it. The voice continued to speak in even tones.

"Listen to my voice. Stay awake, and listen. Help is already on the way, and we will take good care of you. But you have to stay awake, now. Stay awake until help comes."

Mark felt hands rubbing his arms vigorously, then his chest. It was comforting and irritating at the same time, but he started to feel some warmth and feeling return to his arms. He had not even noticed that feeling had left until it returned, and then his skin began to tingle and burn. The blackness in his vision retreated into a more natural twilight, and he weakly beat at the hands mauling him.

"Good. You are beginning to feel again. Concentrate on my voice. Help is coming. It will be here soon. Stay awake. Focus on my voice."

Mark heard more crackling, and then a second figure was present.

"Fire first," said a young woman's voice. It was a statement, but there was a lilt of question in it.

"Yes," the man said. "I will keep him warm until you have made fire."

The woman slipped into the wood, without a single rustle of underbrush. The man continued to rub Mark's arms and chest until Mark grabbed his wrists. His grip was weak, but steady.

The man nodded and then reached into a pouch that hung from a strap around his neck. He pulled out a small package that he quickly shook out into a large, very thin blanket that seemed to glitter in the fading light. He wrapped Mark in the blanket. Despite its thinness, it held his body heat remarkably well.

A few moments later, the underbrush crackled again, and the woman reappeared with a substantial load of deadfall. She stared carefully at the sky for several moments, then chose a spot on the ground and cleared it. She swiftly set up a rude framework of long green branches, unfolded a blanket similar to the one that covered Mark, then fixed it to the framework to form a kind of lean-to. She studied the sky again as she positioned it. She drew a knife from her belt and began to shave thin slices of wood into a small pile, and arranged a cone of small twigs over the shavings. She then did something—Mark could not see what in the dark—and fire flickered in the cone of twigs. It grew quickly as she blew on it, and within minutes, she had a small, robust fire burning.

"We need to move him," the woman said, and unrolled a conventional blanket on the ground between the fire and the lean-to. The man studied the sky, then shook his head.

"With clouds, I can never tell," he said. "You have a gift."

She laughed. "It is no gift to be observant. I saw the last of the sun-glow when I was gathering wood. It was that direction."

He studied her gesture and the position of the lean-to, and nodded.

"This will hurt," he said to Mark, "Are you ready?"

Mark nodded, and the man removed the thin blanket and laid it on top of the conventional one. The cold air made Mark shiver. He tried to sit up, but the man pushed him back down.

"We will do this," he said. His sister squatted near Mark's head and hooked her hands under his armpits, while the man carefully gripped Mark's pants at the knee.

"One. Two. Three." They both lifted, and pain exploded in Mark's ankle as support from the ground fell away. He tried to be silent and strong, but he howled anyway.

And then he was on the ground again, surrounded by radiant heat. The agony in his ankle diminished into an angry, dull throb that kept time to his heartbeat. They swiftly wrapped Mark in another conventional blanket.

"Should we try to splint his foot?" the woman asked.

The man hesitated. He pulled a knife from his belt and slit Mark's pant leg, which had grown tight around the swollen leg. He studied the ankle in the firelight.

"We must remove the shoe first. The swelling will cut off blood, and then the foot will die. If you press here, on the toe, in that direction, it will hold the shoe steady without pressure on his foot. I will cut off the sole, and then we can get the upper part off."

"Don't," Mark said, weakly. They both looked at him in surprise. "They're my good shoes. They cost a lot."

Both of them continued to look at him silently. Finally the man spoke.

"Even good shoes can be replaced. Can your people replace a foot?"

"No," Mark said, reluctantly.

"If the foot dies, it must be cut off, or you will die. You said that you do not wish to die. Have you changed your mind?"

"N-no...." Mark whispered.

"Then the shoe must come off. Do I have your permission?"

Mark thought about the number of hours of labor that his parents had put in to buy those boots. He had never thought about that before. Most days, the days he bothered to come home, he could barely be persuaded to speak to them.

Now, the thought of cutting up his good boot opened a door to a cascade that became a flood: everything his parents had provided for him from the meager earnings of their demeaning jobs. A vision of their faces came, unbidden, unwanted, and he tried to look away, but the picture was in his mind so there was no way to turn: a vision of the last time they had argued, and he had stormed out of his house to live with Danny for three days. He saw the pain in their eyes, and recognized it for what it was. Shame rose like a dirty tide and threatened to drown him. He forced himself to stop thinking about them.

"Cut it off," he said, and closed his eyes tightly. *I will not scream again.*

Despite his resolve, and the care the other two took, he screamed several times. But eventually the boot was off. The man studied the break in the leg.

"This is beyond my skill," he said, and stood. "He must be carried. I will go for help."

"Wait for the light," the woman said.

"It is my debt," the man said.

"Our debt, brother," she said, quietly. "*Our* debt. You cannot make good time in the dark, and you risk your own safety. That does not honor the debt."

The man muttered something under his breath. Then he sighed.

"You are right. As always. At first light, I will go."
She nodded. "I will take first fire watch."

❧

The night passed in a fractured haze for Mark. He slept a little, kept warm by the fire, and his benefactors kept the fire fed. His ankle throbbed continuously, and between crests of pain that woke him, sweating, he dreamed darkly of shadowed forms that rose from cracks in the earth and sank their sharp teeth into his leg.

Sometime during that night's fragmented conversations he learned that the woman's name was Emmaline, and her brother's, Benedict. Each time he woke, they wiped the sweat from his face, and gave him water, but no food. He didn't think he could eat, anyway.

Benedict left at dawn, and by mid-afternoon returned with two other young men, Pavel and William. Pavel carried a large pack on his back. They swiftly constructed a sling from two strong saplings and coarse-woven blankets from the pack, while William and Emmaline extinguished the fire and dismantled the lean-to, carefully refolding the reflective blankets. Emmaline made Mark open his mouth and sprinkled some powder from Pavel's pack on his tongue, then gave him water to drink. The powder was intensely bitter, but his tongue almost immediately went numb and the taste vanished.

"This will make you sleep," Emmaline said, "and it will make the pain easier to bear."

When they moved him to the sling, Mark was already half-asleep, and managed to remain silent even as jolts of agony shot up his leg.

"Where should we take him?" Pavel asked.

"He and his companions came up the old mine path," Benedict said. "We can leave him where it meets the fence."

"The city is empty, there," Emmaline objected. "We saw no people. If he is not found by his people, he will die of thirst as surely as if we left him here."

"His companions will find him."

"His companions abandoned him."

Pavel scowled at Emmaline. "You are suggesting we take him all the way home and tuck him into bed?"

Emmaline set her jaw and scowled back.

"She is right, Pavel," Benedict said. "It makes no sense to move him only so that he can die in some other place."

Pavel and Emmaline continued to glare at each other.

As they argued, Mark's mind drifted, and he found himself thinking of one of his classmates. Gerry. Or Gary. He didn't remember. He had not known him well. But he remembered what had happened. Gary had been scavenging illegally in the I-zone, and the floor in one of the buildings had collapsed. His leg had been shattered by the fall, and when they found him, he was more dead than alive. The doctors had saved his life, but not his leg, and because he had been injured during the commission of a crime, the City Hedge had declined to cover the costs. The bill had gone to Gary's parents, who could not pay. Few could. They'd been forced to choose between exile or indenture, and had chosen indenture. The mother had died within months.

The full gravity of Mark's situation grew clear in his mind. None of them had been thinking when they'd set out to look for the mine. They were supposed to be in school. They were supposed to be inside the city boundaries. It was a prank, a day of cutting class, but by leaving the city, they had committed a crime. He'd been injured during commission of a crime. If he went back ...

"No!" Mark shouted, the drug-induced torpor driven back. The others stopped talking and stared at him.

"Leave me here," he said. "Leave me here! I can't go back. My parents.... Oh God! Oh God!" He started to sob.

Pavel knelt beside Mark, and very carefully, very deliberately, slapped him hard in the face.

Mark gasped involuntarily and stopped sobbing. He tried to sit up, but Pavel put a hand on his chest and held him down. Mark struggled and cursed, interspersed with shouts of pain when he jarred his ankle.

"Stop!" Pavel commanded. "Control yourself, child." Mark had not been called a child for many years, and it stung. Had one of his friends said such a thing, it would have been grounds for knocking their teeth out. Coming from Pavel, it had the opposite effect. He stopped struggling.

"I have given him myco-caine," Emmaline said in the sudden silence. "Its effects can be unpredictable." But her voice sounded uncertain.

Benedict knelt to the other side of Mark. "You seem of two minds whether you wish to live or die, Mark, child of the city. Which is it?"

Mark drew a shuddering breath. "I want to live," he said. "But I can't go back." He explained what had happened to Gary, and Gary's parents.

"If I go back," he continued, "my parents will be indentured. They'll die."

"I do not understand," William said to Benedict. "What crimes have his parents committed?"

"They haven't done anything," Mark said. "They're just not rich."

The four were silent. Then Benedict spoke.

"Do I understand you correctly? If you return with this injury, they will set your bone. But because you have transgressed your people's law by coming here, they will not forgive the debt. They will lay it upon your parents, and because they cannot pay the debt, they will be placed in Dentured, where they will die. And that will satisfy the debt."

"Yeah. I guess."

"So your custom demands that you return and willingly forego healing, suffer pain and lifelong lameness, and perhaps die. To save your parents."

"What? No, they'd go to prison for negligence. They *have* to take me to the hospital."

More silence, as the four glanced at each other in consternation.

"You say they cannot pay the debt because they are not rich," Emmaline said. "What exactly does this mean, 'rich'?"

"Huh? 'Rich' means you have a lot of money."

"You mean hoarded coin?"

Mark nodded, his eyelids heavy.

"Your people *allow* this?" William asked, his tone incredulous. Benedict held up a hand to silence him.

"If they had ... if they were 'rich,' what would happen?" Emmaline asked.

"If they were rich, they could pay for the hospital. But they can't."

Emmaline's eyes widened, as did William's. Benedict stared at Mark without expression. Pavel's face registered disgust, and he turned his head and spat.

"The elders have spoken true of these people," Pavel said.

A long minute passed.

"He must come back with us," Benedict said, at last.

Pavel recoiled in surprise.

"Impossible!" he said. "He is of the city. It is forbidden."

"You heard what he said. He cannot go back. His reason is honorable."

"Let him die here, then." Pavel shrugged. "He claimed the right to die."

"He claimed the right to *live*," Emmaline said, with fire in her eyes. "He prefers death only to injustice, and cannot prevent injustice if he returns."

"These are *his* people," Pavel shouted. "*His* custom. *His* law. It is not our place to interfere."

"It is *my* place," Benedict said, quietly. "I owe a debt."

"*We* owe a debt," Emmaline corrected.

Pavel struggled visibly with this. "It is too high a debt-price," he said at last.

"Let the elders decide," Benedict said evenly, though he was now pale.

Pavel leaped to his feet with a curse, and stalked away. He picked up a branch, and threw it as hard as he could at a nearby tree, then stood for a full minute with his back turned to them.

When he faced them again, his expression was calm, and coldly formal.

"It is your right. Let the elders decide."

&

The shadows were already long when they lifted Mark's litter and began walking, and the drug forced him into deep

227

sleep almost immediately. He woke as they were setting up camp. He watched Emmaline arrange the lean-to structure as Benedict prepared to start the fire.

"Why do you do that?" he asked. His speech was slurred as much by his swollen lips as by the drug.

"Do what?" Emmaline asked.

Mark tried to recover his train of thought. It was difficult to concentrate.

"The blanket," he said. "You look at the sky before you set it up. Why?"

"Skywatchers," Benedict said, bent over the fire that was just leaping up under his hands.

"Skywatchers?"

"Satellites," Emmaline said. "The city-people call them satellites. On a clear night, you can see them in the sky, like moving stars. They are always in the sky to the south. They have tech eyes that see heat."

"Governments hunt us," Benedict explained, "because we will not submit to them. We learned long ago that to stay hidden in these woods, we must shield our fires from the skywatchers, especially the forge-fire. We do not know if they can see single night-fires through the trees, but we are cautious."

"*If* the skywatchers still watch," Emmaline said. "They are tech. Tech is fragile. The elders say the skywatchers must someday fall from the sky, and will go blind long before they fall. Perhaps they are already blind."

"They may be legend now," Benedict admitted, "but it is our custom to hide our night-fires with the silverthread blankets. They also reflect the heat, which is useful."

"What are the silverthread blankets?" Mark asked.

"They are also tech—" Emmaline began.

"You tell him too much," Pavel growled. "He has no need to know these things."

Benedict and Emmaline fell silent.

Mark faded back into sleep, and woke again when Benedict brought him broth. He was desperately hungry, but he felt full after only half the portion. He gave the other half back to Benedict, who finished it. He fell asleep to the sound of quiet voices telling strange stories of the impossible acts of improbable people, punctuated with laughter. Their earlier arguments seemed forgotten.

In the morning, Emmaline gave Mark another dose of the myco-caine, and then once again when the sun was high and sparkled on the rippling surface of a swift-running river. When he awoke the third time that day, it was evening and Emmaline had brought him a bowl of broth.

"We are almost there," Emmaline said. "We hoped to arrive today, but a river crossing sent us far out of our way. We did not want to make you swim." She smiled.

She's pretty. And she's not much older than me.

Mark realized with a start that between the pain and the drug, he had never really taken the time to look at his benefactors. Emmaline had a round, cheerful face with wide-set dark eyes and long eyelashes, a small chin, and dark hair—black in the twilight—woven into long braids that hung to her breasts, bound at intervals with brightly-colored ornaments. Her figure was obscured by multiple layers of loose dun-colored clothing, but it was quite clear that she was female. He studied the clothing—the outer layer was smooth and supple, like skin. He thought it might be leather, though he had never seen real leather. Her shoes were made of the same material. The inner layers of clothing were more like normal fabric, but soft and fuzzy. It looked comfortable, and warm.

Benedict was clearly older than Emmaline, but as Mark adjusted her age downward, Benedict's age came down as well. He was likely only a few years older than Mark. He had the same broad face as his sister, but less cheer—his lips were thinner, and his chin a bit more prominent. He kept his hair in a single braid down his back, bound at intervals, like Emmaline's, with ornaments. All three men wore similar braids. Pavel's was the longest, and had the most ornaments. William's was short, barely long enough to braid, and had only a single ornament. Mark realized that William was probably younger than he was.

As he watched their quiet, purposeful movement, he could not help comparing it to Danny's nervous jittering, or Lovo's sullen immobility. He suddenly wondered what he looked like to these people. Did he twitch and twitter like Danny? Was he as inexpressive as Lovo? And was he as *immature* as he suddenly felt?

All four of the others were clearly adults, even William, but they were unlike any adults Mark had ever known. There was none of the frantic, false good cheer of his teachers at the school. Nor the haunted, careworn expressions of his parents, and his friends' parents.

At the thought of his parents, shame washed over him. He and his friends all held their parents in contempt. Contempt for their poverty. Contempt for their menial jobs. Contempt for their failure. His teachers told them that they lived in a city of bright opportunity where anyone could succeed if they tried, and they'd all understood that their parents had failed because they had not tried. They would not make that same mistake. They were *better* than their parents.

And then Benedict had sawed off his good boot, and forced him to see that, despite their poverty and empty jobs and meaningless lives, his parents had bought him good, strong boots, more than they could afford, so that he could walk freely about the city. It had brought him face to face with the pain his rejection caused them.

The final blow had been the way Pavel had turned his head and spat. It wasn't his parents Pavel had spit out of his mouth. It was *him*. Him and the city and all the values he had been taught. No one had ever questioned those values before, much less rejected them like spoiled fruit. It had completely upended Mark's world.

Mark fell asleep pondering, to the sound of voices and soft laughter.

Emmaline gave Mark another dose of painkiller in the morning before they set out, and he registered only brief, disconnected images of the last part of the journey. There was a wait while Benedict ran ahead to inform the elders and bring back their judgement. They must have consented, for his next image was of a kind of village with many tents and a few temporary structures made of wood. Silverthread blankets were arranged everywhere, always facing the southern sky. There was no smell of woodsmoke, but instead a strange, pervasive, sweet odor he didn't recognize. They went past a place that smelled of hot metal—their forge. Cooking aromas made his mouth water. Adults' eyes were on him, and children, many children, ran after their small procession, shouting and chattering.

He had one moment of full wakefulness, in an enclosed structure where an old woman studied him with distaste, then opened his mouth and put a vile-tasting syrup on his tongue. An instant later, he was unconscious.

He almost-woke to find a dozen people holding him down while an enormous beast chewed on his injured foot, trying to pull it free from his leg: the pain was indescribable. He looked up at his parents' faces to ask, *Why?*

Danny answered, *Because, tube, you've put your foot in it this time.* Lovo grinned like this was the funniest thing he had ever heard. His parents wept silently. Then the world drifted away again.

こ

Mark's eyes opened. His mind was clear, free of the drug, and he felt good. The pain in his ankle had receded to a dull ache, and his face felt only a little puffy. He lay on a cot made of leather, and a soft, fuzzy blanket lay over him: it prickled and made his skin itch. He peeked under the covers, and was surprised to find he was naked. He sat up and pulled the covers away from his foot. His ankle was immobilized by a collection of wooden spars and cloth windings that had been treated with something that made them hard as any fiberglass cast. It was heavy.

Emmaline stepped into the tent, and smiled. He pulled the covers up to hide his naked chest, and Emmaline's smile faltered.

"You are unhappy to see me?" she asked. She seemed disappointed. "I can send someone else."

"No!" Mark exclaimed, as she turned to go. "No, I'm very happy to see you, Emmaline. I just... I'm embarrassed to be naked in front of you."

She turned back, with a puzzled smile. "Your ways are strange, Mark of the city. But I am glad that you are happy to see me." Her eyes were bright, as she pulled up a three-legged stool and sat close to the bed.

"I have a question to ask, Mark of the city. If you were one of us, I would simply ask, but I know that our ways are strange to you. So you must know that this question is an honor to receive. You do no dishonor to answer no, but I would be pleased if you answered yes."

"Um. Okay. I guess? Go ahead and ask."

"Will you consent to make a child with me?"

The blanket fell from Mark's nerveless fingers, and his mouth dropped open. The silence stretched until Emmaline's smile faded. Mark saw the hurt in her eyes at his silence. He closed his mouth, and swallowed.

"No, no, don't—no, I don't mean 'no', I mean 'yes'— Oh, God, no, I mean.... Holy Frack, Emmaline! Wait, just wait, let me get my act together—"

"My question has upset you," she said, tears in her eyes. "The elder said that it would."

"I—look, Emmaline, I haven't finished school, I'm not old enough to get married."

"Married? What is married? Is it a city word for the making of a child? Are you so different from us, that you cannot make a child until you are old men?"

"No, no, I'm sure I could make a child with you, Emmaline. But raising one? I'm not ready for that. I have no job, no money."

"But Mark of the city, I do not ask you to raise a child with me. That will be impossible, since we must carry you back to your city. The camp will move soon. You and I will not raise the child together. We will not meet again."

"You're taking me back? But my parents...."

"They will be fine. You have no further need of medical care, so there will be no money involved, and no one will be placed in Dentured. The elders explained this to us."

Mark opened and closed his mouth several times. It was true. He would still be in big trouble for leaving the city. But so long as he was healthy and no money was spent on his behalf, his parents would not suffer.

"So you're telling me that you just want me to get you— to make a child with you."

"I ask if you would consent, yes."

Mark's mind spun.

"Emmaline, this is—this is so different from how things work in my world! I don't understand the question. Why would anyone ever say no?"

Emmaline seemed baffled by his question. "There are many reasons to say no, Mark of the city. There could be oaths or debts that prevent it. There could be a taint in your line that you did not wish to pass on. You might think me unfit to be a mother, or my clan unfit to raise a child. There might be war coming, and you might not wish to increase the numbers of our clan. You might have received an ill omen. You might simply find me undesirable. These things are obvious, are they not?"

"What about other men who might... object?"

Emmaline laughed. "No man would make such a fool of himself. It is my question to ask, mine alone. Though, since you are of the city, I sought counsel of an elder. She said it would not be ill to ask, but that the question would upset you."

Mark's heart was pounding.

"But why me?"

Emmaline smiled. "Because you were so badly raised, Mark of the city. What you have told us confirms what the elders have told us of your people. Many of us had stopped believing them. We could not understand how any society could be so cruel and senseless. Yet even with such a poor upbringing, your instinct was to die, alone, to save your parents, who had done no wrong. You have honor in your blood. It is a gift that you will pass to your children, and their children."

Mark stared at her, his breath short. "Emmaline, I—I find you very desirable. I would be... honored to make a child with you."

Emmaline beamed. She stood and began to remove her clothing.

"Right now?" Mark squeaked.

"Would you prefer to wait until you are an old man?" she asked, but did not pause.

"Now is fine," Mark said in a small voice. Then he forgot all about questions for a time.

෴

Mark sensed more than saw the figure seated beside the bed, smiled, and murmured, "Emmaline." He reached out and took her hand. It was hard and leathery, with swollen knuckles. He yelped and snatched his hand back, to be answered by a dry chuckle. A gravelly voice spoke.

"For a moment, young man, I thought I was going to get lucky."

"Who—?"

"I am a clan elder. Since Emmaline has chosen to make a child with you, I wished to see for myself what she had chosen."

For a moment, Mark wrestled with the offense of her implied judgement, balanced against the memory of Pavel, turning his head to spit. He closed his eyes and breathed.

"Thank you," he said, opening his eyes, "for fixing my ankle."

She nodded slowly.

"You will do," she said. "As for setting the bone, it was the debt-price for Benedict's and Emmaline's actions. But you are welcome."

"They kept talking about a debt. What was that all about?"

"They never told you?"

Mark shook his head.

"The Earth Avenger," she said.

"I don't understand."

The old woman sighed. "They saw you and your friends, and heard your conversation. They decided to make sport of you. There is an air shaft on the back of the hill. They made sounds into it. They thought it would scare you away from the mine and back to your city. They did not expect you to panic. There were three of you, and only two of them, so they ran with the other two and herded them back to the city. Then they returned to track you. Your broken ankle was the result of their thoughtless action, so they owed a debt of restitution. They thought it would suffice to carry you back to your own people, but it was not enough. So they brought you here, against our custom, but not against our law. A few felt they should be exiled for the offense. But I am glad that you came. Emmaline will bear a strong child from your seed."

"I wish I could stay," Mark said.

She sighed again. "Child, you do not know what you ask. You see us at the end of summer. Our life is good. But winters are bitter, even for those born to our ways. Our clans are not always at peace. Our justice is swift, and hard, and honor can be a brutal master. You are young, but you are already too old to learn our ways. Your place is with your own people."

"Not much of a place," Mark answered, dejectedly. "When they figure out that I was outside the city limits, they'll make an example of me. I'll go to prison. It'll destroy my future."

The old woman chuckled. "Tell them about the Earth Avenger."

"What?" Mark stared at her. "What good'll that do? I'll just sound like a raving Doomer."

"You could do worse than to join the Prophets," she said. "They look after their own, and governments fear them. Not without reason. They are more than they seem."

"You want me to lie?"

The elder shrugged. "Your face appears badly beaten, and you have a serious injury. You have two witnesses—they doubtless have their own stories of being pursued through the forest. Hunters heard you scream, and set your ankle, and saved your life. Where is the lie?"

"But there was no Earth Avenger!"

The old woman studied him.

"So certain, are you?" she asked. "Did you ever *see* what tripped you and damaged your leg?"

237

Mark opened his mouth, but found he had nothing to say.

"Take your story to Master Jerome of the Prophets in your city. Tell him you were advised by an elder of the Circuit. Tell him everything. Follow his advice. He is a good man, and wise."

The old woman rose.

"Now, if you will excuse me, I need to rest. Enjoy your journey home." She chuckled again. "Emmaline will see to that."

࿏

Mark stood at the edge of the city, and watched his four companions vanish into the forest like ghosts.

They had travelled slowly. They still carried Mark, but he was alert and curious. They taught him to stand on his good leg and move about with the help of two wooden crutches. At every stop, Emmaline took him to her blanket. At first, he found it embarrassing. But the others ignored them, and after a while, Mark's embarrassment faded. Emmaline was intent on making a child, and wanted to be sure that his seed caught.

And then, they were here. At the edge of the city.

Emmaline had kissed him thoroughly. She claimed she could feel the child growing already. Benedict asked if the debt was satisfied, though he still had not explained anything about it. Mark told him, yes, many times over. Pavel and William ignored him.

And then they were gone.

Mark turned to face the burned-out ruin of the I-zone.

Find the Prophets of Doom.

But first, he had a stop to make, at home. A debt to pay.

A Mile A Minute

Walter Freitag

This is the story of how Slow Uncle went a mile in a
minute. Or at least, part of him did, probably. And how
Wyatt learned, contrary to his previous lifelong expectations,
that he might have some sense. And how the settlement
southwest of Groves finally acquired a name.

The story started far away from the settlement and from
Groves, and quite a few years back. But for Wyatt, it changed
from a story he'd heard and talked about, to a story he was
going to be part of, one evening in March after finishing his
supper in the refectory. He wasn't on kitchen for a change, so
he was heading for the dormitory porch, looking forward to
spending the grudging remains of the early-spring daylight
planning the summer's prospecting walks. A subtle whiff of
iron in the water of Charter Creek had told him that
somewhere in the upper watershed there was a rust mine.

His idea, to make his own iron hoops for barrels, was a
risk of time and effort. But a self-sufficient cooperage in the
settlement would make many other pursuits, from pickling to

tanning to distilling, more feasible or more profitable. The proctors therefore sanctioned Wyatt's prospecting along the upper Charter Creek tributaries as a suitable pursuit for his scant discretionary time, even though it was uncomfortably close to scavenging. To people living with buried ruins everywhere and work to do, scavenging was considered a vice. At least, when practiced by other people.

Slow Uncle was waiting outside the dormitory, leaning on his good leg. He had other plans for Wyatt's evening.

"The wagon's in," he said.

For Wyatt, this meant an unexpected additional hour or two of heavy lifting in the waning daylight. But it also meant being first to know what goods had arrived from Groves. All in all, a fair trade. Not that he had any real choice.

Slow Uncle was one of the settlement's five proctors, charged with monitoring the younger settlers' plans and progress, with the authority to revoke shares if necessary. He'd arrived in Groves twelve years before, when most of the settlers were tots underfoot, having spent his earlier life on sailing ships. A dockside accident had maimed his leg, driving him to seek landward uses for the carpentry and blacksmithing skills he'd learned at sea.

He was a skillful carver, and he also had a sailor's working knowledge of paints and finishes and an artist's eye for natural forms and colors. The fishing lures he carved not only looked like real fish, they also wiggled and swerved side to side like real fish when you trolled them through the water. More recently, the life-size (give or take) wooden phalli he carved for some of the settlement's young women, to help them enjoy their rights without ending up swived down the creek, looked so much like the real thing that some of the girls insisted they could tell whose was modeled after whose.

That's the kind of uncle he was, worldly and a bit wicked and absolutely necessary, to the bumper crop of third and fourth and fifth children that grew up in Groves in the second generation after the last visit of the blue cough. When Slow Uncle became one of the settlement's proctors, some of the parents muttered about who would be looking after whom, but he hadn't given them cause for complaint. Although, truth be told, that was partly because they were now twenty miles away, and what they didn't know, they couldn't complain about.

In the settlement he'd taken Wyatt on as an informal apprentice, teaching him to assist with blacksmithing and helping him improve his barely-adequate coopering skills. Most of the time, Wyatt still had to pull his weight in the gardens and on the fence lines, and the kitchen and the privies, and martial drilling with the others on Sundays, but the settlers had gradually ceded to Slow Uncle the first claim on Wyatt's time.

The wagon had already been hauled over to one of the supply sheds, the horses by now settling in the stables on the far side of the dormitory. Though it was likely still too chilly for evening romance—or rather, for the bathing that usually preceded it—Wyatt knocked on the shed door just in case. Indoor privacy, like indoor everything else besides eating and sleeping, was very limited in the settlement's early years, making the sheds one of the few options for the settlement's many eager couples. There was no response, so he swung the door open and then began untying the tie lines over the wagon bed. Slow Uncle arrived just as he finished, and the two of them folded back the canvas tarpaulin.

In the settlement's first year, Wyatt had looked forward to the wagon loads from Groves as if it they were gifts or scavenged treasures. But, two years older now, he saw more clearly what they really represented. Reminders of how dependent on Groves the settlement remained. Additions to its growing obligation to parents and older siblings. Commitments to more and greater labor.

The year was too young for the wagon to contain any food. The settlement's supplies of grain, pulses, smoked meat, hard cheese, and dried fruit, sufficient to midsummer, had been meted and delivered the previous fall. Instead, there were bundles of fabric for new clothing to be made, pots of paint for barns yet to be raised, a roll of shinysheet for a solar winter grow-berm yet to be dug, bags of slaked lime for a millpond dam that was presently a pile of stones on the creek bank, and a keg of gunpowder for the next four months of drills for the women. Wyatt took particular note of a heavy bundle of iron hoops, variously sized for barrels, churns, and buckets, that awaited his own unpracticed hand. The staves were already seasoned and the containers would be needed soon. The first dairy cows were due to arrive before the summer.

There was something else in the bed of the wagon, gradually uncovered as Wyatt stowed the other items in the shed. He couldn't identify it at first. In the waning light, it looked like logs or rolled blankets. It turned out to be a massive coil of heavy dark brown rope, as big around as Wyatt's leg, dozens of yards long. It made up a full third of the wagon load.

"What is that?" he asked.

"It's called a hawser. From off the *Eagle* that sails out of Delayed Green. A cable strong enough to hold a ship to a pier."

"And, um, what's it for? I mean, what's it *here* for?"

"Well, as far as the folks in Groves know, it's used cordage to recycle into sixty rope beds for the settlement."

Improved beds would be welcomed by everyone, Wyatt included. "I like that idea. When can we start?"

"In a year. When I'm finished with it."

Slow Uncle had a carefully neutral mind-your-own-business expression on his face that failed to discourage Wyatt's too-necessary question.

"What are *you* going to use it for, then?"

Slow Uncle paused, considering whether to answer. Then his face broke into a slightly wicked grin. "I'm going to go a mile in a minute," he said.

Jeanne had been the most desirable widow in Groves. She was skillful, smart, healthy, and not at all bad looking. Many hopes were dashed—and more than a few kindled, despite the half-dozen years she had on most of the settlers—when she left Groves to join the settlement as a proctor.

Her heart, everyone knew, still belonged to her late husband Marcus, the former railman. In his youth, far away down the Cross Line, he had fired up a locomotive to such a boil, and opened its throttle so wide, that it went a mile in a minute. He did it just to see if it could still be done. It was during a logistics run with just a few empty flatcars, on a straight stretch of track. Even so, it was dangerous and very much against the rules. He didn't lose his job for it because

243

the train stayed on the track and because he and his fireman never told their bosses they'd done it.

A few people in Groves might have called Marcus a reckless fool if they believed his story or a liar if they didn't, but most wouldn't have cared about such a thing at all.

Jeanne cared. She loved adventure stories of spies and doctors and lawmen in old times, with their computers and phones and, most of all, their cars that rushed them from place to place at a mile a minute. Marcus had plenty of good qualities for Jeanne to appreciate, but even so, everybody noticed how she found excuses to mention his outrageous feat in conversation whenever she could. It seemed to somehow give his gray-bearded face a little extra appeal in her eyes. It connected him, however remotely, to those figures from her stories, those romantic renegades of the past.

When Marcus died of a seized heart after only two years of marriage, leaving no children, Jeanne showed no interest in taking up with anyone else. Everyone said they understood, and that she had her rights and more than enough skills to support herself, and it wasn't as though the nurseries and schoolrooms of Groves had been empty of late. But over time, it inevitably occurred to various men and women of Groves, with tedious regularity, that surely Jeanne's lonely life would be so much better with them, or their cousin or nephew or friend, sharing her bed.

The only reason it couldn't be said that she joined the settlement to escape such propositions is that there was no reason to expect the situation to be much different there. And indeed it wasn't, until the settlement's second summer.

Then, out of nowhere, a rumor swept through the settlement: Jeanne had agreed to marry the first man in the settlement who could match Marcus' accomplishment of going a mile in a minute.

Of course she hadn't really said that. She'd said to Dryden, another of the proctors, during a moment of exasperation, that she *wouldn't* marry him *even if* he went a mile in a minute. But that was enough to get the story started, and Jeanne saw an opportunity and made the challenge real. She put additional conditions on it first. "It has to be on level ground, because any idiot can fall off a hill," she told the settlers. "And it has to be a whole mile, in a straight line, not spinning around in a circle or swinging back and forth or some such."

How the thing might be done became an occasional topic of conversation throughout the settlement for months afterward. Most such conversations stalled quickly. Someone would raise the question, and people would shake their heads or chuckle or look off wistfully at nothing. But one morning, while Wyatt and some of his more mechanically inclined friends were harvesting beans, they found themselves talking it out in some detail.

It started when Sticks said to no one in particular, "The whole world spins around in a day, so if you stand in one place for a minute, you're really going ten miles." No one replied, but Wyatt was sure it wouldn't count for Jeanne's challenge.

Zoe turned to Sticks and asked, "How much faster than a horse is a mile a minute, anyhow?"

Sticks didn't know, but Wyatt had asked Slow Uncle, so he knew the answer. "A horse bred and trained for racing, like they used to have at the autumn fair at Headwater, can go a mile in less than two minutes at a full gallop. But our

Rebel, Carla, or Bright Lady would each take more than three minutes."

"Okay, so that's no use."

"Here's something, though," Wyatt continued. "The big teams that haul the stage bus through Groves can run a mile in two and a half minutes. And we're going to be boarding some of those teams when the line closes for the winter."

"But so what?" said May. "However fast the beasts run, that's it. You can't make them go three times faster." Zoe shot a baleful glare toward May at the word "beasts," but May didn't notice; she was whispering something into Fletcher's ear that made him smile.

They talked for a while about the speeds of other running animals, of fish and boats, and of locomotives, cars, and other machines.

Fletcher said, "I think to go really go fast you have to go through the air."

"How would you do that?" asked May.

"With a glider. The how-to is in the Almagest, and a glider doesn't need a motor. Just a high place to start from," Fletcher said.

"That's not on level ground!"

"I bet it would count if I started on the ground, then used a rope with a weight and a pulley to lift me up to the top of a cliff, then glide back to the ground a mile away, all in the same minute," said Fletcher.

They all talked it over and decided some birds likely could glide at a mile a minute or more, but a glider would need to fly more than twice that fast after all the time lost getting its pilot up to the cliff, and that didn't seem likely. Anyhow, the only slopes near the settlement weren't nearly high or steep enough. But the talk about the glider must have stuck in Fletcher's mind, because years later he went to Global and learned the peculiar bells-and-drums language of the Almagest reader, and he found out about gliders and made one. But that's another story.

"If you're getting how-to from the Almagest, why not just make a real car, and a highway to drive it on?" said May. They all laughed, well aware that knowing how isn't the same as doing. That's one of the many meanings of the famous first words of the Almagest: "Ask how, answer why."

Zoe said, "Instead of gliding, maybe something could toss you. I'm pretty sure an arrow flies through the air much faster than a mile a minute. Sticks put his basket down and got his sticks out and did some figuring, and then agreed. "So," continued Zoe, "what if you made a thrower, something like a giant bow, to fire you through the air like an arrow? Not too high, just far."

"But an arrow doesn't go a whole mile," said Wyatt. "You'd need three or four throwers, spaced apart so when you hit the ground from one, the next one's right there to use."

Sticks had been figuring some more, and he said, "I don't think you all understand how fast a mile a minute is. Suppose you fell off the top of the Groves watchtower. Imagine the fall, okay? When you hit the ground, you wouldn't even be going three quarters of a mile a minute."

That tower, made of lashed timbers, was more than twenty yards tall. They all knew if you fell off it you'd be dead when you hit the ground, because Zoe's cousin Selene died just exactly that way when they were kids.

"So to hit the ground at a mile a minute you'd have to fall from a third higher?" asked Wyatt. "Another—let's see—seven yards?"

"No, twenty yards higher. Near twice as high," said Sticks.

"That doesn't sound right," said Fletcher, but in a tone of voice that admitted it probably was right, even if it didn't seem so. Arguing figures with Sticks was usually a waste of time, unless you were really eager to find out exactly why you were wrong.

Anyhow, that put an end to talk of using a giant bow or a gun or anything that would throw anybody through the air.

May had one more idea. "I wonder if the Mayor of Groves still has that motor chair," she said. Mayor DeSoto had bought it for his ailing mother, but it never worked very well, and hadn't seen much use before the old woman's death. It ran off the same batteries that powered the lights of the Town Hall, recharged on dry days by a copper drip grid on the roof.

"He's probably sold the motor by now," said Zoe.

"It doesn't matter. That thing was slower than Slow Uncle anyhow," said Fletcher.

Wyatt said, "It's a machine, though. Maybe there's a way to speed it up, like Marcus did with the train."

"Bigger wheels would make it faster, but then it would need a stronger motor," said Zoe.

"Why?" asked May.

"That's just how things work," said Zoe. "Same as why I'm faster than Wyatt, because I'm also stronger."

"Hey!" said Wyatt. Zoe really was faster and stronger than he was, but that didn't mean there was a natural law saying so, did it?

Fletcher added, "And the stronger motor would need more batteries, and the batteries would make the whole thing weigh more..."

The conversation, like all such conversations, eventually wound down. And there the matter ended.

Or so Wyatt thought, until the evening a forty-yard hawser arrived in the settlement, coiled like a serpent in bed of the supply wagon.

&

Slow Uncle kept his plans to himself, revealing even to Wyatt only what needed to be done at each step. The first step was to untwist the hawser, first one way to make three cables, then each the other way to make nine ropes, then each of those (except for one) the first way again to make twenty-four cords. After all the untwisting, each cord was a hundred yards long and thinner than Wyatt's little finger.

Slow Uncle mostly performed that task himself over the ensuing summer, spending scattered hours of sleep time that he claimed were often sleepless anyhow. Wyatt helped out from time to time. The process was slow and awkward. Each of the smaller strands had to be picked up and passed around the other two, one at a time, over and over again. The freed strands had to be wound up into hanks to keep them separate, and the hanks got cussedly large long before an entire length was unraveled.

Wyatt noticed from the start that the cordage didn't feel like the hemp he was used to. It had a strange greasy texture even when it was completely dry, and it partially repelled water. It weighed less than it should have, and the strands stretched more.

Slow Uncle explained, "The *Eagle* swapped for it at the Midlands, to replace one that got dragged over rocks in a storm. It was the only one they could get, but they knew the appro inspector would fine them for it if she spotted it, so as soon as they got back to Delayed Green an old friend of mine on the crew arranged to swap it to me."

"So, it's petro? Could we get fined for having it here?"

"Don't think so. In a port town, they care about proper cordage and the like. Around here, no one will think to look at it. Bed nets, remember."

"That all adds up to 'yes,' doesn't it?"

"Nothing's sure in life," Slow Uncle said.

Due to variations in their making, some of the cords were a little thicker and stronger than others, and due to their previous usage, some of them were abraded or had stretched sections. Slow Uncle sorted them by strength, strongest to weakest, setting aside the worst ones for other uses. "You can use this one for Thumbs' bed," he said, holding up a length that was frayed nearly through. Thumbs was the strictest, grumpiest, and least liked of the five proctors.

The next task was to splice the lengths of cord together to make one extremely long cord. Slow Uncle made Wyatt do most of that. "Splicing line is a useful skill," Slow Uncle told him. "Only it takes doing it about, oh, twenty-three times to get the hang of it." He showed Wyatt how to unravel the ends of each of two lengths of the cord, and then weave them together end to end. When it was done right, the two lengths would be joined into one with no knot, just a finger's length of thicker line in between, looking all of a piece and as strong as the cord itself. But it was easy to make a mistake, to miss a tuck or pull unevenly, and have to start over. Slow Uncle would accept no imperfect splices.

Five unsuccessful attempts into the first splice, Wyatt needed a change of subject. "A mile in a minute, and it sure looks like we're making a rope a mile long."

"About a mile and a third, actually. Have you figured out the rest of it?"

"No," said Wyatt. Thinking back to Fletcher's glider idea, he added, "You could tie one end to a wagon, and the other end to a big rock, then all you need is a mile-high cliff to drop the rock off of."

"That's closer than you might think," said Slow Uncle. He gestured at the rope ends still in Wyatt's hands. "Don't bother unweaving that splice. You've fatigued the yarns trying. Cut it off and start fresh."

❧

The post road through Groves, bearing the stage and most of the other trade and traffic the town saw, ran northeast toward the County Seat at Global, and south toward the seaports. A rougher road, little used, followed Charter Creek downstream to the east, to Ambler Falls and the Monday River. The Charter Creek watershed to the southwest of Groves had always been Groves land, but it was untraveled and barely used, except for occasional hunting and trapping.

More recently, though, a change had come in Groves. After generations of struggling just to keep from withering amidst fevers, blights, and local wars, the town had thrived and filled up. Gratitude for this good fortune was tempered with concerns for the future. There was talk of mouths to feed, of loss of pasture land to food crops and forest land to pastures, of staying sustainable, of the hazards of eggs in one basket should one of the devastating fevers return. And there was a crowd of young men and women all of age to start families of their own, threatening to increase all those problems.

The settlement was one portion of an answer.

The settlement would be a community project, not a haphazard colony of independent families in homesteads. The living arrangements would not, at first, be suitable for infants, and the workload would be too high to allow time for child rearing. As part of their agreement with the town, the settlers pledged not to conceive any children during their first years.

All of the settlers would also drill in arms, and make up most of Groves' levy. Should the County call the muster, the settlement's plans would have to be set aside, but fewer households would be broken, and fewer children orphaned.

Accordingly, the settlement's compact affirmed the rights of age of all the settlers, but required that couples who got pregnant would forfeit their shares and return to Groves, where a child could be cared for. Some doubted whether anyone would be left in the settlement after a year, but the midwives were optimistic that they'd instructed the young people thoroughly enough. "For once, the boys will have to learn to do something in bed besides snore and make babies," Alderwoman Adams had said. Though few others spoke of it so directly, this experiment was part of the search for a more durable answer to the new threat of crowding, perhaps more important than the settlement itself.

But to Wyatt, in the first two years of the settlement, the child rule had as much relevance as a rule against leaping to

252

the moon on Wednesdays. Not counting proctors, the settlement had nineteen young women and thirty-three young men. As the youngest and one of the smallest of the men, he saw little opportunity for romance. Or rather, he didn't recognize the opportunities that came his way for what they were. He was vaguely aware, for instance, that Zoe's frequent teasing just might really be flirting, but he wasn't ready to chance it. Jeanne's challenge was only interesting as a how-to problem to solve. He certainly wasn't ready to marry anyone.

He could understand how Slow Uncle was attracted to Jeanne, though. So, he worked willingly on the cordage and kept their secret.

That summer, the settlement's third, saw many changes. The settlers fenced pastures, built the dairy barn, expanded the stables, improved the worst parts of the road back to Groves, and added more coops, hutches, and gardens. They would need no cheese or peas from Groves that winter, and less meat and grains. They planted the first few orchard trees, and started a vineyard. Wyatt even found his rust mine. How that happened is definitely another story, though.

One thing the settlement still lacked was a real name. The settlers simply couldn't agree on one. Some called it Upper Groves, but most of them actively disliked that name. Early on, Thumbs suggested naming it after the first crop to yield a filling meal. When that proved to be the product of the mushroom cellar, a few settlers had used the name Edible Fungus for a while, but that didn't last long. A variety of other names, from Charterville to New York to Rivendell, had been tested out and failed to catch on. By that third year, most of the settlers were resigned to it forever being named Settlement by default.

જ

It was the first light of dawn, a cool April morning following overnight rain. It had been more than a year since the hawser had arrived. Now, Slow Uncle and Wyatt and a number of co-conspirators were out in the far western section of the lower pasture, a mile west of the settlement's buildings. The stretch of land was unusually flat; possibly, some thought, because it had once been a highway following the creek valley. But it did have a slight rise along the way. Looking back from where the settlers were making their preparations for Slow Uncle's attempt, only the roof of the dairy barn could be seen.

During the winter, Slow Uncle had built the remaining items he needed. Key among these were two blocks, pulleys inside wooden cases that guided the long line through them. Slow Uncle had shaped them carefully, trying out a few different designs to make sure the splices could pass through without catching.

One of the blocks was fastened to the trunk of a lone-standing tree a half mile from the farthest end of the pasture. The other was fastened to the rear of the bed of the sturdy supply wagon.

The stronger end of the long line was hitched fast to the wagon itself; it then passed through the block at the tree, then back to the wagon and through the block on the wagon bed. The rest of the line would trail behind the wagon, attached to Slow Uncle's strange conveyance. However fast the horses pulled the wagon, the far end of the rope would be pulled forward three times as fast.

254

Slow Uncle had demonstrated this to them using a length of twine tied to one finger, then wrapped around a finger of the opposite hand, then back around the tied finger and back again past the opposite hand. Sure enough, when he separated his hands a yard, three yards of the twine had been drawn up.

Sticks' position was a few yards back from the tree. His task would be to count the time, using a pendulum that he'd taken all the way back to Groves, on some pretext, to calibrate with the town clock. A flag signal from Fletcher at the mark exactly a mile away, at the moment Slow Uncle passed, would start his count. One minute was one hundred twelve swings.

The rest of the line was carefully stacked, in ten distinct coils, in the sledge that Slow Uncle would ride. The sledge was the strangest part of the whole apparatus. It was shaped much like a boat, but lower and flatter, two yards long and a yard and a half wide but only half a yard high at the peak of its "bow," where a small iron cleat waited to hold the towing line. On its underside it had five parallel keel-like runners, polished smooth, that curved up toward the front. Smooth thinner planks filled the spaces in between. Inside, the sledge had ribs like a boat, and a cradle of crisscrossed ropes stretched between its sides. During the ride, Slow Uncle would lay prone on the cradle, holding onto two handles tucked up under the bow, his good foot wedged against a thicker rib near the stern.

What the sledge didn't have was wheels. Slow Uncle had insisted that any wheels he could beg, borrow, or make would either be too small, too heavy, or too fragile. The sledge would glide directly over the rain-softened ground.

Hitched up to pull the wagon were two teams of the stage horses, eight horses in all, and their tackle, borrowed for the purpose during what was one of the final days of their boarding period. Zoe, who had been grooming and exercising the teams for two winters now, would be driving them from the front of the wagon. She knew the horses and had rehearsed the run. They would only have to run half a mile.

"It's either too many horses, or too thin a rope," Wyatt had advised Slow Uncle when he heard that part of the plan.

"It would be, if there were a heavy load at the end of the rope," Slow Uncle had explained. "That's why the sledge has to be light. "

They hitched the sledge by a tow rope to the settlement's chestnut mare Carla, to draw it back east to the starting point near the buildings. As they departed, Slow Uncle called out to Sticks and Zoe, "Remember, when the long line gets moving full speed, it'll be about the most dangerous thing you've ever seen in your life. It might not look like it but it will be. Don't fucking touch it. Do whatever you have to do to stay the fuck away from it."

"Uncle!" said Wyatt. He'd never heard him use sailor's cant outside the smithy before.

"I needed them to pay attention," Slow Uncle explained.

Slow Uncle rode standing up in the sledge, carefully inspecting the ground for any rocks or debris that might have been missed, while Wyatt, walking alongside, with equal care paid the rope out behind them onto the wet grass of the meadow. Tight and straight, because any loop or snarl that got drawn up into the blocks would snap the line or worse. It took half an hour to go the mile Slow Uncle hoped to retrace in one minute.

256

Fletcher and Jeanne were waiting at the starting line, a mile from the tree and a half mile from the barn. Jeanne had a nervous look on her face. Wyatt couldn't tell whether she was afraid Slow Uncle would succeed, or afraid he would kill himself trying.

"You could call this off, Jeanne. If you don't want me to do it, say the word."

"When you've already gone to so much trouble? Wouldn't think of it," Jeanne replied. Wyatt realized that though she was nervous, she was also excited. Her words sounded rehearsed. Wyatt guessed that Slow Uncle had had this conversation with her before, more than once.

Fletcher was ready with his signal for Sticks to start counting time, a yellow shirt tied to a two-yard pole. The tree, wagon, and horses were visible in the distance behind them, but the small rise was in front of them still, and hid the gate at the east of the pasture, closest to the barn, where they would start. The challenge was for a mile, but the additional quarter mile between Fletcher and the gate would be needed for the horses, line, and sledge to get up to speed.

They continued on to the gate, where they untied the sledge from the tow line. May was waiting there, with a bow and a red-streamered arrow that would signal Zoe to start the horses.

Wyatt hauled the sledge into position. Without the line or Slow Uncle in it, it felt very light and flexible. He gave it a test push forward and, though it stuck to the ground at first, once it got moving it slid surprisingly easily.

There was still some extra line coiled in the bow of the sledge, and the last few loops had tangled down among the cords of the cradle. Slow Uncle stepped in to retrieve the snarled coils.

"What are you doing? What is going on here?" The voice was behind them. It was Dryden, striding across the barnyard with Thumbs right behind him and a few dozen curious settlers trailing along.

Slow Uncle dropped the line and turned around as the proctors stepped close. Thumbs and Dryden had no idea what they were looking at, and no one knew how to begin explaining it. Dryden, though, immediately and literally seized on the one thing in the scene he could understand: the unauthorized use of militia equipment, the bow and nocked arrow in May's hands. He said, "Put that weapon down," and not waiting for her to do so, grabbed at the belly of the bow. May's fingers were still wrapped around the bow string. When she let go of it a moment later, the bow flexed weakly and the signal arrow wobbled up into the air.

It went mostly sideways, only a few yards up, but far enough.

Thumbs was yelling questions at someone, but Wyatt just stared at Slow Uncle with his jaw open and his face gone pale for a good long time, knowing what was about to happen but not ready to believe it. A good long time, because nothing did happen at first. It turns out, it takes a while for bad news to get from one end of a mile-long rope to the other. More than five seconds. More than ten, even. But less than fifteen.

That should have been plenty of time for Slow Uncle to jump out of the sledge, except for three things. One, he wasn't much for jumping; two, the loose cordage was still all around his feet at the bow; and three, he was hoping Zoe hadn't seen the false signal. At least, that's what Wyatt later figured Slow Uncle was hoping, because he thought he heard him saying the word "maybe..." when the line twitched and started lifting off the ground in front of the sledge. The tautened line began moving slowly forward, and some of the coils around Slow Uncle's feet snaked up, tightening on his leg. At first the line slid smoothly past the cleat on the bow, but when the tangled loops reached the cleat they caught in it. Nothing else happened for another second, then the sledge jerked ahead about a yard, slackening the rope ahead of it and pulling Slow Uncle's feet out from under him. The sledge stopped, and an instant later the rope pulled tight again. There was another jerk, and another short pause. Then the thing started off for real.

With that first tug, Slow Uncle lost his balance. He landed on his back on the cradle, inside the sled, his feet still in the bights of rope near the bow, his head just short of hanging off the stern. He tried to grab the cradle to pull himself upright but he lost his grip as the sledge started forward again, and instead, his arms wedged between the taut cords and stayed there. Then off the sled went, and off Slow Uncle went, face up, feet first, and searing the morning sky with a streak of sailor's cant of a sort never heard in the settlement before or since.

Nowhere near a mile a minute. Not at first. For a few dozen yards, May, Thumbs, and Dryden, running in pursuit of the sledge, could even keep up with it. But as it went, it went faster and faster, leaving them all behind as it drew toward the top of the rise. From farther ahead, Wyatt began to hear the hooves of the horses, two teams now pulling at a trot for all they were worth, and speeding up.

Wyatt had the presence of mind to mount up on Carla before giving chase. Carla wasn't saddled so he couldn't chase very fast, but at a trot he gradually overtook the others, and he had an excellent view of everything that happened next.

The sledge was approaching Fletcher and Jeanne at the start of the mile. It was going very fast and still speeding up. Mud and water sprayed out behind it. Jeanne was yelling, "Let go!" but Slow Uncle didn't, or more likely, couldn't.

Fletcher, intent on the starting line and his flag, hadn't noticed anything wrong yet. He raised the flag smartly the moment the sledge went past, then dropped it in surprise as he saw what was happening.

Onward the sledge sped. The tow line was making strange noises, an eerie whine that went up and down in pitch each second. There was some irregularity to the sledge's motion; it surged ahead and then lagged, surged and lagged, in time with the changes in the line's pitch. Slight changes in the ground also made it bounce up and down in a different rhythm, slightly at first, and then more, like a stone skipping over a pond.

It was going fast now. So fast! Feet first or no, Wyatt thought, Slow Uncle was going to do it! The line howled.

But then, a quarter mile or so past the starting mark, the sledge started to veer from side to side.

Wyatt blinked in surprise. How could that be happening? The sledge was only being pulled from the front. What would make it go sideways? Then he thought of Uncle's clever fishing lures, that would wiggle from side to side all by themselves in the current of the creek. There was something about the weight in the sledge being in the wrong place, or pulling the wrong way. The sledge was flexible. Uncle was supposed to be holding those handles, was supposed to be braced against the stern rib.

The sledge veered right one final time and then way to the left, almost to the south fence line. There, the ground dropped away a little bit, so the sledge went a little farther left, tore through some dead brush, and then, going a mile a minute, hit an old piece of half-rotten log that was half-sunk into the ground.

Wyatt saw it all very clearly.

The log propelled the speeding sledge a yard up into the air. There was a terrible splintering noise, delayed by distance.

As it rose the sledge flipped upside down and began collapsing on itself, the shattered frame crushed by the tension of its own cord cradle.

For a moment the tow line went slack, just as Slow Uncle began falling free under the inverted craft, except for the line still tangled around his ankle.

The tow line snapped taut and yanked the now-falling sledge forward again. Slow Uncle's leg jerked forward with it. The rest of Slow Uncle didn't. He went one way, and his leg another.

Slow Uncle touched down and rolled along the ground until he splashed into a puddle and came to rest, face up or face down Wyatt couldn't tell. The wreckage of the sledge, still pulled by the rope at something like a mile a minute, sped away westward, making crunching and cracking noises, spraying mud from the ground, and shedding pieces. From farther beyond, the sound of the galloping hoofbeats continued.

By the time Wyatt reached Slow Uncle and dismounted, the distant drumming hooves had stopped. For a moment, the morning was silent.

Slow Uncle lay on his side by the puddle, covered with mud and bits of dry brush. He looked as limp as a wet shoestring, and his eyes were closed.

"Uncle!" yelled Wyatt. "Hey, Uncle!" He wanted to yell, "You alive?" but figured it would be rude if he was, and pointless if he wasn't.

Then as Wyatt came up closer, Slow Uncle rolled onto his back, and groaned.

"I think a rib's broke," he said. "And my leg's gone."

"By now, that leg's half a mile away," said Wyatt, looking at the broken scraps of leather harness on Slow Uncle's left thigh, at the stump where his leg was usually attached.

"And probably the worse for wear," added Slow Uncle.

It had been Slow Uncle's masterpiece, that wooden leg, carved and painted so perfect you could hardly tell it from the real thing.

Truth be told, though, it had been heavy. Awkward to use. Everyone thought a crutch would have been easier to walk on. But Uncle would rather be Slow Uncle, and look whole.

&

Wyatt torqued the tension shaft behind Slow Uncle's leg with the wrench, then slipped the pawl into place. Slow Uncle shifted his weight to test it out, and nodded with satisfaction.

The leg looked nothing like a real leg. It had a strut sticking right out of the front of the hinged knee, with four taut brown cords stretched over it like the strings of a violin. That gave it just enough flexibility to make Slow Uncle rather less slow than he'd once been.

"Can I ask a question, Uncle?" Wyatt said as he hung the wrench on the wall of the smithy.

"Sure."

"Okay. Why?"

"I've been waiting for you to ask that, Wyatt. 'Ask how, answer why,' but it always looked as though you were intent on the how without thinking about why. I was even a little disappointed."

"I thought I knew why," said Wyatt. "I thought you wanted to marry Jeanne."

In the four months since the mile-a-minute adventure, Jeanne had romanced, however briefly and cautiously, three men. None of them was Slow Uncle.

"Did you think Jeanne would have just up and married me, even if I had gone the whole mile in a minute? This isn't a teevee tale, Wyatt."

"Well, I thought maybe she wanted to anyway." He smiled, struck by a notion. "She at least should have kissed the leg. That did go a mile in a minute, as far as anyone can tell."

Sticks had dropped the pendulum when he saw the sledge come apart, and had run uselessly toward the horses, with no way to signal Zoe to stop. The leg, as Slow Uncle had predicted, had ended up cracked and useless, but it did pass the tree before the horses slowed. No one would ever know for sure whether it had really gone a mile a minute.

"So, now that you know better, why do you think I did it?" Slow Uncle asked.

Wyatt thought about it some more. "It seems like... well, this might sound funny but it's almost like you did it to *free* her, somehow."

Slow Uncle smiled and nodded his head. Then the smile faded again and he turned away.

After a long pause, Slow Uncle turned back to Wyatt and spoke, slowly. "The thing is, Wyatt, we're all still caught by the past, a little bit," he said. "Jeanne's hero stories. Scavenging. The Almagest. Marcus and his mile a minute on the railroad. My leg too, I suppose. We have a chance for a good life here, but there's still parts of the past we're tangled up in without even noticing. Sometimes you have to look closer at something you're holding onto, and see it different, maybe have a laugh about it, before you can let it go."

"Done with you for today," he added. "Is it nearly suppertime? Go on now."

Wyatt stood up, then paused as Slow Uncle spoke again. "The past is read-only, like the Almagest. We have to put our own mark on things."

Wyatt just nodded. As he reached the doorway, Slow Uncle said, "You have sense, Wyatt. Or you will someday soon. I mean real sense, not the kind that means following every sensible rule you hear. Remember that."

Slow Uncle picked up a chisel and turned to his work.

Wyatt, of the village of Uncle's Mile, went out into the midsummer sunlight, heading toward the stables, looking for Zoe. There was another question he'd had on his mind.

When it Comes A Gully Washer

N. N. Scott

Every year since I could remember, after the harvest but before the autumn storms set in, Crazy Uncle Robert came down from Chicago to dig for music in the ruins of New Braunfels, Texas. Our father called him crazy, but brother Rolo and little Claris and I thought him the best of men. He brought us gifts, strange toys and even books from Chicago, and sometimes plate recordings of the songs we had salvaged the previous year, if any had been recovered from the old black disks that we unearthed in the dark tunnels with such care. He would set a plate upright in the spring-driven player that Rolo and I fought for the honor to wind, and music would come out of the horn wailing, or thumping, or in strings of notes that went up and down like birdies, as Claris said. It was strange music. Neighbors would stop by on their way, and a few even walked the five kilometers from Crane's Mill to have a listen; it was one of the small occasions of the year. Some years the local bajo sexto players would pick up one of these ancient tunes and make it live again for a few months at gatherings where people were shucking or baling,

265

then it would be forgotten. But better than music, in my opinion, was Uncle Robert's radio.

It resembled a small valise with a handle and latch, but when opened it revealed a brass plate with two black knobs, other switches and a small brass pointer painted red, that moved across a range of etched lines with numbers. The antenna was a marvelous thing that came in a bag: white aluminum rods that screwed together, five meters tall when assembled, with guy wires of braided steel and a kite-shaped head of aluminum slats. Uncle Robert would set it up outside against the mud brick chimney of our house, and run the wire in through a window. He had a solar battery to charge it: four long jars half of dark glass and half of metal, that had to be set in the sun all day so the radio would work. Then at night, after the dinner things had been cleared away, the most necessary chores done and the others begged off for the evening, the three of us would squat beside him on the dirt floor of our home, watching with fascinated eyes as he sat cross-legged coaxing strange tapping clicks from the speaker, clicks that were voices from hundreds of kilometers away.

"News from Chicago," he would say with a smile, and translate for us public information releases from the National Head Office of the Grange: railroad schedules, barge dockings on the Mississippi and the Inland Canal, bandit control reports and the like. One evening after listening to the clicks for a while he said, "The malefactors who burned down the Dagon House in Cincinnati have been caught after a fight, and will be put on trial."

"What's a Dagon?" asked Rolo.

"Central food storage, kiddo. You want to be a bandit hunter when you grow up?" We all cried yes, even Claris, which made him laugh. But after the news ended he kept on fiddling with the tuner, running the pointer with slow care back and forth across a portion of the range, with the headpiece to his ear. Other sounds started coming through, much fainter, broken by static and the whooping, sizzling noises that Uncle Robert called 'the song of the sky.' He let us listen.

"Who's speaking now?" I asked.

"They're far away," he said. "Montreal maybe, or New Haven. Sometimes London comes through on this band. But judging from what time it is, I'd say this is coming from out west, beyond the desert and the mountains. Some peak in the coast range, where they've set up a tower." The lamplight slid round the rims of his spectacles as he leaned forward, turning the dial. The whispering sounds trickled through.

"So what are they saying?"

"Nothing you need to know," said our father from the table, where he sat mending harness by a kerosene lamp. "Contradictions, rumors, ridiculous fables and lies – or else the inside business of the Grange, which is no concern of ours. Shut it off, Robert. You're keeping them from their chores."

Uncle Robert looked up at his older brother. "I serve the Grange as well, Arilan. It might be my business too, along with the rumors and lies."

Father pushed the point of his awl into the leather with care, then drew it back a bit to loosen the thread so he could feed the working end through the gap. It was a good awl and very old, the kind with a pierced needle that carries the thread in a channel, and makes what is called a factory stitch. If it ever broke the needle would be hard to replace, but as my

267

father would say, it hadn't broken yet. He liked well-made, practical things. "The only business of the Grange that matters in this county," he said, "comes through the town receiver in Crane's Mill and is posted in the meeting hall each month. Price of beans, price of wool, purchasing schedules, freight rates, tariffs at the border in San Antone. What other news does a farmer need to know?"

"How about the weather?" suggested Robert.

Dad sniffed. "The weather. There's the Almanac, and also a thing called stepping outside and looking at the sky, as a man ought to know how to do. And to have patience when it don't rain, and to know what to save when it comes a gully washer." He smiled. "And you haven't told them yet that you can't understand a word of that clicking, anyway."

Robert stiffened. "Not this kind, of course. It's in code."

"But you said you know the code," said Rolo, to dad's further amusement.

Uncle Robert thought for a moment. "What I meant is, well, there are different kinds of code. The clicks can be interpreted into human speech – I can do that. Right now this one's saying..." He paused to listen. *"Aphor ... pocrase ... delin ... taneer ...* and so on. But once you've got the words, you still don't know what they mean. It's another code beneath the first, like a blanket laid under a quilt. And when you get down to the message itself, it might be in a language you don't know. And even if you get through that and understand it, as your dad said, it might be untrue. Sometimes the message is intended only for one person in the whole world. Sometimes they just broadcast nonsense to confuse us.

"Who's them and us?" I asked.

"If it's coming from beyond the western mountains, who do you think?" said dad. "Brother, shut it off." Robert pushed a switch and the sounds died away.

Years passed. Robert would come each autumn from the train station in San Marcos, riding a borrowed horse or driving a hired wagon if he was bringing salvage frames. Every year dad would tell him to stop wasting his time on foolish things and not to put ideas into our heads, but every year they went together to dig for music, the most unlikely of projects for dad. He and Robert had purchased a joint lease on the digging site from a Mexican landowner in Nuevabrón, and dad rationalized it by saying that the lease was a valuable interest and shouldn't be left to neglect, or the owner might assume it had been abandoned and sell it to someone else. Despite their differences, he always went with Robert. Dad could be stern, especially to children who neglected their chores, but he tried to see the good in people, as the Scriptures advise. He treated mother with respect, and he had taken in Aunt Juana, who was no relation of ours but an old lady with a bad leg who had come into the country years back from somewhere out west, and could not manage a farm on her own. About the only thing Aunt Juana ever said of herself – and this with an air of distinct pride – was that she had been "born in Hondo, on the good side of the town." That most likely wasn't true, but dad never pressed her on it, and she shared the work with us as part of the family, a great help to mother.

The year I turned fourteen and dad let me drive a team and I started to think of myself as something like a man, Uncle Robert didn't arrive when we expected him. A week passed, and then another. The clear hot sky of September began to curdle into the unsettled hazy sky of October. A sultry dry heat pressed the land, and brittle leaves hung stiff on the old hackberry tree beside the barn. Dad took to standing in the evenings by the fence gate watching the sky, and would come back grumbling that the rains would come before that fool of a brother showed. Then Robert arrived one evening after sunset, on a horse that looked as though it had come much farther than the three-day ride from San Marcos. On another horse beside him was a woman.

He introduced her as Leah, and offered no last name. She was taller than any of us except dad, of a brown complexion with long straight black hair and pale, hazel green eyes, a straight nose and a stern, sad face. Like Robert she wore brown travel clothes and a grey-brown cloak that had seen heavy use. Robert spoke quickly, and both of them looked exhausted. We all found her fascinating and Rolo peppered her with questions, none of which she or Robert acknowledged. There was some discussion with dad in the yard, as I held the reins of Leah's horse and the rest of the family stood about, in the mixed light from a lantern on the porch and the rising moon.

"Leah's a hydrologic engineer," Robert explained, "seconded to the Port of Morgan City for a three year term. Her work doesn't begin until December, so I invited her to join me and see my old home country and what we do in our diggings. From Nuevabrón she can cross the Guadalupe and head east through Seguin, and Buddhagosa and Houston. I'm sorry we didn't write in advance. I'd have wired from one of the stations up north but I know you don't get into Crane's Mill more than once a month, so... anyway here we are."

It wasn't clear whether this story was completely fabricated, or just a highly edited version of the truth. Dad, having watched them both while his brother explained, tersely welcomed Leah, asked mother and Aunt Juana to take her inside and help her get clean, then went with me and Robert to the barn, leading the horses. Robert talked incessantly while we worked, about what luck it was that he had brought extra salvage frames the previous year, though in fact he always brought a double load on alternate years. He checked the frames, each made of two square boards of hardwood pressed together, padded on the inside surfaces with felt and secured by four brass thumbscrews at the corners. He wondered aloud how much time we'd have to dig before the rains came, and suggested that we ought to get on our way soon. Dad made noncommittal responses and I dealt with Leah's horse, noting several small wounds of the sort that come from being driven through brush, a partly cracked shoe and other signs of heavy use, none of them critical.

With the horses fixed we went inside for dinner, and it was an uneasy meal. Mother had laid on extra hominy from our none-too-plentiful supply. Leah, cleaned up and wearing a fresh shirt, spoke vaguely of her travels and seemed unresponsive, though genuinely thankful for the food and care. It came to me that she didn't speak American very well. Uncle Robert continued to talk with fervor about one thing after another, mother said only what was needed for politeness and dad spoke little. Aunt Juana kept her small red-rimmed eyes on Leah, looking almost angry, or as though waiting for some kind of apparition.

The next day would be Holy Services and market day at Crane's Mill, and there was some talk of early preparations.

When Robert heard this, he suggested that the rest of us should go while he and Leah would stay at the farm to rest. Dad said, "No, I can't have that." He set down his cup of chicory with decision. "Half the county knows she's here, I suppose. There'll be talk if you and her don't show."

"I actually don't think so, Arilan. We were very discreet leaving the train at San Marcos."

"You left no train," Aunt Juana broke in. "You came from the west, and cut off from the old highway at Smithson or some such place to deceive us. You and this woman."

"Abuelita please," said mother.

After a silence dad said to his brother, "You forget what it's like, Robert, living as you do in a huge town of a hundred thousand people. People here notice travelers on the road, even if they don't let you see them watching. It'll be the first thing spoken of after the service, and that's if Doctor Peterson doesn't preach the sermon on it. I don't want people to think I'm keeping secrets from my neighbors. Your life is your own, and you are family, so you and Leah are welcome. But if you stay in my house you will go to Holy Service."

That evening there was no music, and no radio. We did our chores. Leah and Uncle Robert sat together on a bench by the table, now and then speaking in low voices. The next morning before dawn I checked their horses, much improved by rest and feeding. Leah's horse with its cracked shoe bothered me, but the crack didn't go much into the iron and otherwise the shoe wasn't badly worn and the nails looked tight, so I left it. We started as the sun rose. Leah and Robert rode beside our wagon, which was loaded with several bags of cabbages, pot-herbs, chiles and onions from our garden, bundles of Aunt Juana's mending and embroidery, and a dozen big sacks of tepary beans from dad's principal crop – the portion that he hadn't transferred to the Grange agent for sale in Chicago.

The trip to Crane's Mill was uneventful and despite dad's exaggerated concerns, Dr. Peterson's sermon in the meeting hall was of the ordinary kind: reminding us of the sorrow of those who have turned their faces from the Face of God, of the joys of reunion, and of the majesty and mercy of our Lord. "For He is manifest to us as the sun, if we would only see," he declared, holding the Scriptures aloft while his great beard waggled in a way that had always made me struggle not to laugh. "Manifest in his Book, in the book of creation round about us, and in the faces of the poor among our brothers and sisters. *Lo,* He says, *whichever way you turn, am I not before you? Did you think Me heedless, or unaware?*"

After the service the people filed out for market, and now came questions about our visitors who had, in fact, been seen the day before on the road to our farm. The women gathered around mother with trivial gossip and attentive faces, as though expecting her to suddenly bring forth a new baby. The men, including two local Grangemen in their Service Day sashes and cockades, quizzed Leah about her work and sought her views on re-grading the low-water crossing at Bear Creek. She spoke reservedly, but with enough confidence to make me wonder if she might actually be an engineer, and whether dad and Aunt Juana had misjudged her. But what with helping mother, keeping Claris under control and messing with the other boys my age who had also come to town, I forgot about it. As afternoon drew on and we prepared to return I noticed that Leah, Robert and their horses were gone.

As we neared home about sunset we saw the antenna standing, not by the chimney as usual, but against the side of the barn. Shadows of evening lay across the ground, darkening to blue as the sun departed. After the others had got down and taken their things, dad gestured to me to leave the wagon and team, and follow him. We approached the barn, not exactly sneaking but not making any more noise than we had to. Leah and Uncle Robert were inside, working the machine.

Through a crack between two boards I saw them, sitting with a candle lamp nearby. She held the earpiece to her head, listening and speaking from time to time, and sometimes he spoke back. Their words I could not clearly understand, for they spoke the Business English of Chicago. It sounded muddy and full of extra sounds, though I knew even then that it is only a more elaborate version of what we usually talk. I caught fragments: "inconvenient for central" ... "three or more" ... "one week". Then in the midst of a string of speech she said the word that Robert had not uttered on that evening years before, when we had listened to the strange sounds coming from beyond the desert and the mountains, the word that felt like an unfriendly hand on my neck: "*Calorwash.*"

I looked at dad, but the expression on his face told me nothing. He whispered, "Open the door," and I rolled it back for him. As we entered, I saw beside Robert's hand a piece of equipment I had not known he carried: a brass box with something that looked like a little hammer mounted to the top of it. I had once seen a thing like that in the Grange office in Crane's Mill, when dad was receiving mail. It was a Morse key, illegal to possess on pain of imprisonment, except for authorized agents of the Grange. Robert's nervous expression had settled into a more determined mask of urgency. To my father he said, "You're back. We need to leave tomorrow for Nuevabrón."

"Hold it," said dad. "You mean for digging, or just to get her out of the country?"

"Both," said Robert. "The Mexicans haven't agreed to let her cross into San Antonio. Five or six days, they said – they have to get word back to their capital. It's complex. But it isn't safe to stay here."

"All right." Dad turned to Leah and to my surprise spoke in Business English, which I could make out better than before, hearing it in his familiar voice at close hand. "Lady, it would help me to know as much as possible about your situation, and who is coming after you. How dangerous is this for my family?"

She replied with the careful precision of one who speaks a well-learned foreign tongue. "Mister Kommerson, I feel deeply sorry for the trouble this has caused. I would not have come this way, but I was nearly waylaid in Dallas, and could not take the main road. Your brother has done more than he was asked, much more."

"I don't doubt that. My brother is a good man and a dedicated servant of the Grange, but he sometimes lacks discretion. How badly have you put yourself beyond the pale, Robert?"

"Your family will not be pursued..." Leah began, but Robert put a hand on hers.

"I knew what I was doing. I'm sorry to have come this way, but there was no helping it. Leah is – or was – a person of some standing in the Federal Republic of California, Oregon and Washington. She came east in secret to negotiate

275

a territorial understanding with the Grange, about certain lands, on behalf of a faction in that country. She crossed the mountains at Idaho pass and traversed Dakota and the Six Provinces, but by the time she reached Chicago the situation had changed. The Shasta-Klamath faction is no longer in a position to negotiate. Every inland town north of Sacramento is in flames, Red Bluff and Redding are cut off, and the Calorwashian army air corps has begun striking Klamath Falls. It's over." He drew a ragged breath. Leah said something to him in another language that I didn't understand at all, and he answered, "Perhaps not, but it seems so."

"There's no need to go into those details," said dad. "What about here and now?"

Robert collected himself and continued. "In the current circumstances, Leah's presence in Chicago had become an embarrassment. No one at the Central Office wanted anything to do with her. I was instructed to accompany her south toward Mexico on the pretext of getting her over the border, but actually to hand her over, in Fort Dallas, to certain other operatives who would meet us there. I... chose not to do that." His eyes were steady. "We tried to go west, but the Calorwashians also have people out looking for her. So now we really are going to Mexico, if we can get over the *frontera*."

"And you think you can?"

"There's a chance. I've had contact with someone in Monterrey. We may know in a few days, in a week. In any case we need to get as near as we can to Nuevabrón, where the old highway fords the Guadalupe. That's where they'll meet us, and take us south. The Mexicans won't come up into the hills, and there's a good chance the Grange would hesitate to pursue us in force, near a town that is under Mexican influence. They've tried to shift the frontier there more than once."

"And the Calorwash?"

"We can't plan for everything, Ari."

My dad thought about this and asked other questions, mostly logistical; he wanted to get this danger away from his home as soon as possible. Then he said, "I'm sorry I made you go into town today, Robert. I was proud, and it made matters worse." Uncle Robert only shook his head, saying nothing. As though just noticing my presence, dad said, "Hector, we need to load the wagon and get on the road as soon as possible."

We packed that night and left before dawn, me and Rolo with dad in the wagon, Leah and Robert on their horses. Mother, Aunt Juana and Claris stayed behind, with dad's rifle and their promise not to open the door to anyone they didn't know. We drove east by small dirt roads, following the gullies and moving slow. All day we watched for signs of pursuit, but saw only rocky hills, dry creeks, scrub oak and juniper. Starved and bony range cattle browsed on thorns or rested in the bush. The air was still and heavy. Hawks circled high above, black specks against the white blurry sky. The wheels of the wagon trickled dust into the air as they rolled.

After two days we crossed Bear Creek and struck the paved road that runs southeast from Canyon to join the military highway, its wide concrete surface threaded with grass-lined cracks and partly scavenged for building material, though the Grange imposes severe penalties on anyone caught doing this. On the evening of the fourth day we came down from the brown hill country through the canyon of the Comal Stream, and saw the green lands of eastern Texas rolling away to a distant, dark horizon. The Guadalupe River curved southeast amid groves of hackberry and sycamore overgrown with kudzu, its water reduced to a green-brown trickle at this season. The town of Nuevabrón, descendant of old New Braunfels, lay clustered around its ford a few kilometers away, where concrete wreckage from the highway bridge had been dragged to make the river shallow.

We crossed the Comal Stream and made camp at our lease in a flat, juniper-forested valley about three kilometers across, where the old town lay buried under ten meters of earth and rubble that had washed out of the highlands during the Catastrophe. The active leases were scattered over an area roughly five hundred meters square, where it was thought the ruins underground were most densely built. Farther out you could dig for a month and only strike one house, if that. Leases were marked by hanks of twine on trees, lines of rocks and occasional hand-chiseled signs on logs, warning interlopers away. Some camps were active. We saw Henry and Zekiel's wagon from Canyon; they had been digging there more years than we, and always claimed to be on the point of finding the town bank. But when we arrived, no one could be seen above ground.

Robert set up his radio, and with Leah he listened at sunset, their appointed time, but heard nothing from Mexico. Night fell among the junipers, and bats flickered to and fro. We ate and slept uneasily, each with his own thoughts. Rolo snuggled me closer than I preferred, though it wasn't cold.

In the morning we took the horses to the Comal, then set about opening the dig and cutting juniper limbs for timbers.

By midafternoon we had pulled up the lid of rock-covered logs that closed our shaft and I was the first one down, gingerly negotiating a twisting rope ladder, with a lantern in one hand. At the bottom of the shaft a tunnel just tall enough for me to duck-walk in, though dad had to crawl, followed the surface of the old blackstone road, crossed a sidewalk and ran along a brick wall to a break that might once have been a door. Once inside you could stand, for this was the special part of our lease.

This building, unlike all the others that anyone had found here, hadn't completely collapsed when it was flooded and buried in the old days. Its concrete ceiling still held, though buckled and broken and pierced by juniper roots. Above a two meter layer of earth and rubble was another meter and a half of musty-smelling air. Rolo and I thought this the most secret place in the world, and always made a point of walking around in it with the lamp on the first day of the dig, searching the streaked brown ceiling for thin hanging daggers of pale dripstone that could be snapped off and sold for medicine in Crane's Mill. The air, however, gave us headaches, especially on the first day. The main practical benefit of this empty space was that it could be used to store earth and rubble shoveled out of our excavation, until we opened a new trench and the earth could be shoveled back again. Salvagers in the other leases had to haul their tailings to the surface, something about which they were generally lazy, packing it along the walls of their tunnels and risking death by collapse and suffocation.

The next day we worked in the bottom of a trench, in a part of the room where Robert had found recorded sound the year before. In earlier days he used to speculate whether this building had been a store, a warehouse, a museum or what. "We know quite a lot about how people lived back then," he would say, "but what we know should make us cautious, whenever we lack explicit documentation. They had a weirdly large variety of highly specialized businesses and operations. How it all worked is a mystery, and we are always finding things we can't explain." He would theorize like that, or tell stories of strange things dug up elsewhere, talking as he worked until some unusual item came up against the trowel, but this time he spoke little and worked with a kind of wooden intensity, his mind elsewhere. Leah sat and watched him in the lamplight.

That morning we unearthed only rubble, broken plastic and small disks of a kind that Robert said were worthless, as they looked a bit like records but contained nothing that could be played back. About noon we struck a patch of dark soil; that was a good sign. Soon the first black disk came to light, covered with grime. Robert seemed to regain a little of his old spirit at the sight, and dusted it gently with a shaving brush as he told us to bring a salvage frame. He slipped the blade of his knife in around the edges of the disk and began to coax it free, but it fell to pieces as he raised it. Beneath it was a thin layer of dirt and then another disk – a whole stack of them – but each one broke as he tried to lift it out. "My hands aren't clever today," he said.

"Let me try," said dad, who rarely worked with the disks themselves. The first one broke under his touch but the second came out whole, and we got it safely pressed in the frame, with the thumb screws clamped down. By noon we had nearly twenty, and Robert's disposition had improved. "I can't wait to get these back," he said, as though forgetting that he wasn't returning to Chicago. "I want to play them for you, Leah."

She smiled in a careful, weary way, like the smile a sick person gives to reassure the one looking after them. "They are beautiful, but I need to go up now to the sunlight. This air makes my head hurt."

"Ah, okay, should I..."

"No, don't come. I can go alone." She said something else in her own language, and he nodded. She took a candle lamp and moved toward the exit tunnel. Robert, excited by the disks that were coming up, returned to the work, eager now to try his hand again. I noticed dad looking after Leah, then at me. He made a motion with his head toward the tunnel.

"I gotta go up too, and take a piss," I said. "You okay, Rolo?"

"Mm," said Rolo, half asleep.

I hurried through the tunnel to the entrance shaft, and not bothering with the ladder, climbed the rough timbering that supported the walls. When I got to the top at first I saw no one, just the ash of our breakfast fire, our camp baggage and horses, with an unfamiliar horse standing near them. Then someone who had been crouching by the entrance laid hands on me, dragged me out and threw me to the ground with expert skill, slammed a knee into my chest and put the cold mouth of a pistol against my jaw.

I looked up into the face of a stocky, weatherbeaten man with a straw-colored mustache, wearing a stained brown hat with a rounded crown, a worn leather jacket and a filthy shirt, riding pants and boots. A welted scar ran down the side of his head, across where one ear had been. He said something to me in that same unknown language—Calorwashian, I suppose—but I couldn't have answered anyway because I couldn't breathe.

Leah spoke from somewhere nearby, in a tone of command. The knee and gun relaxed enough for me to get my breath, and turn my head to see her standing by another man, a little taller than herself and with the same brown skin and long black hair, a family resemblance perhaps, though I've since wondered about that. He wore no hat but was otherwise dressed much as the man who held me. I smelled tobacco; the stocky man had thrown down a half-smoked cigarillo when he lunged for me.

Leah came to me. I have rarely seen such a transformation in a person. Her eyes shone and her face, for the first time, looked purposeful and alive. At her touch the man let me go, though he stayed nearby with gun drawn. She knelt beside me and spoke in her odd manner. "Hector, you don't owe me anything. I owe you. But I owe your uncle more, who is a good man, a good Grange man. I want to make it easier for him. Tell him you saw me ride with these men towards the town, the big river, Nuevabrón. He must not follow. It would be very bad. Do you understand?"

"I understand," I said.

She reached behind her neck and unfastened something, then drew out of her shirt a fine silver chain hung with a flat jewel, black but glossy as a mirror, set beneath a little pane of crystal in a frame of malachite. She put it in my hand. "Keep this, and tell no one. When you see him next year give it to him, from me. Next year, you understand?" She smiled again briefly, like one who knows the secret to a magic trick. "We dig these up in our mountains. Maybe it holds more music than this whole city that is buried, or maybe other things. You understand?"

I held the jewel, still warm from her body, and lied. "I understand."

"Maybe you do." She rose and went to the tall man, speaking. He nodded. She went to get her horse.

"Leah," I said, "your horse has a crack in its right front shoe. You need to get it fixed soon."

The taller man heard me and laughed, saying something in a tone that suggested that wouldn't be much of a problem. He gave me a mock salute, then in a different tone spoke to the stocky man, who rolled me over and tied me hand and foot. With my head sideways against the earth I saw Leah mount her horse. She looked back and raised her hand in farewell as she rode off west, toward the hills. The others followed. The sound of their hooves had faded away long before anyone came up from the dig and found me.

I told them what Leah had asked me to, and Uncle Robert and dad had an argument, saying the worst things I ever heard them speak to each other. Rolo cried, and dad threatened to knock Robert down if he tried to go into Nuevabrón after them. Robert stammered and paced, and cursed, and stood gazing downstream in anguish, as I burned with shame to see him looking in the wrong direction, because of the lie I had told. Three times he started to go, then stopped, and hung his head. Dad left him alone to work it off. An hour later a party of Mexican soldiers, well-armed and well-horsed, came up the trail from Nuevabrón and questioned everyone they found, though they wouldn't say what they were looking for. I said nothing while dad and Uncle Robert pleaded ignorance. The Mexican officer wasn't fooled, but as his questions started to become more probing, another soldier came riding down the western trail, saying that signs had been found farther inland. Their horses kicked up dust as they left.

We ate in silence, laid out our packs and blankets, and slept. The next morning dad and Robert debated what to do, along with Henry and Zeke who had come over from their lease to hear our news, and another pair of lease holders who had arrived during the night. The risk of being caught on the road by the soldiers was weighed against the risk of staying. The new arrivals said three people had been seen riding fast to the west on the military highway, and that someone had stolen a horse in Panther Springs. Dad gave me a look on hearing that, and later took me aside among the trees. I told him everything, to my great relief.

He nodded, just a little. "You did all right. Don't show anyone that thing she gave you. If I were a practical man I'd have you bury it here, but..." He sighed, looking toward camp. "Just don't show it to anyone. Not for a year, like she said, and then only to him. Can I trust you?"

I said he could. "Is Uncle Robert going to be all right?"

Dad rubbed a hand in his beard. "There's an even chance. He's failed the Grange, but this is an awkward case; they won't want to see it go to trial. If he tells them she tricked him, which I think is true, they'll probably just give him a reprimand. He's lost all chance for promotion, but when did my crazy brother ever want that?" He winked, and I felt better, though that wasn't really the answer to the question I thought I'd asked.

"All right," dad said when we returned to camp. "It's time to load and go. We've worked our lease for this year, we've dug up enough of Robert's old rubbish, and the sky is looking ugly. Pull out the tools, close the shaft and bury it good, and let's be gone before it comes a gully washer."

Contributors

Matthew Griffiths is a New Zealand engineer and environmental planner who currently lives in Australia working on environmental management. He loves reading and writing, especially about his twin interests: global sustainability and China. At other times he plays guitar with more enthusiasm than skill. He and his wife have two children.

N.N.Scott received bachelor's and master's degrees from the University of Texas and has since lived abroad. "When it Comes A Gully Washer" is his third published work.

Joseph Nemeth grew up in Cheyenne, Wyoming, USA at the height of the Cold War with the former Soviet Union, and never worried much about The Bomb, assuming that nearby Warren Air Force Base was ground zero for at least one Soviet ICBM, and that it would all be over before there was time to duck and cover. He attended the University of Wyoming, earned a Master's degree in physics from SUNY at Stony Brook, and has spent the last three decades writing computer software. He is a classically-trained violinist, pianist, and composer of several classical works, including the Missa Druidica, a five-movement musical setting for the seasonal rites of the Order of Bards, Ovates, and Druids, of which he is a member. He has been writing fiction since his early teens, but has only recently ventured into the world of publishing. He lives in Colorado with his wife, whom he regularly reminds is the best woman in the world.

Martin Hensher was born and brought up just outside London. Somewhat mysterious circumstances allowed him to attend two of England's most august universities, and - more incredibly - to subsequently find gainful employment.
He learned about collapse close up, working in Kazakhstan and Turkmenistan shortly after the fall of the Soviet Union - and then learned a little about preventing collapse during six eventful years' work in post-apartheid South Africa, where his two older children were born. He now lives with his wife and four children in Hobart, Tasmania, where he is very much minded to stay if they'll have him.

David Trammel is a moderator at the GreenWizard.Org website, where he helps people learn how to make the changes in their life to survive and prosper in the coming Post Peak world. Stop by and join the community.

Diana Haugh's first novel, *Dawn at Dunnelson, 1999,* was well received and still draws good reviews even though it is now out of print. Her short stories have won awards, such as the 1997 First Prize from NPR's WITF for *Speaking Out, 2000* Past President's Award from Harrisburg Manuscript Club for *The High Cost of Living*, and Honorable Mention from Apprise Magazine for *Stube's Right Eye.* She draws on her Hispanic culture and life in Pennsylvania's coal country to create the strong themes of community that frame all her works.

Artist, Graphic Designer, Home Designer/Builder, **J.M. Hughes** is the author of several short stories and novels most of which remain unpublished. The author resides near Southworth, Washington on the Olympic Peninsula with his wife and daughter.

A native of Mount Desert Island, Maine, **Calvin Jennings** studied media theory and production at the University of Southern Maine before relocating to Los Angeles in 2008, where he worked a variety of jobs in film production, distribution and casting. While Calvin is still engaged in film and video work he has, since 2010, turned an increasing portion of his energy into fiction writing, which he uses to explore topics of history, culture and spirituality. He is currently in the final stages of writing his first full-length novel.

Grant Canterbury is a naturalist and writer who grew up exploring landscapes wild and settled in Alaska and the American West. His stories have been shaped by both the imaginative sweep of science fiction and the recombinant complexity of the natural world. Currently he is working on a novel of exploration and magic in the Renaissance. He resides near Portland, Oregon, with his family and quirky spaniels. See **canterburia.blogspot.com** for irregular project updates and posts.

Tony f. whelKs is the fiction-only pen name of a fifty-something writer living in the rural East Midlands of England. Initially trained as a pharmacist, he has worked in electronics, communications and renewable energy, then spent some years as an activist with a variety of environmental NGOs. He is also an amateur radio operator and permaculture gardener. His fiction was first published in the satirical periodical 'Guernsey Attic Press' in the 1990s, but writes non-fiction newspaper and magazine articles under his real name.

Walter Freitag is a programmer, lab technician, game designer, DIYer, skeptic, and lifelong SF nerd. His first published work was a text-based computer game about exploring the stars. He's now pursuing more conventional forms of fiction, and more challenging views of the future.

Rachel White works in youth services at a public library. Stories fascinate her, especially as they relate to the future of industrial society. A native of Delaware, where she studied anthropology, she now lives in Washington, DC.

20404732R00181

Made in the USA
Middletown, DE
25 May 2015